Racing Luck

REBBECCA MACINTYRE

Palmetto Publishing Group, LLC
Charleston, SC

For information regarding special discounts for bulk purchases, please
contact Palmetto Publishing Group at Info@PalmettoPublishingGroup.com.

ISBN-13: 978-1-944313-80-7
ISBN-10: 1-944313-80-X

Prologue

Danni Scott stood in her greenhouse, immersed in the watery light of the Highland sun, clipping snippets of herbs for the oxtail soup she was cooking. One of Colin's favorite dishes, it was a peace offering. They would have it for dinner tonight, whenever he got home. She'd said some hurtful things on the phone. That he didn't care their newborn son had died only weeks before. That he loved racing and his cars more than he loved her. That she was leaving him.

She still loved him. But, when he said, "I love you," on the phone, she'd simply hung up. That was cruel, and something he did not deserve.

After an hour of tears, she'd gone back to the bedroom and unpacked her suitcase, called British Air and cancelled her reservation. When Colin got home, they would talk, just like he said they would.

She washed the herb cuttings in the big kitchen sink then dropped them in the pot. The lid firmly in place, the soup would tend itself now.

With a little sigh, she rinsed her hands and started toward the sitting room, and her computer.

An odd flash of light caught her attention. She watched through the window as her brother-in law's car turned in the driveway. The gravel made a strangely loud crunching sound.

The case clock in the hall chimed four.

Why on earth was Edward here?

Not that she minded. He and his wife, Jane and their kids often dropped by, but not when Colin's race was on. Danni wouldn't watch the damn thing with them or anyone else.

Through the window, she watched as Edward put the car in park and just sat in it for several seconds, as if he could not manage to get out.

Something was wrong.

Half way to the door, a chill gripped her stomach, stopped her breath, surrounded her heart.

She wanted to back away, leave, never hear whatever Edward had to say.

"No", she whispered. Despite the cold slithering up her spine, she jerked the door open.

Edward stood on the other side, his face drawn and pale. He held out his arms. "Danni."

She stepped back. It couldn't be. She hadn't had the chance to say she was sorry.

Edward took a step inside. "Danni, I..." he choked back a sob.

In a single heartbeat, Danni's world crumbled. She'd not told Colin she loved him, she still loved him. Edward's arms around her were the only thing that kept her upright. "Oh, Danni" he said, "there was an accident."

Chapter One

On the second Saturday in December, Danni exited her car, and started toward the entrance of the restaurant south of Denver.

The evening had started out a bit rough. She'd hoped to be early. Instead, she couldn't find her keys. Probably because they were right where she'd left them, in her purse, not in the evening bag where she'd put her ID, credit card and lipstick.

She'd backed out of the drive way, gone half a block and remembered the sticky note she'd left on the front door, reminding her to take her checkbook to pay some friends for the cookie dough she'd ordered from their kids for school. After a u-turn she'd gone home, ran inside, got the checkbook and started once more toward Sedalia.

If she had half a brain she'd probably lose it.

This would be the first MG Car Club Christmas party she'd been to in the more than three years since Colin died. It was time to face it. Her friends would be warm and supportive, and if she fell into little pieces, they would understand.

The storm had begun late in the afternoon with freezing rain, then snow. The parking lot was unavoidably treacherous. She should have worn boots and changed into dress shoes. Oh well, too late now.

Danni carefully minced her way toward the door. Without warning or any way to stop the inevitable, her feet slipped forward without the rest of her body. She landed hard on her back and rump. Damn it!

She lay there, taking stock. Was anything broken? She seemed to be ok, just the wind knocked out of her. Great. Just great. What an ignominious start.

"Are you all right?" An unknown, masculine, baritone voice asked.

Danni looked up and nodded. Snow fell silently. Big, fat flakes landed on the shoulders and dark hair of the man who knelt by her side.

She added mortification to her list of emotions. This night just got worse and worse.

How come he didn't fall?

Gently, he took her hand. "Let me help you," he offered in a soft Southern accent.

Carefully, she got to her feet, as he steadied her.

Thank goodness on one else had seen her fall flat on her butt. It was embarrassing enough that a total stranger had witnessed it.

"Here, take my arm," her rescuer said.

Danni murmured, "Thank you."

He guided her safely across the lot, then followed her through the door.

"Thank you again," she said without looking at him. Head down, she hurried off to the ladies room, glad she did not know the man.

Danni shrugged out of her coat, then brushed it off. No rips or tears. Her shoes had somehow survived. She took some deep breaths, and then left the quiet of the restroom.

The private dining room of the restaurant glistened with lights and candles. Greenery hung over the doors and windows. Outside, the snow sparkled in the reflected light. It seemed to shimmer with the very essence of Christmas. She wandered in slowly, stopping to chat.

Danni's best friend, Sally Williams, waved a hand in the air. Danni made her way to the table. She knew everyone there, except for the man talking to Sally's husband, Mark.

Oh no, it was her savior from the parking lot. Please, she pled with herself, don't blush from sheer embarrassment.

Impeccably dressed in a fashionable tux, the stranger was a little short, maybe five-eight, with longish, dark brown, nearly black hair. He turned toward her.

Eeh gad. He had moss green eyes and long dark lashes. A straight nose, dark expressive brows, a firm, slightly square jaw, and perfectly shaped lips that combined to make made a devastatingly handsome man.

Mark said, "Ashley, this is Dr. Danielle Scott. Danni, Ashley Jenkins."

"Dr. Scott," Ashley said politely, and held out his hand. "I believe we met in the parking lot."

Danni swallowed her humiliation, reached out, and when their hands touched, his fingers engulfed her hand. They were warm, strong, with little calluses along the palm. Though slender, an aura of subtle strength emanated from him.

"Call me Danni." She managed to say. "Mark likes to impress people by pretending I am a neurologist or something."

"A doctor of what then?" he asked.

"History. And historically speaking, Ashley is rather an unusual name for a man, now. I take it your mother was a fan of <u>Gone With The Wind?</u>"

He'd probably heard that one a few million times. "Sorry, that was a ridiculous question." She hoped her face wasn't too red.

"I've heard it before." Ashley's charmingly lopsided grin revealed straight white teeth. Who the hell was she kidding? He was gorgeous.

Her stomach fluttered in a warm, wonderful, nearly forgotten way.

His smile let her know her awkward question had not bothered him. "And why would Mark make up stories about you?"

"Because, he enjoys bedeviling people." Danni smiled at Mark, then leaned conspiratorially toward Ashley. "I have seen that innocent looking man start a food fight, in a restaurant."

Mr. Gorgeous placed a hand over his heart in faked horror. "Really? I would have never suspected."

"I would suspect just about anything," Sally said, walking up, a bright smile on her face, directed at Mark. "But then, I've lived with him for better than fifteen years."

Danni laughed, and Ashley did too.

Her friends had taken it into their heads that she needed a boyfriend. A woman her age did not need a boyfriend. Much of the Thanksgiving conversation with them, and her parents, had revolved around the status of her non-existent love life.

Tonight, the ladies milled around on one side of the square table, the guys on the other then, as they took their seats, her friends nicely maneuvered things so Ashley would sit next to her.

He pulled out the chair for her and smiled again.

Her stomach warmed as she said, "Thank you." Lust was a wonderful thing.

Ashley decided Mark's description of Danni as cute hadn't done her justice. She was diminutive, with short, wavy, bright blond hair, and china blue eyes set in a heart shaped face. Her dark blue, velvet gown had long sleeves, a deep V in the back and a scoop neck. It showed off a curvy figure and complemented her fair complexion. She was thirty-three, Ashley knew, because Mark had told him.

Obviously, Mark was trying to put Danni and him together. Ashley was game. He had no trouble finding a date, if he wanted one. But, the morals clause in his contract made him very particular.

Until Mark had mentioned Danni, Ashley hadn't considered the car club as a potential place to find a woman who might be interested in a little romance.

Trying for conversational tidbits, Ashley asked her softly, "Why are we sitting this way?"

Her blond brows rose. "Division of topic. The guys talk about cars, and we talk about everything else." Her voice was melodic, full of texture, like slubbed silk.

"Maybe your topics will be more interesting."

She gave a polite shrug. "Oh, we roam into cars too, but we don't discuss camber, the weight of the cam shafts or proper tire pressures for MG's."

His concentration on Danni was disrupted by the arrival of the salad, so he turned back to Mark and the other guys. Curious about her, he continued to glance at Danni out of the corner of his eye.

The Club was a fun group of people who enjoyed driving little British cars. Ashley had a lot in common with the people at the table. They had MG's and raced vintage sports cars.

Right after he'd moved here, in September, he'd joined the club. Since their meetings were in the middle of the week, he'd even made a couple of them.

Once the local vintage race season got started, maybe he could make a one or two. He'd like to. Mark had suggested Ashley join them in Las Vegas or Phoenix. He certainly knew the tracks. The hard part would be getting a car there. Maybe he could borrow a ride?

He refocused on the conversation just as Doug Cook asked, "How do you fix under-steer Ashley?"

"Depends on whether or not I want the car tight."

"There's a nice enigmatic answer."

Ashley smiled and shrugged. "A little tight, maybe take a half pound of air out of the front right. A lot tight, make a wedge, maybe a track bar adjustment, get some more pressure on the rear tires," Ashley answered. "Part of it depends on the track, what we're doing and when the problem happens."

Mark said with a smile, "That was clear cut. But the guru has spoken. Will you loan us your pit crew?"

Ashley leaned back. "Only if you pay them."

Chuckles answered him.

They had grown accustomed to him rather quickly. It was a nice change. They respected his opinions but didn't treat him like he was very different. But, when they discussed driving they were all ears.

He joined in both of the conversations, the women's and the men's. He had to admit, the division of the table was a simple solution to an old problem.

Mark had told him about Danni. But, why hadn't Ashley met her before?

Danni asked, "What do you do Ashley?"

So, she hadn't heard him talking to the guys. His standard answer sprang into mind. "I'm a pilot." Most people didn't believe him when he'd told the truth, so he used a partial truth. He was a pilot. He just didn't do it for a living. "What about you? I presume you teach?"

With a small smile, Danni said, "I do research for other people. My... husband's..." she said the word as if it had stuck in her throat, maybe a nasty divorce? "...travel schedule was demanding. Since I went with him, no time to teach. Though I may do it some day."

Danni paid him polite attention, but no more than that. He was used to single ladies, and some married ones, angling to be seen, or take a tumble into bed, with him. He avoided the married ones all together and was careful about the single ones. He couldn't afford bad publicity. Danni wasn't married and didn't seem overly interested. That made her...intriguing.

Dessert was placed in front of him, some chocolate creation. He watched Danni's face as she savored every bite. "Do you like it?" he asked.

She rolled her eyes, then licked her lips.

He doubted she had meant the gesture to be seductive, but it was.

"Delicious," she said.

Yes, he'd bet she was delicious. He'd like to find out.

"Are you a chocolate fan, Ashley?"

It took a mental detour to go from the shape of her lips to the question she'd asked. "Not really. I like it, but...I would just as soon have key lime pie."

To cover a sudden case of nerves, he took a sip of his wine, then asked, "Are you staying for dancing?"

"For a little while. I have a long drive home," she answered.

More curiosity rose. "Where do you live?"

"Arvada, though technically, it's unincorporated Jefferson County."

Close. Near enough for some excuse to drop by? The prospect made him smile. "So do I. Up by Standley Lake."

"That's in my neighborhood."

No invitation. No batting of eyelashes. No innuendo. He wasn't sure if he was pleased or miffed. Women did not ignore him. Partly because of his looks, partly, because of what he did. But, this was a woman he wanted to get to know.

The music started. "Where do you live?" he prodded, almost shouting over the music.

She told him. Her address was only a mile or so from his place.

In the silence between songs, he asked, "Dance with me?"

She blinked a few times, as if she were trying to understand his question. Her smiled dimmed a little. Was there a way to politely withdraw his invitation?

A bit hesitantly, she said, "Yes."

The flash of worry he'd felt dissipated. "Good."

He reached for her hand, and tentatively, she took it. Her fingers were cool. The brush of her skin, tantalizing. Though she wore high heels, the top of her head just reached his shoulder. She had to be about five foot or so, maybe a little taller, but not much.

First dances were awkward, spent learning how much your partner knew. She moved very well, confidently. If he gambled, he'd bet she'd had lessons. They made it through without a misstep.

Then, a good, slow song, At Last, by Etta James started. He suppressed a smile. What luck.

He gathered her up. She fit nicely against him. They had made only one turn around the floor, when suddenly, she pulled out of his arms and fled.

What the hell? How could she just walk off? Confounded and angry, he followed.

In the bar, he caught her. She stood a foot away. "Danni?" He winced at his tone, sharper than he'd intended.

Her head was down. Her shoulders slumped and rounded.

Something was wrong. "Danni?"

Touching her shoulder as softly as he could, he willed her to turn. She did. He half expected tears, instead, he saw determination, a touch of embarrassment and something else. What, he wasn't sure.

"I'm sorry, it's... it's not your fault. Sometimes I just...have a difficult time." She shook her head. "I don't want to hear that song."

Still confused, he said, "It's a nice song."

"I know." Danni looked down. "I had it played as the first dance at my wedding reception."

A hammer hit him in the stomach. Sorrow was what he had

seen in her eyes. He slid his hand down her velvet-clad arm. A wedding ring circled the ring finger of her right hand, an old fashioned gesture of widowhood. His grandmother had done the same thing.

He watched as Danni took several uneven, deep breaths.

He wasn't good at comforting, but he wanted to try. "Let me take you home. We'll come back tomorrow and pick up your car."

She shook her head, pulled her hand out of his. "No. I have to work through this."

They stood by the wall, close, but not touching.

How fresh was her grief? She looked almost on the edge of tears, but determined to hold them back. After another minute she said, "That's twice tonight I have embarrassed myself in front of you. I hope I haven't ruined your evening."

Maybe he could tease her into a better frame of mind? "You haven't ruined my night. I thought you fell rather... gracefully, and you're the best dance partner I've had all night."

A tiny smile appeared. "I'm the only dancing partner you've had tonight."

Ashley shrugged with a smile. "I'll get your bag, and you can freshen up, or would you rather go?"

She looked away, her upper teeth biting her lower, full lip.

"If you stay, I'll let you dance with me again," he teased some more.

She glanced up, her eyes bright with a touch of humor. Something stabbed him, something good.

"How could I refuse such an offer, especially since you dance rather well."

"My mother would have been very disappointed if I hadn't finished my lessons." It was one of the few things he was now glad she'd insisted on.

Danni flashed a small smile.

He was inordinately pleased about making that smile appear.

"Would you bring me my purse, please?"

Ashley went back into the party. Sally watched him pick up Danni's bag, then, with a worried frown, she peered beyond him, looking for Danni. "Is she all right?"

He nodded. "Upset over that song."

Sally touched his arm, and nodded her head in understanding.

Danni waited for him in the long hall, near the restrooms. The walk gave him time to look her up and down again. She was pretty, not classically beautiful. She held out her hand with a shy smile and took her handbag. At only a few inches square, it couldn't hold much.

"If you'll excuse me, please." Danni turned, then closed the restroom door behind her.

Well, Ashley thought, so far, so good. She gave no indication she knew who he was. He got tired of women--people--who wanted to meet him, or be seen with him, just so they could say they had.

Danni was an attractive, intelligent woman. Her friends clearly thought she was ready to date, but was she?

Only one way to find out--ask. He didn't want to scare her off. Patience, he needed patience. Sometimes you have to let the race come to you.

Danni reappeared, took a half step back and cocked her head to one side. "You didn't need to wait for me."

"My mother taught me a gentleman waits for a lady." She didn't resist when he took her elbow, then walked beside her back to the party. A thread of desire tugged low in his groin.

"Your mother seems to have taught you a lot."

The statement banished lustful thoughts. "She tried." She had taught him manners, between her visits to the charities, the country club, and the society functions she wanted to be seen at. Being seen was probably more important to her than actually doing anything.

"And what part of the southeast are you from?"

Ashley glanced at Danni. "Guess."

Her blue eyes sparkled with merriment. "Okay. Not Deep South. Your accent is too soft. No twang or bite to it and no drawl. Sooo, Kentucky?"

He shook his head. "Nope."

At the threshold of the private dining room, she turned to look up at him. Lord, she had beautiful eyes.

"Virginia?"

After another second, he managed to answer her, "Yeah. But what part?"

Her shoulders dropped, as she rolled her eyes. "I'm not that good." A grin appeared.

He couldn't help smiling back. "Richmond."

Obviously pleased with her guess of the correct State, she stood up straighter, tipped her nose up, and looked absolutely adorable.

Resisting the urge to kiss the tip of that little nose, he said, "Come on. Let's dance."

That's what they did for the next hour.

Despite a desire to dance only with Danni, manners overrode and he partnered a septuagenarian sweetheart and all of the ladies who sat at the table with him at dinner.

Danni sat down, took the last sip of her wine, then said, "Well, my feet have had it."

Ashley noticed her nail color perfectly matched her toenails, as she wiggled them in her impractical, open toed shoes.

Considering her ease on the dance floor and her ignominious fall in the parking lot, those beaded high heels had to be slippery. He chuckled. "My feet are tired too, and I'm not wearing heels."

She looked up at him, eyes full of mischief. "You might look good in heels."

"No thanks. But, if you'll give me your claim check, I'll get your coat."

"Deal."

While he waited for the coats, Ashley looked out the windows. Snow fell heavily. No question now, he would follow her home. She probably drove well on snow, but he would feel better knowing she was safe.

As he held her coat for her, he said as much.

"You don't need to do that," she said.

He shrugged. "It's not out of my way. Besides, if I slide off the road, you can rescue me."

She grinned and relented.

Cold air, filled with snowflakes, hit them in the face as soon as he opened the restaurant door.

"Where's your car?"

She glanced around, as if a bit lost, then pointed with her head. "The Audi convertible."

White with a blue top. She had good taste. After delivering her to her car, without so much as a slip, he got in his custom Corvette Z06 and followed her out of the lot.

Heavy flakes streamed toward his windshield. He dimmed his lights, to reduce the reflection, allowing him to see further.

The wide track of the 'Vette made up for the car being rear wheel drive. The fact he had all weather, instead of high performance tires on it, helped too.

He got used to the conditions, leaving half his mind free to wander. Why hadn't Mark mentioned Danni was a widow? What had happened to her husband? How long had it been since he died?

As she turned into the driveway, the headlamps of both cars illuminated a big, older ranch style home. The snow made large lumps of some type of shrubs or bushes that lined the fence. A huge tree, its slim, naked branches bent to the ground, guarded the sidewalk.

The garage door lifted, she stopped her car next to a dark

green, late fifties MG A sitting like a sleek beast on one side of the oversized space. She got out of her car and waved, not good-bye, but come in.

Ashley drove up the slight slope to the end of the drive. He joined her just inside the door that led from the garage into the house. Considering the washer, dryer and sink, it must be her laundry room. It smelled clean, without a hint of bleach or detergent.

She looked composed, much as she had through most of the night. "Thank you."

"You're welcome," he said. "And, thank you for making my evening so enjoyable."

A shy smile answered him.

He felt almost like a teen-ager, wondering what happened next. Hell with it. He leaned down, slipped his hands to her cheeks, and brushed her lips with his. Her mouth was soft and giving. She tasted faintly of chocolate and red wine. He did not kiss her long or hard, but the contact was enough to shake him.

Defying the urge to kiss her until they were both out of their minds, he dropped his hands. "Good night."

She blinked a few times, her mouth opened just a little, then, her voice cool, she said, "Good night."

Not sure if he was intrigued or insulted by her outward calm, or just stunned from the pure lust he felt during their kiss, Ashley half turned away, then turned back. "May I call you?"

The corners of her mouth turned up a fraction. "Yes, you may."

Still confused over her reactions, and his, he drove home. He looked her up in the Car Club directory. Her phone number was in it, along with her email and snail mail address, one here and one in...Scotland?

Chapter Two

Sunday morning, Ashley felt even more like an idiotic teenager. He hadn't asked someone on a date, someone he would really like to be with, in a while. That afternoon, he picked up the phone and with slightly shaking fingers, dialed her number. She answered on the third ring.

"Would you like to catch a movie, maybe have some dinner?" he managed to ask without sounding like a fool.

There was a pause. She was probably thinking of some polite way to say no.

"Sorry, I was untying my shoes. And yes, I would like to go."

His anxiety disappeared. "Great."

"Come over and we can decide what we want to see."

Danni opened the door. Ashley stepped into a wide, deep, entry hall. Green marble tile paved the way to the rest of the house. She looked small in the big room, fresh and appealing in loose fitting jeans and a red sweater. It was a good color for her. Pink booted slippers were on her feet.

He nodded at her footwear. "You were untying your shoes

when I called?"

She frowned for a second, then her brows arched up along with her lips. "I wore lace up boots to church this morning. Then I put these on."

He grinned. "You going to wear those to the movie?"

Her answering chuckle came from deep inside her, a warm, sexy sound. "I hadn't planned on it, but it's not a bad idea. Nice and warm." She moved farther into the house. "Come on in. You want something to drink?"

"No, thanks."

One hall went behind him and to his right. On his left, a set of glass French doors opened into a huge dining room. She led him through an arched opening into another big room. A computer sat to one side, surrounded by floor to ceiling bookcases. A flat screen TV hung on one wall, above a gas fireplace. The furniture was mission style, the colors warm. It all combined into a comfortable, cozy look.

She sat on one end of a long couch. "Please, sit down."

He picked up a newspaper, rather old fashioned of her, that lay open on a table and sat next to her. A spicy scent tickled his nose. Her perfume. What would she do if he leaned in...

"What do you want to see? There are a bunch of new movies out."

Her question jerked him right out of most of the thought of kissing her. Their heads together, he wondered when would the time be right time for another kiss?

They picked a film that started in about a half hour.

"Let me put on my shoes, then we can go." She disappeared back the way they had come.

Alone, Ashley looked around the room again. A group of pictures hung on a wall. In the center was a photo of a blond man. A face Ashley recognized.

Danni Scott was the widow of Colin Scott, a Formula One driver from Scotland who'd died in a freak track accident just over three years ago.

Damn. This certainly complicated things. Ashley's stomach sank. Should he tell her?

A date! She had a date! Despite her protestations about not wanting to see anyone, she was unexpectedly excited.

Danni pulled on her warmest snow boots. Good traction. She didn't want to fall and embarrass herself for a second time in front of maybe the most handsome man she'd ever met.

Somehow, last night she'd maintained a normal façade, despite the attention he'd paid to her. She didn't want to look like an over-eager teenager. As attractive as he was, he probably had dates falling out of trees. She grinned at the image of women falling out of the fronds of a date palm.

His kiss had been very warm, wonderful, too short, but he <u>had</u> kissed her. In her laundry room. What the heck had she been thinking?

Then when he'd asked in such a gentlemanly way if he could call her, it had been hard not to smile.

She put on her long leather coat and found Ashley in the hall, near the front door, waiting patiently. "I'm ready," she said.

His smile seemed a bit subdued, like a thin cloud passing over the sun. He opened the door. "After you."

A sky the color of slate promised more snow. It never lasted long, and came often enough to satisfy her need for four seasons. It was just too cold in Scotland this time of year. Though, it held its own stark beauty.

Ashley opened the door of the car for her.

She raised her brows. "Your mother teach you to open doors, too?"

He grinned. "No, my grandmother."

Danni smiled as she slid into the leather seat. She knew women who were offended by a man opening a door. Didn't bother her. She never thought less of a guy who acted like a gentleman.

She'd not ridden in a Corvette Z before. The only thing between them was the console. His shoulder nearly touched hers.

This man was interested, in her. To her surprise, she was interested in him.

She chattered away about the wildlife, the greenbelts and trails around the area. She pointed out the bald eagles nest in the big cottonwoods on the north side of the lake.

"Really? Do you see them often?" he asked.

She nodded. "Yeah, especially in the spring and summer. It's a nesting pair. If you spend some time watching them, you'll see the immature ones practicing."

His eyes still on the road, he asked, "What are they practicing?"

"Diving, hovering. The first few times is actually pretty funny. They look totally awkward. Then, the next time you see one, it is incredibly graceful."

After getting a grip on her nerves, she watched the snow as she tried with all her might to remember how to behave on a date.

She managed to look at his face. A very slight smile turned up the ends of his lips.

Then, after he smoothly shifted into fifth gear, he softly laid his hand on top of hers.

Oh my, oh my. How good it felt. Touching. She missed it even more than she missed sex. The simple pleasure of the warmth, the soft caresses, of being near. She soaked in the touch of his hand.

At the theatre, Danni was amused by the reaction of the young girl behind the ticket counter, who took Ashley's money while looking at him as if he were an especially good dessert. Ashley had seemed oblivious.

The film was a light romantic comedy, good fare for a first date. In between little bites of popcorn, he held her hand lightly through the movie. It had felt wonderful, more than wonderful. Did he realize the affect he had on her? Probably. Very handsome men knew they were handsome.

She spent the hour and a half in the darkened theatre wondering about him. They had had little time to talk, and there were so many things she wanted to know.

As they left the theatre, she'd muttered, "Excuse me," then pointed with her head toward the women's room.

He gave her a lopsided grin. "Me too." The grin had faded into a frown. "Only, I think I'll use the other one."

He had a quirky sense of humor. She liked it.

Necessary things done, she checked her make-up, freshened her lipstick and zipped up her coat. Ashley waited for her near the outside door. Men always finished first.

He asked where she wanted to eat.

"I am not particular. There's an Italian place, a sushi bar and a sports bar just around the corner. What about you?" She really didn't care where they went, as long as it was quiet enough to talk.

"I would like a steak. You know the place over by Flat Irons?"

She did. It was a favorite meeting place for her and her girlfriends. "Sounds great."

He took her hand again. Oh, how she liked it.

"I do have one question."

"What's that?" She smiled and looked at him.

In the glow of the overhead lights, reflecting off the snow, his boyish expression was apparent. "How do I get there from here?"

Danni issued her instructions. Ashley laughed. "Those may be the most succinct directions I ever heard."

"I used to run rallies with a friend, and some with my husband."

Ashley nodded. "That explains it."

She managed to say <u>my husband</u> with out a hitch. Certainly, an improvement in her state of mind.

"How do you do research? I mean for other people?"

"When you read the credits on a documentary or in a book, that say <u>research assistant</u>, that's me."

"Do you have a specialty?"

After several minutes of answering his questions, Danni decided Ashley was one of those people who could make others talk about themselves. She knew precious little more about him than she had twenty minutes before.

There was a short wait at the restaurant. The place reminded her of a really good pub in England or Scotland, one small room after another, with dark wood paneling, comfortable seats, and a friendly atmosphere. If it were a little closer to her house, the place could become a habit.

The next <u>date</u> predicament raised its ugly head. She had no idea what to order. He had money, but some men were, rightly, offended by dates that only asked for the best.

He didn't seem to be the type that would appreciate an offer to go Dutch.

Over his open menu, Ashley looked at her. "What would you like?"

Prevaricating, she said, "I am not sure yet."

"Well, I am going to be a glutton and have the New York Strip. You like oysters?"

Danni nodded. His comment solved the <u>what to order</u> dilemma, clearly, whatever she wanted.

The waiter appeared, and openly stared at Ashley.

"We'll have half a dozen oysters as an appetizer and a bottle of the Gruet Blanc de Noir."

"Very good, Mr. Jenkins."

They knew his name? He gave it when they came in, but for a waiter to know it? "You must come here a lot," she said.

Ashley grinned and shrugged. "I do. I just hadn't driven here from the theatre."

Danni chuckled. The reminder about asking her directions reminded her of something else. "You know about the Glenwood Rallye the MG club sponsors?"

He nodded. "I heard about it at a meeting. It sounds like a lot of fun."

"Do you think you'll give it a go this summer?"

He sighed, the smile slipped away. "Probably not. My schedule won't allow it."

Just as Danni started to ask why, the waiter reappeared, presented the bottle of champagne and poured. Danni took a sip then set her glass down on the cherry wood table.

Ashley touched her fingers. "What I told you, about what I do, is true, as far as it goes."

She uncurled her fingers from around the stem of her glass.

"I really like you." He tugged her fingers into his.

Why did she hear a great big but coming?

"But, I saw your husband's picture."

Danni's stomach did a slow roll just as the waiter delivered the oysters and then disappeared.

Ashley still held her hand.

"I am very confused," she said.

"I saw Colin's picture and realized who you are."

"You knew Colin?"

Ashley's lips thinned as he shook his head. "No, but I know who he was, and what I am."

What in the world was he talking about? "I don't understand. Is something wrong?"

An unseen hand pressed against her, feeding her conviction that something was wrong--with her.

He let go of her hand, stood, then slid in next to her. While the heat of his body so close to her was comforting, she had no idea what Colin had to do with Ashley.

He placed one hand beneath her chin and turned her to face him. "There is nothing wrong with you, it's me."

She blinked. "I haven't noticed anything wrong with you."

A cautious, sad smile crossed his face. "The waiter doesn't know me, only my face and name. He's probably a fan."

"A fan?"

"I'm a race driver, Danni. Stock cars. I finished second this year. I've won three championships. Last night, I'd hoped you didn't know who I was. But now, I realize I should have said something."

Danni's heart thumped loudly, hammered in her chest, rang in her ears. "I didn't know. That you were a racer, I mean." Like moving through deep water, nothing seemed to work as fast as it should, especially her brain.

The first man she had been interested in since Colin's death, and he had to be a driver.

Shit.

"Danni?" his voice was soft.

He sat still beside her. Quiet. Pensive.

She looked at him. Really looked at him. Despite the tone of his voice, she expected to see the self-confidence he seemed to exude. Instead, it looked like he was waiting for bad news.

"Do you want to go home?" he asked.

"That's two nights in a row you've asked me that question." Still angry, with what she wasn't sure, she made a quick decision. "No, let's stay. I want the petite cut filet, rare."

"Okay."

She needed to collect herself. "Let me out, please."

He slid away from her and stood, offered his hand. For some perverse reason, she took it.

"Save me some oysters," she said, and with as much composure as she could muster, walked away.

A damn driver! Ok, calm down. There were worse things. There were. There had to be. She understood why he would not tell her who--or rather what--he was, if he thought she didn't know.

The world of Formula One, the world she knew from experience, was different from stock cars, but she was sure stock car drivers were followed through garages, onto pit roads, at hotels, everywhere. It was difficult to know who was interested in you and who was interested in being seen with you. Especially with successful, and therefore usually wealthy, drivers.

And, when the man could a model for GQ, even more so.

She looked at her reflection in restroom mirror. Try to be logical, for once, she thought.

Ashley didn't know many people here. He was single, drop dead gorgeous, and probably just looking for a date, a friend, maybe an affair, before the race season started.

She took a deep breath. Despite her great friends and family, she was lonely.

Every touch today had thrilled, and filled that abandoned, lonesome, part of her. A portion of her wanted to have some sort of a relationship with him and just not worry about it. Another part shrieked warnings. With a swallow she choked down her anxiety.

Oysters, champagne, a good steak and a handsome man awaited her. Time to stop panicking and try to enjoy the rest of the evening.

She checked her eyes and her lipstick one last time.

Couldn't she just not like him? No, she answered her own question. She'd liked him from the second she'd met him, well, after their informal meeting in the parking lot.

Who was she trying to kid? She'd liked the way he looked even then. He'd been polite, helpful and he hadn't snickered or anything.

Damn it!

After she jerked the restroom door open, she counted to ten, took a deep breath, regained her composure. She spotted him in the booth, head lowered, a frown furrowing his brows. He looked... lonely.

Ashley watched Danni walk away. So far, this had gone about as well as a bad handling car at Daytona.

If she decided to stay away from him, he couldn't blame her, but that wasn't what he wanted. She was attractive, interesting, had her own money and understood his business probably better than he did.

So, that was good. Right?

He hated arguing with himself.

People could think Ashley's life was glamorous, and to an extent it was. On the other hand, the schedule was staggering, the travel, murderous. Regardless of the safety improvements, it was still dangerous. Thanks to that, and his distrust of most people, Ashley kept most of his relationships casual. He'd always avoided the temptations of the willing women who hung around the tracks. He'd known Danni twenty-four hours, and she was temptation itself.

He stared at the semi-liquid gray bivalves lying on the plate and wanted to feed them to her, kiss her and throw her onto the nearest flat surface. He'd felt drawn to her from the moment he saw her fly backward onto her backside in the parking lot.

Why? He had no idea.

He twirled the stem of his champagne glass slowly between his fingers. One evening in a group, and now half way through what had to be considered a shaky experience, and he was afraid. He wanted her to stay. He wanted to know her better. He shrugged his shoulders, tried to rid his body of the anxiety, while he wondered what she would do.

Suddenly she was there. She offered the barest hint of a smile as she slid into the booth, opposite him.

"You didn't have any of the oysters," her melodic voice was soft.

"I waited for you."

She chewed on her lower lip. "Come sit over here."

As unexpected as the offer was, Ashley's stomach tightened. He moved to her side. Pure, unmitigated lust tightened his body.

Maybe he would get to feed her oysters.

He picked one up, slid a knife under it, making sure the membrane was severed, and then asked, "Tabasco?"

With another small smile, she nodded. "A few drops."

He obliged, then touched the edge of the shell to her fingers, she took it and then he watched her lips as she opened her mouth. The oyster slid in. She bit down once, then swallowed.

Watching her eat could be habit forming. He had to distract his unruly libido. He picked up another oyster, prepped it, and enjoyed the salty flavor as it slid over his tongue and down his throat. It made him want to taste something else salty sweet.

He dropped some Tabasco on another oyster and gave it to her.

"Two is my limit, unless they're cooked," she said.

"Leaves more for me." He was about ready to believe the old tales about shellfish as aphrodisiacs. He was half hard, just from watching her.

"So, you're from Richmond, and your mom taught you to be a Southern gentleman."

Mention of his mother dampened any stirred feelings of lust. He swallowed then said, "She tried. She's from Georgia."

"And that explains your name."

He chuckled. Sometimes he wondered if his parents had named him Ashley just to make his life difficult. If they had, it worked. Ashley Wilkes may have been the idol of Scarlet in <u>Gone with the Wind</u>, but most people thought of Ashley Judd or at least a girl, when they heard the name <u>Ashley</u>.

"Tell me about your family," he asked, hoping to avoid the topic of his own.

She shrugged. "We're pretty normal."

The rest of the evening was spent in superficial discussion. He was afraid to dig too deeply. She seemed wary of showing any emotion other than pleasant companionship.

Dinner was good, but did nothing to satisfy the hunger rising inside him, for her.

By the time they started home, the snow had stopped. The thick, white blanket cast its own ethereal light and sheltered the ground hidden beneath. The contours of the land provided shading and shadows. If he hadn't been driving, he would have stopped and just stared at it.

He didn't think Danni would appreciate parking. He suppressed a shudder at the thought. High School. Dating. Being thirty something and dating was almost worse.

The roads were a bit slick. He concentrated on driving while Danni tuned the radio to Christmas music. The drive was silent other than Danni as she hummed or sang along. Last night he thought her voice sounded rich. He'd been right.

Safely at her house, he escorted her to her front door, where she pulled him just inside. "Thank you, for dinner and everything."

"You're welcome." Afraid to do too much or say something that would scare her off, he said, "I would like to see you again."

"I need a little time to think," she said.

Ashley swallowed. If she couldn't handle what he did, it was best to end things now. No one else had ever lasted past a few dates. But, he wanted this to be different. He wanted to leave her with a promise, something for her to think about, to show what he thought.

He slid his hands around her waist, pulled her up against him, let the desire out and kissed her with all the power he could put in a gentle touch. Then, he teased her with his tongue. Her mouth opened and she kissed him back.

It took all his concentration not to pull back in surprise.

Mouth molded to hers, he tried to pull all reluctance out of her. He wanted her, and wanted her to know it. Unless she was numb from the waist down, she could feel his growing erection. This was going too fast, even for him.

Slowly, he pulled away, and caught his breath.

With his thumbs, he traced her cheekbones. "I'll call?"

She nodded, then rose up on her toes and brushed her lips against his. Another surprise.

"Drive safely," she whispered.

The frigid air felt really good. Maybe he should walk home? No, a cold shower would do.

Somehow, he drove a mile with his cock aching and his mind on his bewitching neighbor.

Physically stunned, mentally shaken to her soul, Danni stumbled into her bedroom and tried to make her mind work. She had to think, had to think if she wanted to see him again.

Oh, yeah. She wanted to see him. But, could she deal with it? The emotional baggage was more than she wanted to lug around.

When he kissed her, it was as if some electrical current flowed from him to her, from the top of her head to her toes. He left her body warm and wet, wanting.

She slipped on a nightgown, then wandered into the great room. With the back of her hand she pushed the drape away. The snow was a gleaming white quilt, blanketing the landscape. The nearly full moon peeked through the rapidly flowing clouds, filling the night with light. A beautiful, cold, winter night.

She'd swear her lips still tingled from Ashley's kiss. Was it just sexual combustion? Should she see him again?

Turning away from the window, Colin's picture stared at her, silent.

Should she see Ashley when every thought of his profession reminded her of the fear that had slunk around her spine and lodged in her stomach through the years of her marriage?

The fear had been there, eating at her in Australia, Malaysia, The Ring, Monte Carlo, Brazil, the U.S. Grand Prix--wherever they were. The Formula One cars would flash past, and over the whine of the engines, she listened for the sound of a crash she prayed would not come.

She stared at the photo, trying to recall the timbre of Colin's voice, the scent of his skin. It eluded her now.

For a week after his death, she'd held his pillow, buried her face in it, breathing in his scent, yearning to feel his body beside her. But in the chilly hours of the night, he was only a phantom.

She was alone.

And, it was her fault.

In the years since, she'd prayed Colin had forgiven her. She hadn't the heart to forgive herself.

Two days later her phone rang at ten o'clock in the morning.

"Hello?"

"Did I wake you?"

How completely depressing. Danni, after finally falling asleep, spent the night in sensual dreams, and now, instead of her dream talking to her, it was her father.

"What do you think?" she asked, not bothering to hide the sleep--or the smile--from her voice.

"More than likely," he laughed.

"Most perceptive of you. How are you?"

"Oh, we're fine. Just wanted to call and see if you were doing all right."

Danni sat up, stretched her toes until her ankles popped. "I'm fine. Do you want to shop for Mom sometime this week?"

Married for over forty years, her father could not manage to Christmas shop for his wife without his daughter. What did he do before she was old enough to go with him?

"In a couple of days, when the snow has melted a bit."

"Sounds good to me."

"Danni, is anything going on with you?"

She would swear he had ESP. She'd been debating with herself for forty-eight hours. Should she, shouldn't she. What she should do was talk to her dad. He understood her better than anyone, maybe even better than she did.

"Not really, why?" she lied.

"Don't know," his inflection was quizzical. "I just thought maybe you'd met someone."

He was downright spooky. "I sort of have, but I haven't decided if I really want to date him," she confessed.

"You have a good head on your shoulders." He paused, then said, "Just remember honey, not everyone you care about will leave you."

If she'd had a mirror, Danni was sure she looked like a fish gulping for water.

Before she could think of anything to say, he said, "Well, I'll talk to you later. Love you."

That fast, he was off the phone.

Conversations with him were the antithesis of the ones Danni had with her mother, who could talk for hours about not much of anything. Her dad talked for two minutes and encapsulated the universe.

Giving up on understanding how he did it, Danni went back to the bath, turned on the shower. When the phone rang again, she almost ignored it, then rushed into the bedroom and picked it up just before voice mail would have taken care of it.

"Hello?"

"Good morning, Danni," said the voice she'd been dreaming about.

Chapter Three

Her spirits lifted. That feeling answered some of her questions. "Good morning,"

"I'm going for a walk. May I stop by?" Ashley asked.

"Sure. Give me a little time. I just got up."

"An hour okay?"

"Yeah." She smiled and hoped he would hear the teasing in her voice. "May I ask a question?"

"Sure."

"Do the other drivers give you a hard time about your name?"

He burst out laughing. "Only when I lose. I'll see you in an hour."

"Coffee or tea with your scones?" she asked quickly.

"Coffee, with my... whatever they are," he answered.

"Scones. I'll see if I can find the coffee pot. See you then."

Coffee pot? Where had she put it? Still nude, she went to the basement and searched her storeroom.

Ten minutes later she found the thing. She'd need it for Christmas anyway. She grabbed the bag of coffee out of the freezer. She had no idea if freezing it actually kept the coffee fresh, but it did keep the container out of her pantry.

She bolted up the stairs and practically ran through the

shower, did her hair, got her make up on, then stood and stared at the clothes in the closet.

He was coming for a cup of coffee, for heaven's sake, not a cocktail party. Jeans were fine. She slipped on a pair, then pulled on a long sleeved, pink, v-neck shirt. She dug her toes into a pair of warm, hard-soled slippers and charged into the kitchen.

Measuring spoon in hand, she glared at the coffee bag, and its lack of instructions. She never touched the stuff, consequently she only made it a couple of times a year.

The doorbell chimed. She nearly jumped out of her skin. "Coming!" she called out.

Mr. Gorgeous stood at her door, spectacular looking in jeans, leather jacket and sunglasses.

Butterflies appeared in her stomach.

After shedding his coat, he followed her into the kitchen. A laugh shimmered in his eyes, and one dark brow rose. "I see you found your coffee pot."

"Yeah, now if I could remember how much to use, I'd be a happy camper."

He took the spoon from her hand and picked up the grinder. "I think I can handle it."

She watched his nimble fingers as he went through the simple motions of making coffee. His hands would be strong, as would his body. They had to be to drive well.

His brilliant smile appeared. "Not many people lose their coffee pot, so I assume you don't drink it."

Danni smiled back.

"How do you get your caffeine?" he asked.

Waving her hand like a magician, she lifted the cozy off her teapot.

"Tea?" he sounded a little incredulous.

"With milk."

A very fake looking shudder shook his shoulders.

Pointing her chin at the big island worktop, and surrounding chairs, she said, "Take a seat."

While she got out the clotted cream, butter and lemon curd, she asked, "How was your walk?"

"Cold, but good."

If he was typical of the men she had known in the race world, he had a work out regimen. "Part of your exercise routine?"

"Yeah."

"What else do you do?"

"Weight training, biking, running. I work out--five, six days a week and have a personal trainer come in three times a week."

"Scones and coffee shouldn't ruin your diet." Coffee ready, she poured him a cup, got her tea, then sat in the tall swivel bar stool next to him.

"Thanks," he said, then took a sip. "You get your kitchen plan from the Iron Chef set?"

Danni smiled. The kitchen was her favorite room in the whole house. "Nope. But I like to cook."

He wrapped one hand around the big mug. His hands fascinated her. Quit staring and talk, her manners told her. "When did you move here?"

"September. Though I'm only here a couple of days at a time, until now."

"You had to wait until the race season was over?"

Her cup made a slight tic as it touched the granite surface. If he noticed her slightly shaking hands he didn't say anything. Score one for him.

He nodded. "It's a long haul. Testing starts in January, and the last race, Homestead, is the weekend before Thanksgiving."

She sighed. "And if you want the championship, you better not miss much."

Ashley nodded. "Not any."

Danni sucked in a deep calming breath, then, tried to put her jumbled feelings into words. "I've known you what-- four days?"

He nodded, his expression calm, waiting, and she wanted to kiss him. She might not be comfortable with what he did, but she liked him. "I -- do want to see you. If you want to see me." How horribly embarrassing, like she was begging for attention. Maybe, said a little voice in her head, she was.

A small smile turned up the corners of his mouth. "If I didn't want to see you, I wouldn't be here."

He leaned toward her. The butterflies in her stomach took wing. He brushed his fingertips along her cheek.

His lips were warm, the kiss tender. After far too short a time, he pulled away. Something softened in his green eyes.

"Do you have plans for the day?"

It took a second for her mind to work. She shook her head. "I have rehearsal tonight."

His frown was instant and curious.

She shrugged. "I sing some at my church here, and tonight is rehearsal."

Ashley felt a twinge of disappointment. He'd really hoped to spend the evening with her. He doubted she'd rearrange her life for him, though other people often did.

You're a singer?"

"Voice was my minor in college. I still dabble."

"I'd like to hear you sometime."

Her brows went up. It was charming. More so, because she didn't seem to realize it.

"Christmas Eve, I'll do <u>O Holy Night</u> all by myself."

Usually he spent Christmas trying not to argue with his parents. But they were out of the country on an extended vacation. He'd planned to go to Richmond and hang out. That plan had just gone in the scrap heap. He would stay here.

"You know," she chuckled, "I met Colin in a bar."

Ashley mentally blinked, trying to decide which part of her statement confused him the most, the complete change of subject or the sudden mention of her late husband.

She bit her lower lip and looked down. "I'm sorry. That was rude."

He wanted to know more about her. He shook his head. "It wasn't rude. But, what does singing on Christmas Eve have to do with meeting him in a bar?"

A sheepish grin made her eyes twinkle. "After I finished my master's degree, I felt like I'd been in school forever. So, I traveled around Europe. I picked up extra cash singing in bars. I met Colin at the pub near his house."

Now Ashley understood. "Did you know who he was?"

She shook her head. "I didn't know he was an up and coming, titled, wealthy guy. He was just...a guy. I think he liked that."

Something else Ashley understood. He swallowed the last bit of the tasty scone, which turned out to be savory biscuit type thing.

Talking about her dead husband made him uncomfortable, so he found another topic. He remembered a detail she'd mentioned at dinner. "So your dad was in the Air Force. What was it like, moving around all the time?"

Suddenly, she looked a lot more relaxed. "It wasn't too bad. But when I started high school, mom wanted me to have more stability. So, she got a teaching job here and we stayed put while dad roamed the world. After he retired, it was nice to have him home, even if I was grown." A chagrined look quirked across her face. "Then, I got married and started spending half the year in Scotland. That is where I got my doctorate," she said.

"In Scotland?"

She nodded. "University of St. Andrews. I worked on my

dissertation at tracks, to keep occupied."

There it was again, the hesitation and discomfort with the word track or race. So, he changed the subject again.

"I want to know more about your research career, what you do. Don't you publish?"

"I have some articles out there. But mostly I work for other people." She gave a self-deprecating shrug. "It's fun and the computer doesn't care if I am here, or in Scotland."

"The computer is how I finished my engineering degree last spring."

She grinned. "Congratulations."

"I'd only finished one year of college before I started driving full time." Much to his parents' dismay.

"With your schedule, finishing a degree is a feat. Your parents must be very proud."

Hardly. A knot appeared in his stomach. He stopped his usual reaction to the word parents and took a deep breath. "I guess."

An odd expression crossed her face as she tipped her head to one side.

"May I ask you something very personal?" she asked.

"I suppose."

"Why aren't you tripping over ladies who want to be with you?" His stomach untwisted.

He did, frequently. "Because, I am never sure if it's me, or if they want to be around racing, or with a driver. It's made me... picky."

She nodded, slowly. "Well, you don't have that worry with me. I been there, done that, and have the T-shirt." Her smile faded. "It's nice to know that someone is more interested in who you are, rather than what."

She certainly was intuitive.

"Driving is part of you, of who and what you are, but it's not all of you." Her face held a new seriousness. "You love it, don't you?"

"The competition, the adrenaline rush, being just on the edge of control, the speed. Yeah, I love it."

She looked up at him, blue eyes glistening. "Loving what you do is not altogether a bad thing."

"No, it's not." He wanted to make the sad look on her face go away. A warm, nervous quiver started low in his body. Hell with it, he gave up fighting. He kissed her, touched his tongue to her bottom lip and she opened her mouth. Hunger grew. For her, her company, her laugh.

His stomach growled, loudly. She lifted her head and laughed.

"I'm still hungry," he said. For more than food.

"How about pizza for lunch?"

They went to Randi's, a little neighborhood pizzeria. Danni swore they had the best pizza on the planet.

It had been fantastic. Ashley didn't want to go home. Not yet, and not alone. A grocery store in the strip mall had Christmas trees in the parking lot. Inspiration struck. "I think I want to put up a tree."

She glanced at him while she unlocked her car doors. "Real or artificial?"

Ashley thought about it. "Real. Want to take me shopping?"

"Why?" She eyed him suspiciously over the roof.

He shrugged. "I don't have any decorations."

"Nothing?" she asked.

He shook his head. "Nope."

Her expression turned incredulousness. "Nothing." She turned out of the parking lot onto Ralston Road.

"I was never at my house for Christmas." He'd never had a reason to decorate.

Danni made a face, like she has just bitten into a lemon, then rolled her eyes and said very clearly, "Men." She shook her head and sighed. "How tall a tree?"

"I don't know."

"Okay, let's figure out what we need." She looked at him. A slow smile lit her face. "You are in trouble now."

Hours later, he had a stand, lights, garland stuff, ornaments, a tree topper, a tree skirt-—who knew you needed a skirt for a tree?-- and, was a few hundred dollars lighter in the pocket. It had been worth it. Danni had smiled and chatted and made him laugh. He'd talked too. His usual reserve had checked out and was long gone. That surprised him.

It was dark. That made it tough to pick out a tree. And it was damned cold.

Danni stopped at the gate of his driveway and punched in the security code he gave her. "I'd wondered who'd bought this place. You left all the old trees. I like that."

The compliment made him happier about keeping them. "The land is what sold me."

"The house looked like it was falling down. Did you have to raze it and start all over?"

"Yep." He shook his head, catching his laugh. "The house was a pit. Rot, mold, flood damage, you name it. I wanted to save it, but it was too far-gone. The architect and engineer made blueprints of the existing house. There were old photos from 1876, right after it was built. We used those to copy the original elevations. The contractor salvaged everything inside they could, made copies of the original details, then tore it down and started all over again."

"You basically reconstructed the original house?"

The project had excited him almost as much as a win at Indy, and still did. "Yeah. Only bigger. It's what I wanted. Victorian-Prairie. Wrap around porch. Widow's walk. Observatory. The whole thing."

The tires crunched over the gravel of the quarter mile long drive way. "It was under construction for what? Two years?"

"Yeah, and worth every moment, and every penny. Everything, even if it looks old, is new." Even the 80-inch HDTV was hidden behind the doors to an old library cabinet he'd found in Charlotte.

"Where's the garage?" she asked.

Somehow it didn't surprise him that she would ask that.

He shook his head and chuckled. "Which one?" He pointed with his right hand. "The carriage house, about fifty feet behind the house, was in good shape. We built an apartment-guesthouse into the second story. We only had to clean up the ground floor, upgrade the plumbing and wiring--

Danni's laugh interrupted him. "And put in air conditioning and heat, so you wouldn't have to suffer."

"How'd you know?"

"We did the same thing."

They had so much in common. For her, some of it had to be very unpleasant.

"Big boys and their toys." Danni sighed. "The barn behind my house was converted to a detached garage. I've let some members of the car club store their cars there."

She didn't have to say it. It had been Colin's domain.

Not wanting her to dwell on the similarities between him and her late husband, he went on, "Behind the carriage house is a barn, that's a barn."

"You have horses?" she sounded almost shocked.

"Not yet, but someday. I like to ride."

"Me too. We could never find the time to do much of it."

The F1 season had fewer races, but they did a lot more travel-ing. It was hard to do anything except travel, do the appearances, practice and race.

It's what you did if you wanted to win.

Danni parked at the top of the drive. After several trips to empty the car, he gave her the grand tour. They roamed through oversized the three-story house. She asked all kinds of questions. Ashley wondered what she thought as he reviewed his choices, trying to see it through her eyes.

The furniture was either antiques or reproductions. While it looked right, it didn't feel like home. He hoped it would just take time.

Danni made him feel at ease in a way he'd never felt with a woman, with anyone, at least not this fast. And, he had no idea why. But, he liked it. No, he liked her.

"How did you get started racing?"

In another turn that surprised him, he answered her, "My grandfather. Started racing carts on weekends when I was eight. Grandpa helped me with the cars, picked me up from school with the racecar loaded on the trailer. We stayed in a camper on his pickup. Ate sandwiches my grandma had packed."

Those memories were like a warm blanket on a cold day.

"I took accelerated classes in high school, graduated when I was seventeen, started college the next fall. But I raced every weekend. What I earned, and my grandparents, funded it. I was running dirt track, sprint cars."

Then came the hard part. "When I turned eighteen, my parents delivered their ultimatum. Full time college, no racing, or no place to live. So I packed up and left."

He hadn't bothered to tell them he was leaving.

Danni remained quiet, her open look inviting him to continue.

"I had a bit of money, so I bought the truck, trailer, racecar and camper from my grandparents. I lived in it for a while."

They had offered to give him the rig, but he'd turned them down.

"Lucky for me, I signed a contract with Evan Murphy for a full time ride when I was nineteen. I made the Cup series only three years later." Saving the embarrassment of either going home or asking his grandparents for money. "I haven't looked back."

Danni leaned forward, touched his hand. "Nor should you." She chewed on her bottom lip for a second. "When did your grand-parents die?"

The question came from nowhere, like a blade that cut through him, sharpening the memory of the loss. "My grandfather when I was twenty four, Grandma three years ago. How'd you know?"

She squeezed his hand. "If they were alive, you'd still live in Richmond."

The words stopped him dead in his mental tracks.

Damn it. She was right.

More uncomfortable from her intuition than her comment, he turned the tables. "Why did you stay in Denver?" he asked

Slowly, she turned the pop can in her hand. "Colin wanted me to be able to spend time with my family and friends. He started Vintage Racing with the locals when he wasn't racing something else."

She looked... wistful. Too tempted to resist, he leaned closer and kissed her cheek. "I am not quite that bad."

Her brows lifted. "Good thing." She looked at her watch. He glanced at the clock. Nearly six.

"I have to go," she said.

He had hoped she would forget about her rehearsal.

"I want to see your TF first," she said.

Bundled up against the cold, he flicked on the lights in the carriage house. His pale blue MG TF sat close to the near wall.

"Is that the camper?" Her voice held a note of surprise. "You've kept it all these years?"

"Keeps me humble." It reminded him of what he'd gone through to get where he was.

Ashley guided her through the space, past his SUV, the

Corvette to the MG.

"It's really nice," Danni said. "It's my favorite MG, after my MG A of course. Do you drive it often?"

"Not enough. But someday..."

"So, it is ready when you are."

With his hand at the small of Danni's back, he led her back around the house and to her car. It gave him an excuse to touch her. He didn't want to let her go, but the day was over.

"Drive safe," he said. He slid his hands into her hair, bent down enough to kiss her.

The light weight of her hands wrapped around his waist. She opened her mouth under the pressure of his kiss. He soaked in her warmth and kissed her until he felt her shiver.

"What are you doing Monday?" he whispered.

Her head cocked to one side. "Why?

"I have to do a photo shoot. Come with me?"

"Maybe."

He realized how badly he wanted her to go. It would be a lot more fun with her there.

"Well, think about it. You will go tree shopping with me day after tomorrow, right?"

Her grin a bit bemused, she nodded.

Once her headlights disappeared down the drive, he zipped into the house. How to spend the remaining hours of the night? He moved furniture around, making room for the tree he didn't have. Called his business manager, his PR rep Terri, talked to his crew chief, Kenny Morgan, to his long time friend and spotter, Cade Smith, to Evan Murphy, the team owner and to his teammate, Josh Pierce.

Phone calls exhausted, he surfed through the sports channels, looking for anything to hold his attention. Pro Rally reruns? Nope. No football on, he didn't get to watch much of that. He worked on

Sundays. He stopped flipping as one of the history channels caught his attention. The show was about ships. Danny said she was doing research on eighteenth and nineteenth century ship design. Maybe he would learn something. He did, after all, understand engineering.

It was going to be a long time until the day after tomorrow.

The phone rang. Danni jumped. She glanced at the time in the tiny box at the bottom of the computer screen. Just after two. Not four. Four. The time when bad news is delivered.

"Hi, dear."

Danni sighed and smiled as she shook her head. "Hi yourself, Mom. What's going on?"

"Oh, nothing," Laurie Hopkins answered. "Just thought I would call and see how you are." That was the standard opening line for every phone call.

"I'm fine. I'll be over as soon as I finish up with the Portsmouth Naval Museum online."

"That sounds interesting."

Danni shook her head, not falling for the ploy. "I'll tell you all about it when I get there. See you soon. Bye." Sometimes that was the best way to get off the phone.

She shook her head again as she remembered the conversation they'd had in October. It had been the anniversary of Colin's death. She doubted her mom had realized it when she called. It was the same conversation they had every fall.

Danni always came to Denver for the holidays, and every year, her mother would call her in Scotland and ask if she was coming home. It would be comical, if it were someone else's mother.

Danni would say, "I'll be there in another week or so. By the way, that will be a month before Thanksgiving."

"I wish you would stay with us." The disembodied voice would say, with just a hint of pleading. It was the other thing that was said every year.

"Mom, I have a house in Denver, I don't need to stay with you and Dad." If she had, there would have been matricide.

"I wish you could spend more time here. After all, you don't have any family in Scotland."

No, she had peace and quiet in Scotland and Edward, Jane, their adorable four-year-old daughter, and precocious six-year-old son, and Colin's parents. She loved them, her house and her neighbors in the village.

Sometimes Danni wondered if her mother's major goal in life was to make her feel guilty. The best way to fight it was ignore it.

Danni put her hands to her temples and pressed gently. She loved her mom, but sometimes wondered what planet she'd been born on.

Unfortunately, Danni thought she came from the same planet.

Even when she was alone, her thoughts would chase each other around in circles or take huge leaps from one topic to something that seemed completely unrelated. Maybe that was how she could read three or four books at a time, and keep track of all of them?

Blinking to refocus, Danni refined her search for early steam powered naval vessels. She'd always thought of them as a middle nineteenth century development, but they weren't. There were steam powered dredges in operation in the 1820's. As subject matter, she'd thought this would be pretty dry, but it hadn't been.

Pretty dry...about ships. How come she could never come up with a pun that good when she was talking?

She hit the print button, getting the bibliographic information she needed.

Ashley didn't seem to mind her conversation, even her abrupt changes of topic. He found her humorous. At least he smiled and laughed at the appropriate moments.

Talking about himself so much had surprised her.

When the light in the carriage house had shown so brightly on the old camper, something in her heart had twisted. Keeping him humble? Maybe. It proved what he had done, on his own, without any help. Prove it, to whom?

How did Ashley handle the attention of big time stock car racing? Interviews, appearances, sponsor meetings, charity functions, surrounded by people, when in essence he was a solitary man?

So solitary he'd bought a house half way across the country from the race shop, his friends and connections. Was it what he said? That he needed a place away from all the demands? It almost made no sense. Staying in Denver even part of the time wouldn't make his life less hectic, but more so.

During the quiet of the night, Danni's thoughts returned to the question of why she wanted to see Ashley.

He was devastatingly attractive. She wanted him, in a physical sense. Who wouldn't?

He was wonderful company, funny, engaging, intelligent, though he played down that aspect, and attentive. She enjoyed being around him.

Okay, so what was wrong with him?

Self centered. One simply had to have a good-sized ego to have the confidence to drive a car at two hundred miles per hour. Danni had not seen that particular side of him, but she knew it existed.

His career was all consuming.

What was she afraid of? The terror that had ruled her when Colin stepped into a racecar? Or, the haunting knowledge that somehow she'd caused that wreck?

At ten in the next morning, Danni shut down her computer and called Ashley. He appeared in his SUV twenty minutes later.

Time for the Tree Cutting Expedition.

She kissed him on the cheek at the door, and drew him inside. "Do you have some old sheets?" she asked.

Even his frown was handsome. "No. Why?"

"Wrap around the tree, keep it from drying out too much during transport and protect the roof of the car. How about a saw? And tie down ropes?"

"Those I have."

As she went down the hall toward the bedroom, she glanced over her shoulder. "You aren't hopeless then."

The linens were in the closet in the master bedroom, next to the bath. She threw a couple of older sheets over her arm and turned. He had followed her.

They were in her bedroom.

An odd enchantment swirled around them. He stood still, eyes intent. Her heart thumped loudly as she looked at him.

Maybe they could forget about Christmas tree cutting? No, no, no. Too soon, her brain screamed.

She moved past him briskly, breaking the sensual tension that had nearly overwhelmed her.

"I think you've been on these expeditions before," he said, voice sounding normal, from a foot behind her.

"My folks and I used to do this every year when my Dad was home."

"So, you're a knowledgeable tree hunter."

She heard the laughter in his voice and smiled in return. "You have to be very careful. Evergreens are notoriously sneaky."

"I have this sudden vision of killer Christmas trees," he said.

They drove north, to Red Feather Lakes.

Ten miles north of town, she screwed up her courage and asked, "Why did you move to Denver, really?" She wasn't sure he would answer, at least not fully.

"I'd been here on vacations. I like the mountains and outdoor stuff and frankly, it's a beautiful city. There's plenty of good racing around. But it's not a hot bed of rabid stock car fans."

"This is frightening. You're making perfect sense." she teased again.

He glanced at her, saw the slight upturn of her lips, then turned his attention back to the road. "My address in Richmond turned up on the Internet. People drove by and honked, shouted. Most were harmless, but not all. It was hell for my neighbors."

"Won't someone do some digging and post it again?"

He pointed at his chest, self-aggrandizing. "I am a corporation."

"Really? You don't look fat enough."

He liked her peculiar sense of humor. He laughed quietly. "I formed a corporation years ago that has nothing to do with my name. The corporation purchased the house here and bought a more secluded place in Richmond, where I stay when I'm there."

"Aren't your parents in Richmond?"

Less than a mile a way. "Well, yeah, but I don't think they miss me."

Danni frowned.

They lived in Windsor Farms, and now, so did he, and still they didn't see much of each other.

He could almost hear her mind working. She and her parents were close. He was as far from that as possible, without committing a criminal act. Shrugging, he said, "They don't really approve of what I do."

She leaned back, a puzzled frown pulled her brows together. "Why not? You're successful, wealthy. What's not to approve?"

Deeper hurt surfaced, but without thinking about it more he answered, "I'm beneath their dignity. They'd feel better about it if I drove Grand Touring Cars or Formula, but I don't. They think the average stock car fan is an ignorant redneck, sucking on a can of beer. I guess they think the same of me." Damn it, it still upset him.

She smiled softly and touched his hand. "We both know otherwise."

"Doesn't matter. It's what they think, and I can't change it." He drew a deep breath. "It's funny, they wanted to have a party for me when I got my degree." He swallowed bitter bile. "They didn't offer any celebration when I won my first Championship, or the second or the third. Only my degree was worthy of celebration."

"What do your folks do?"

"My dad is the CFO of a pharmaceutical company and my mom..." What was she? "My mom is a professional social climber."

Danni's brows rose dramatically, her fingers covered her mouth, but he saw a hint of a smile. "I don't think I've heard anyone described that way. I'll have to remember it." The humor faded. "I'm sorry."

With a shrug, he said, "It's not like it was horrible. More like they forgot I was around. Dad worked a lot and Mom did her best to make sure he was successful, and appeared to be. So, I went to all the right schools, joined the right clubs, did all the right things..."

"Like dance lessons for those society type parties." She grinned. It lifted his mood. "Yeah." He nodded. "Like that."

At the ranger station they bought their permit.

"One tree or two?" Ashley asked her.

"I have an artificial tree." She grinned. "I'm allergic to ever-greens. I used to sneeze through every Christmas."

Ashley laughed.

The ranger gave them a map. Ashley stood silently beside her, not saying a word, while the ranger gave her directions, too.

Back in the car, he asked, "Why did you ask for directions? The map is a good one."

"Because, I am spatially challenged." She fastened her seatbelt. "Maps and I do not get along."

The barest sliver of a grin appeared at one corner of his mouth. "Spatially challenged? Is that what it is?"

"Yep." She managed not to smile. "At least I don't spend hours at a time driving around in circles."

Ashley leaned toward her, a devil-may-care look in his eyes. "So, you are a road course kind of woman?"

Danni didn't know what to say, so, she decided for once in her life, she'd stay quiet.

"Good thing I'm good at those, too," he said.

Faster than she could think, his mouth was on hers. The kiss didn't last long, though somehow, it seemed filled with a promise of something more.

Without a single wrong turn, they reached the cutting area, where Danni suggested they find a tree close to the road. Ashley found a ten footer fifty yards away.

Not exactly her definition of close.

She tried to talk him out of it, then gave in. "Ooohkay, but don't say I didn't warn you."

Ashley cut it and Danni admired the view, of him, as he worked. The tree whistled through the air and landed with a soft thud on the foot deep snow.

She put on her gloves. They both grabbed a part of the trunk and pulled.

Huffing for air, they stopped after about twenty feet. "Didn't I say something about 'close to the road'?" Her hands were on her hips, but she smiled.

Ashley grinned at her. "Well, yeah, but how am I supposed to believe a woman about distances?"

"I think I'm offended. I'm the experienced tree hunter."

He gave her a bow. "I yield to your expertise. Ready to go?"

She lifted her end--the top--of the tree. She remembered doing this with her parents.

Last night, while she'd helped them decorate their tree, Danni didn't mention Ashley. Her mom would start making wedding plans and her dad would ask fifty questions about him, where he came from and worst of all, what he did.

While she and her mom had finished the tree decorations, her dad had fixed dinner. He'd been in charge of the turntable and CD player. Christmas music had flowed through the house. They sang along more often than not. She loved them deeply, even if they drove her crazy. Sometimes she forgot how much fun they could be.

Suddenly she thought of Ashley. She had a hard time comprehending how a child could feel forgotten in his own home. He'd said it hadn't been that bad, but Danni couldn't stop the image of a lonely boy who'd grown into a lone man.

"How you doing?" Ashley asked, interrupting her thoughts, as Danni twisted her body to put both hands on the tree trunk.

"Wonderful," she said, her voice dripped with sarcasm.

"Good. Stop for a second."

Danni let her end down, and looked at him. Breathing hard, he grinned then winked.

"Isn't this fun?" she teased.

"You didn't adequately describe this marvelous experience," he said, dryly.

"It is marvelous." She smiled. "When you cut the tree closer-to-the-road."

He laughed.

It took them another half hour to get the tree back to the car.

Danni stripped off her gloves, jammed them into her coat pockets, wrapped the tree in the sheets, and secured it with some bungi cords. Then, they lifted the tree up.

Ashley had the job of tying it down.

She unzipped her coat, to let in some cool air, then leaned over, her hands in the fresh snow.

He stood on the open door frame, busy with bungi's and rope.

It wasn't fair to hit a man with a snowball while he was perched on the doorsill, but who said a snowball fight was fair?

The snow exploded out of its loosely packed, baseball-sized configuration, smack in the middle of his chest.

His mouth slightly open, he looked down at the spot she had hit. His eyes got very round. He moved so quickly, she had no time to prepare.

He tackled her, back into the snow. "Now, you are in trouble." Straddling her, he flung loose snow at her with both hands.

She picked up as much of the fluffy white stuff as she could and rubbed it in his hair.

"Unfair! You're wearing a hat." He laughed.

"I know how to dress for a snowball fight!"

"Oh yeah?" He pulled her hat off, crumpled it in one hand. "How about for this?"

He slipped one cold hand under her neck.

"Ack."

His weight shifted, moved over her. His face was flushed, whether from the cold or something else, Danni didn't know.

In a heartbeat, his mouth was on hers, and he kissed her, long, slow, and sumptuously. She closed her eyes, bathed in the heat of his body and the chill of the snow.

"I think I could like tree hunting," he murmured. He held out his hand to her, she took it, and he helped her up.

She didn't let go. She stepped closer, wrapped her arms around his neck, and kissed him. Her tongue dipped into his mouth. She nibbled on his lower lip. She wanted to wrap him around her. Finally, she leaned back. His arms supported her as she ran her fingers along the line of his jaw. Dark stubble tickled her fingertips.

He turned his head, kissed her palm. The tiny touch sent a shiver down her spine that warmed every inch of her.

If they had been at her house, or his, she knew she would not stop.

"Not that I mind kissing you, but we should go," he said quietly.

He opened her car door. Before she could step on the running board, he lifted her off her feet and set her gently on the seat. The feel of his hands on her waist, under her knees, strong and gentle, was enough to make her sizzle.

Grinning, he put her hat on her head. "I don't want you to get cold."

"I'm not cold, now," she complained, very half-heartedly. She had never made love in a car. Would it be very gauche to ask him to slide in beside her, or crawl into the back?

He got in, turned the key, and looking ahead said, "Thank you for coming with me, it really has been fun." The smile that lit his face made her feel as if she were glowing.

The drive home was mostly in companionable silence, with the Trans Siberian Orchestra on the CD player.

They turned into his driveway. Danni wanted to stay and help him decorate. It would give her an excuse and she really did enjoy it. But, she wouldn't invite herself. No matter how badly she wanted to.

"Will you stay for dinner?" he asked.

Maybe he was reading her mind.

Chapter Four

$\mathcal{D}$anni stared straight up for about half an hour then rolled onto her side, and glanced at the alarm clock. Almost two. She had been in bed since midnight.

The first hour had been spent re-living the evening. They'd set up the tree, put the lights on, had dinner, poured a bit of wine, then finished the decorations. She'd enjoyed every moment of it. They had turned off the lamps, curled up on the comfy couch, cuddled together and watched the lights on the tree blink. He had not pressed her. He'd barely traced his fingers along her breasts.

Ashley drove her home, walked her to her door, kissed her goodnight and left.

Damn, but the man could kiss. Her toes were permanently curled.

Danni licked her lips, in a valiant, though futile effort to regain the sense of him touching her.

She had spent the last hour thinking about <u>him</u>. There was no doubt she liked him, wanted to be near him.

Fear lurked in the depths of her brain. It was stupid, beyond stupid, but there it was.

She thought of Colin, of the sudden emptiness. The inability to say <u>I love you</u>, one more time.

Ashley wondered if Danni was asleep, peaceful in slumber. He was wide-awake. After he got home from the quick trip to her house, he had plopped on the couch in front of the television. He hadn't moved since then, except to shift his weight.

Danni had entered his life a week ago. Now, he had a hard time getting through a day without calling her, or seeing her. At some point, every day, she danced through his brain.

What was wrong with him?

Women were something he enjoyed for a while, then, moved on. Yet, right now, when he thought about where he would be in a few weeks, or months, Danni was in the picture in his mind. <u>That</u> had never happened before.

He'd had one focus in his life, drive as fast as he could on a track. Usually, by Christmas he itched to get back, ready for the season to start.

When they talked about racing, he saw anxiety, nearly fear, wash across her face, and fill her eyes.

He couldn't blame her. She lost her husband to racing.

How did he feel about her?

Confused?

Oh, yeah.

Pleased to have drawn her attention, spend so much time with her? That, too.

If they were to go on, he needed to know if she could deal with what he did.

Suddenly, he knew he wanted their relationship to continue, badly. Wanted to be with her. Hold her. Talk to her. Make love to her.

As Ashley turned onto the entrance road to Jefferson County airport Danni asked, "Where are we going?"

"Las Vegas."

"What!"

"It's just for the day."

"But Ashley..."

He took her hand, led her up the steps of his jet. His pilot stood just at the door. "Good morning." Gray haired, gray eyed, divorced and serious about his flying, Pete Morris was the perfect private pilot.

"Pete, this is my friend, Danni Scott," Ashley introduced them, and noticed Pete's appreciative, if subtle, appraisal of Danni.

Ashley hoped his proprietary hand on Danni's back answered Pete's perusal.

"You want to take the controls today?" he asked.

"Not today."

Pete gave a quick nod. "Flight plan's filed. Pre-check is done. We're about ready to take off."

"Great." Still holding Danni's hand, Ashley tugged her into the passenger compartment. He'd been apprehensive about this, not sure how she would react.

"Yours?" Danni glanced around him at the interior of the jet.

"The first really big purchase I made."

She sat, and fumbled a little with the seatbelt. "It's a lot easier with your own plane."

It was not a question. Had Colin had a plane? Was that what was making her, if not nervous, upset?

"Thank you for coming with me." He squeezed her hand.

Her brows pulled together in a suspicious frown. "Why did you want me to?"

"I...didn't want to go alone." That much was true. Might as well be honest. "I wanted to spend some time with you. It is just for the day."

The wrinkle above the bridge of her nose slowly smoothed out, and her eyes took on a twinkle. "I suppose you really weren't devious." A tiny smile turned up her lips. "You just didn't bother to tell me the photo shoot was in Vegas."

Ashley shrugged. He'd been afraid if he told her everything, she might not have come.

"You've done these before?" It was less question than comment.

Danni nodded. "Some, though not as much as you might think. I didn't usually go to the team shoots. The team is a big deal in F1."

Ashley thought for a few seconds more, staring up at the ceiling. "I would think that could be a marketing advantage."

A deep, soft chuckle drew him back to face her. "I can just see the Ferrari team hawking beer in German, Italian, and English."

"And translated into how many more?" Ashley added with a smile.

"Oh, couple hundred." Her smile widened.

He raised his brows. "I should know, but I don't. Is Formula One really that big?"

"Only thing bigger is soccer. There's something like four hundred television networks that cover it. It's just not huge here. It's one of the reasons F1 would love to get an American driver. Gather some interest."

"And the reason American stock cars would love to get a European driver," he said.

Danni nodded. She understood the sport very well.

"The debacle at Indy did not help F1's cause in the States. Nothing like having most of the teams refuse to race because of tire issues," Danni said.

Ashley shook his head. "We would never have let that happen."

"So what is the drill for today?"

Ashley noted the quick change of subject. She was knowledgeable, intelligent and conversant on almost any topic. She never talked about racing for very long. "Well, we fly in to McCarran, get picked up by the PR folks, go to the shoot, have some dinner, go home. Unless you would rather eat in Denver."

She leaned close and kissed him. Soft. Quick. He could smell her perfume. He wanted to run his hands up under the fabric of her purple sweater. Instead, he drew a breath through his nose, drinking in her scent.

"It depends on how windy it is in Vegas," she said. "I hate that dry wind."

It took him a second to understand what the hell she was talking about. Dinner. That was it. He kissed the tip of her nose, then tried to relax.

They spent the flight time in conversation interspersed with comfortable silence.

Near the end of the flight, Ashley stiffened his backbone and told her the thing he'd held back. "You should know," he said, as he watched her face for reactions, "the shoot is at the track."

Her face became almost a blank, then she looked away.

"No driving or anything, just pictures, me and the car."

Something invisible, three or four feet away from her on the floor, had her complete, unblinking attention.

"Danni?"

Her blue eyes were round, wide. He touched her cheek. "I know racing bothers you. I thought something like this might help."

Danni felt so comfortable with him most of the time. Part of her resented him for realizing how much racing disturbed her; another part was grateful he did.

The morning went much as Ashley predicted. A PR guy named Gerrard met them at the airport. If he was trying to impress her, he failed. Miserably. He worked for the jeans company who proudly displayed Ashley's name and face, and butt, on their ads.

It was still early morning. The sky was clear with a line of thin, white clouds. The wind was tolerable. They drove west to the Las Vegas Motor Speedway. Danni swallowed the growing lump in her throat and did her best to look calm.

The limo cruised to a stop. "Here we are," Gerrard pronounced. She rolled her eyes at his obviousness. As if they couldn't tell they had arrived at a giant set of grandstands surrounding a big oval track.

The driver opened the door, and standing a few feet from the car, Danni saw one of the tallest women she'd ever met. She was about six four, thin, with very long brown hair, clipped at the back to keep it out of the way.

"Hey, Ashley, welcome to Las Vegas." The voice was feminine and almost soft, as if she were trying to compensate for her height.

She was Ashley's publicist, Terri Fuller, and she quickly took over.

"We've set up by the garage."

Danni's heartbeat thundered in her ears as she walked with Ashley down and across the track, following Terri. It looked different from what she was used to. Oval, high banked, without a kink or turn in sight. No noise of voices or the growl of engines. Still, mingled with the winter air was the smell of oil, gas and tar. She could swear she smelled exhaust.

Ashley gripped her hand just a little tighter, as if sensing her tension.

Breathe, deeper. Now was not the time to hyperventilate. It wasn't a freaking race, just a photo shoot. Advertisements. Jeans encasing Ashley's rather great looking butt.

She could do this.

Did she want to?

Danni could feel Ashley's gaze. It was open, inquiring and said are you okay, almost as if he had spoken aloud. She managed a small smile.

"It'll only take a few hours," he said.

One of Ashley's racecars sat in front of one of the empty garages. Her stomach twisted.

"It's a show car. Doesn't even have an engine."

Danni blinked at his calm statement. "No engine?"

"Nope, only an old car body, I probably raced it a couple of years ago. We take out the engines and use the body for appearances and stuff."

He was trying to reassure her. It was--sweet.

She tried to calm down as the advertising agency and the photographers hauled Ashley away for makeup and clothes.

"Have you known him long?" Terri asked as she pointed Danni to a place where they would both be out of the way.

Danni shook her head. "No. He lives down the street."

Terri smiled, then chuckled. "The new house?"

Danni nodded. "How about you? How long have you known him?"

"About eight years. Our firm has several drivers on the client list. As busy as he is, he's easy to deal with. Where did you meet?"

Danni answered and found as they talked that she relaxed, a little. And, she liked the tall, older woman. Danni had gotten her breathing close to normal when Terri said, "I have to admit I was a bit surprised to see you get out of the limo. Ashley rarely brings anyone with him."

Nearly shocked, Danni said, "Really. That's a surprise. I would think, with his looks..." She remembered what Ashley had said about being picky.

Terri smiled and nodded. "Yeah, you would think so."

She might have said more, but at that moment, Ashley came out of the trailer they used for a dressing room. He looked gorgeous.

They shot photos of him walking around the car, as if checking it out, leaning against it, signing autographs.

Through the process, Danni focused on staying calm, breathing deeply, and maintaining her conversation with Terri.

"Okay, everybody take a break," the lead photographer shouted to the area in general. There were sodas and snacks in easy reach. Ashley waved Terri to him, had a brief conversation, then once again, disappeared with several other people, into the trailer.

Gerrard, still trying to be officious, joined Danni and Terri, attempting to impress them with his vast knowledge of everything and everyone who was anyone.

Mentally, Danni ran through the list of people she knew, whose names she could drop, but she'd never been one to do that unless very hard pressed.

She was getting close, though.

Gerrard bobbed his head, and asked, "So, Danni, what do you do?" His tone insinuated that as a small blonde, she was only capable of being a bimbo. It wasn't the first time, and it wouldn't be the last.

In her best-cultured voice, she said, "I do research for projects- -books, television, film."

His shoulders wiggled some more. "How did you get into that? Sounds rather specialized."

"She has a PhD in history from the University of St. Andrews, in Scotland," Ashley's voice rang through the garage, though he stood only a few feet away.

"Oh, well. How nice."

Danni almost did not hear Gerrard's response. She was too busy staring at Ashley. The driver's suit covered him from neck to foot, designed to snugly hug him.

For protection.

They used to be called fire suits.

Fire. Wrecks. She closed her eyes, took a deep breath.

"You okay?" Ashley's voice was soft.

She opened her eyes. He crouched down in front of her.

Pulling together the threads of her tangled brain, she managed to nod. "I'm fine."

His eyes narrowed, focused sharply on her, then relaxed. He might not believe her, but he wasn't going to press it.

With a quick smile, he got up, strolled to the car, and they started shooting again.

Danni wasn't sure she could watch. She wished she'd brought a book or something to occupy her while Ashley got in and out of the car, posed beside it, got spritzed with water, and messed up his hair, looking like he'd just pulled off his helmet.

She didn't want to watch, but could not look away.

Something warm touched her wrist. Terri's fingers lightly touched Danni's arm.

Terri said, "They're almost done. We've got a late lunch put together in one of the suites, you want to go now?"

They were simply taking pictures, but her pulse still thudded in her ears and she felt half sick. How big a coward was she?

She could just leave. She had the excuse.

No. She was stronger than this. "I'll wait."

Danni was certain the other woman had sensed how disturbed she was, or maybe Ashley had told her, but Terri didn't say anything else about it.

When they had finished with the pictures the crew pushed the car onto the waiting platform of a tractor-trailer rig, then the lift whined, taking the car up into the top of the transport.

Ashley had likewise disappeared, undoubtedly to change back into his street clothes.

"You know," Terri's voice caught Danni's attention, "it should be illegal for any man to be that good looking, and that short."

The tension broke, drained away. Danni laughed. "He's not short."

Terri grinned. "My hubby is six eight. Ashley is short."

"You are probably nicely..." Danni frowned, searched for the right word. "Balanced. You know, one not too much shorter than the other."

"Well, I think you and Ashley could be nicely balanced."

Danni did something she hadn't done in a long time. She blushed.

Lunch was light, a meat and cheese tray, salad, soda and wine. The food looked appetizing, but she wasn't hungry. Her stomach was still too nervous. She popped open a diet soda as Ashley poured a glass of red wine.

"No, I'm not flying," he told Terri with a smile.

Ashley mingled with the people from the clothing manufacturer and the photographer, who apparently had worked with him several times before.

Danni tried to stay in the background, but noticed several people glance her way more than once. Especially the women.

After about an hour, Ashley asked if she was ready to leave. She was, more than ready. Gerrard had, thankfully to Danni's thinking, disappeared with the corporate types. Terri walked to the limo with them, said good-bye, and left them on their own with the driver.

"You want to stay here for a bit? Or go home?" he asked.

"Home, if that's ok with you."

In the car, he slipped his arm around her. "I'm sorry if you were uncomfortable."

Snuggled into his shoulder, she felt warmer and calmer.

Colin hadn't normally noticed her discomfiture. Or, if he did, he chose to ignore it. He had not been unkind, just not comforting.

"I'm okay, really. By the way, you look really good in those jeans."

Ashley tossed back his head and laughed. "Glad you think so."

They spent the flight back cuddled together on the seat, essentially a couch, with seatbelts. One of the really nice things about private planes, no bothersome arm rests sticking you in the back.

Under Ashley's soothing, light massage, Danni drifted.

"We're landing." His deep, silky voice woke her. "Feel better?"

Danni nodded as she snicked the seatbelt into place.

"Where you want to eat? It's just before seven."

Despite heated kisses and wandering hands, he had yet to do what he really wanted, put her in his bed.

He hoped the time would be soon. He'd been afraid of scaring her off, so he'd kept the brakes on. Maybe it was time to shift gears?

The effect she had on him was so bizarre. Pleasing her made him feel good. Being with her, made him want to spend more time with her. Her smile made him want to smile.

In a quiet corner of the Burns Pub, she asked, "Why did you move to Denver? Really?"

He'd moved to a different neighborhood in Richmond, then pulled up all stakes and fled halfway across the country . Had he fled?

He realized there was something deeper. "I told you I wanted a change?"

She nodded.

"With my grandparents gone, except for convenience, there was no reason to stay."

Her head tilted to one side. "You must have left behind old friends."

"I did, but it's not like I never see them or talk to them." He spoke more to them now than when he lived a short drive away.

"And, I have made new friends."

She smiled softly.

It warmed his stomach, but his mind still churned over the ideas her question had provoked. "Sometimes, it feels all-consuming. I don't have much else in my life. Maybe I thought by changing things so much, I could separate it more."

"Your personal and professional life?"

"Yeah."

She looked away, down at some spot on the table. When she raised her eyes, she stared directly at him, as if she could see something he couldn't. "It's a part of you, you know." She shook her head. "A person can't do what you do without it being a part of them."

That was true, and they both knew it.

They sat in silence for a few minutes. He wished he knew what she was thinking.

Their entrees arrived. Between bites, she asked, "What are you doing Christmas Day?"

He shrugged.

"Come to my house?"

He'd heard a bit about her Christmas plans. He shook his head. "You have your family and friends coming over. I wouldn't want to intrude."

Everything about her seemed to soften. Her eyes sparkled. "You wouldn't be intruding. Please, say you'll come."

How could he possibly say no? "I'll be there."

A pleased smile turned up the corners of her mouth. He wanted to kiss her, just there, at the edge of each side.

He wanted a lot more than that. "I have some new decorations. I want your approval."

"Can't hang garland or something without supervision?"

With a chuckle, he said, "I've been thinking I would have a

housewarming or something. Maybe around the first of the year."
He'd been planning it for about the last thirty seconds.

"That would be fun."

After it popped out of his mouth, it did sound like a good idea.

At his house, he took her coat, as she said, "So, show me these decorations."

Ashley pointed with his head toward the wall of the sitting room, where over the fireplace, he'd hung a wreath.

"That's it?" She grinned.

He felt a pinch of guilt and shrugged. "I suppose I was looking for an excuse to bring you here."

Her laughing smile disappeared. "You don't need an excuse."

Ashley wrapped his arms around her and stared down into her face. "Stay, stay with me."

She laced her fingers around the back of his neck, her hands cool against his skin. He pushed his luck a little more, bent down, brushed her lips with his.

He kept one hand at the small of her back, as he cupped the back of her head, pressing harder against her opening mouth.

Never had he wanted a woman this badly. Maybe he could just slide through her skin?

So she had time to object, he moved his hand slowly along her spine, around her waist, up, brushed the tips of his fingers along the top of her breast. She moaned. The sound tightened every nerve in him. Encouraged him to touch firmly, squeeze, ever so slightly.

Without breaking contact with her lips, he pulled her sweater up, slipped his hand under it, lifting it.

Her skin was warm and soft. Ashley fluttered his fingers across her stomach and felt her muscles tighten. The tip of her tongue brushed along his lower lip. Energy flowed from her touch through his balls and to his feet.

Touching her through the silky fabric of her bra, he found the conveniently placed front fastening. It was easy to open, even with one hand.

It came apart and she sighed.

The swell of her breast filled his palm.

Wanting much more, he stopped kissing her, dipped his head, pulled her nipple into his mouth with a small tug.

Her fingers dug into his hair, pulled him closer. He accepted her offer, took more of her.

She was delicious. He slowly released her, she groaned as he turned his attention to the other breast.

"Not yet."

The quiet words stopped him. He let go and looked at her face.

A sensual smile lifted one side of her lips. "You have entirely too many clothes on."

He nearly ripped his shirt off. But, her fingers were a bit chilly as she opened the buttons and ran her hands under the fabric, neatly brushing it off his shoulders.

She pressed her palms against his chest. He held her hands against him and kissed her.

Easily, he lifted her into his arms and carried her.

No protest, no questions, she leaned her head against his shoulder.

With his foot, Ashley pushed the door to his bedroom open, set Danni down on the bed, then looked at her as he toed his shoes off.

She gazed at him, openly curious, perhaps even admiring. He liked that, knowing she wanted him as much as he wanted her.

He untied her shoes, slipped them from her feet and dropped them on the floor.

Her feet were small. He'd never noticed. He ran his finger

along the instep, she jerked. So, she was ticklish. That was worth remembering.

He crawled onto the bed.

Half naked, she reclined on his bed. Her breasts were round, generous and perky. He gathered her up, let his hands roam over her back, sides and those luscious breasts while he kissed her. He wanted to slide into her fair, soft skin, drown in her warm body.

He unbuttoned the top of her jeans, pulled down the zipper, subconsciously holding his breath.

What if she changed her mind?

The pants loose, he slipped one hand down the front, felt the satiny slide of her underwear.

Danni's hands moved over his back and shoulders. Everywhere she touched, tingled.

He wanted her clothes off. Hell, he wanted his clothes off.

He needed to slow down, a diversion. He slipped off the bed, walked to the fireplace and flipped the switch, starting the gas fire.

"Nice ambiance." Her voice ran like silk over his skin. A tremor rippled inside him.

Wanting to touch every inch of her, he slipped her socks off. Caressed her toes, rubbed them gently.

"Don't you dare tickle me."

"No?" he teased.

She shook her head. "No."

There were too many other things he wanted to do anyway. "Okay." He wrapped his fingers around the hem of her jeans. "How about this?" He pulled.

"Eeck," she squeaked, then lifted her hips with a wicked grin.

He tossed her pants on the floor. He unfastened his jeans and let them fall.

Only their underwear remained, a final barrier between them. What little he wore felt as though it would strangle him. He hoped he would not be in anything for long, unless it was Danni.

The antique walnut, four-poster bed, creaked as Ashley once more put his knee on the mattress. She turned a little toward him, and opened her arms. It was all the invitation he needed.

He wrapped her in his arms, rolled her on top of him.

She wiggled. "Oh my." She stared straight at him. "With this, I bet the other guys don't tease you about your name."

It was excruciating. "They've never seen me in this... condition."

Her chuckle increased the pressure on his now painful erection.

"They would be very envious." Her hands continued their dance on his skin.

He had never thought about it. Could barely think, but answered, "Really? Do women think guys compare? Like in the bathroom or something?"

With her face inches away from him, her brows drew together in a tight frown. "You mean you don't?"

"No. We might stand next to each other, but we don't check each other out."

The perplexed look on her face nearly made him laugh, but, only nearly. He ran his fingers into her hair, let the soft strands slide through, then pulled her head down to kiss her again.

Easily, he darted his tongue into her mouth. Without any real thought, without taking his lips from hers, he let his hands wander over her, felt the heat and weight of her pressed against him.

Her hands touched his sides, caressed his arms and shoulders, ran down his hips, while she moved her tongue in and out of his mouth.

Alluring. Seductive. So good, it was so good.

He reached for the elastic band at the top of her bikini panties as she did the same to his boxers. In near unison with him, she tugged. He lifted his hips, gave her room to slide the cotton off. She moved up just far enough to let him slip the satin down her hips.

With a few kicks of their feet, they were, finally, naked. The shapeliness hinted of in her winter clothes bloomed in flesh. She was beautiful.

Touching her skin became an obsession, every inch of her. Then, he glided his hands along her soft inner thighs, felt her wet heat, and had to get inside her.

Her mouth was only a breath away, when reality crashed in. "Danni? Are you..." With a mental shake, he moved far enough to reach the nightstand, and discover with one hand, in the top drawer, the box of condoms.

Ashley had never had unprotected sex in his life. After his grandpa had told him about the wonders of sex, he'd said, 'you get a girl pregnant, I may beat you senseless, you get some disease, I'll tell your grandmother.'

With a grin at Danni, he hurried to open the package.

Her soft, warm hands held him, helped him put the condom on. Damn. He was going to embarrass himself if he wasn't careful.

In almost one movement, he turned her onto her back, her thighs shifted to either side of his hips. He pushed inside her silky, wet heat.

His body tightened as she raked her nails up, along his sides.

As gently as he could, he said, "Stop that. I want this to last a long time. You do that much more, and it won't."

"I'll remember that," she murmured against his cheek, but she rested her hands on his low back. "That better?"

Almost past the point of coherent thought, much less speech, he said, "Much. Just no nails, baby, please."

She lightly bit his ear lobe.

So much for speech.

With a flex, he pulled back, then slid in again. The heat of her body drew him deeper, enveloped him. He put his hands under her, held her up. Inside she was tight and wonderful.

He felt, more than heard, her groan, as he pushed down, deeper, until he was hard against her. This time, her moan held almost a hint of pain.

He opened his eyes and looked at her face. "Are you alright? Did I hurt you?"

"I'm fine." One corner of her mouth turned up. "You are kinda big."

She tipped her hips up, took him in a little more and stole his breath. It took him a few seconds to regain some composure and start a rhythm.

The movements and sounds she made guided him, let him know what she enjoyed. Like a perpetual motion machine, she moved, her hands, legs, and hips. It drove him crazy with need. Close to orgasm, he knew he couldn't hold out much longer.

Her eyes were closed, her mouth a round little "o", with that strained look that only came with sex.

"What do you need?" he asked.

"Just a few more."

He drove into her as hard as he dared, kept his rhythm as she'd wanted, and was rewarded when her inner muscles went into spasm around him, more wet warmth encircled him as she clenched and released over and over.

The pressure she created in him was too much to hold back. He came.

Slowly, he collapsed against her. Kissed her shoulder then her neck. After about four deep breaths, he shifted a bit to one side, Danni still close against him.

"You didn't need to move." Her eyes half closed, her face relaxed and he noticed, with a touch of pride, sated.

He rested for a minute or so. Now that he wasn't working so hard, the air felt cool. He sat up and pulled her beside him, then slid the covers over them.

Danni nestled against him. He stroked her hair, marveled again at the softness, as her breathing deepened, relaxed, into sleep.

He might not have had a regular girlfriend, but he was far from a monk. Sex with Danni had been incredible. He'd like to think he wasn't completely selfish, but he couldn't remember ever being so concerned about what his partner wanted.

This had gotten very serious, very fast.

Danni woke, warm and comfortable. She blinked a couple of times before she could focus. There was no way to see a clock as Ashley's chest and shoulder blocked all view.

The fireplace provided a flickering silent light. She leaned her head back. The shadows of his beard made Ashley look rugged, instead of just classically handsome. It did not detract at all.

A slightly urgent feeling told her what must have awakened her. She tried to wriggle out of bed without waking him, but his arm and leg were a dead weight on top of her.

After a push, he rolled with a slight sigh onto his back. She slipped away, remembering where the bathroom was.

Necessary things finished, she shivered as she glanced at the clock. It wasn't even midnight. Unsure if Ashley was awake, she slipped quietly under the covers.

She had no more put her head on the pillow, facing away from him, when Ashley cuddled up behind her, spooning her. "You're cold," he murmured.

He kissed her, just at the base of the nape of her neck. She shivered again, not from cold. The length of his body pressed gently against her. He slipped one arm under her neck, the other warmed her hip. She snuggled closer to him.

Colin had been the last man who had touched her. Never had she thought of herself as wonton. She'd not ever had casual sexual relationships.

This was not casual either.

No, she thought, this was wonderful, but temporary. He would go off testing, and she would remain in Denver. Ashley could be a sometime lover when he was in town.

That was still safe.

Chapter Five

The morning sun was bright, even through the heavy drapes of Ashley's bedroom. Danni had long since become immune to the noises of a Chinook wind. He abruptly glanced toward the window, every time it shook in the gusts.

"Is this normal?"

Danni nodded, her head rested on the pillow, where she'd been indulging in looking at Ashley.

"The wind?" she asked, as innocently as possible. She felt mischievous and slightly naughty, and more content than she had in a very long time. Who knew one night of great sex could improve her mood so much?

"Yes, the wind." His warm fingertips drifted down her hip.

"This time of year, yeah. The down slope winds are warm."

"I'm warm right now."

Then he proved how warm he was.

Lying beside her, he said softly, "I need a shower. How about you?"

Her skin still tingling from his touch, the thought of hot water sounded delightful. She nodded.

Ashley crawled out of bed and started the water.

It took Danni a couple of seconds to get the courage up to get out from under the covers. She'd just spent hours with this man, naked. Why the sudden sense of shyness?

With a strengthening deep breath, she threw back the covers and joined Ashley. The shower was big enough for a small party. Jets rained down from both sides.

"We do live in a semi-arid climate," she teased.

He made a circle with his fingers, indicating she should turn around, her back to him. "They are low flow shower heads," his tone matched hers.

Danni smiled and relaxed a little as his hands, slippery with soap, massaged her shoulders and neck. "Feels good," she muttered. Ashley moved, and water beat against her.

"Hold still," he said.

Suddenly, his fingers were in her hair, shampooing. "Hmmm," it came out as a groan.

Ashley chuckled. "Glad you're enjoying it."

He must have sensed her disquiet, because everything he did made her more comfortable. They soaped and scrubbed each other, enjoying the touch, without it flowing into sex. Danni grew more at ease.

The water off, he opened the big glass door. Pulling a towel off the rack, he shook his head, as a gust of wind rattled the window set high above the old-fashioned claw foot bathtub. "This is not a day to be outside. They have a small dog warning out?"

"What?" she asked as he stood behind her, wrapping the towel and his arms around her.

"You've never heard that expression?"

"No."

"Must have lived a sheltered life."

His arms disappeared. "Small dog warning. Winds so strong it'll blow your dog away."

Danni shook her head, laughing. "That's awful."

"I'll bring your clothes in."

She glanced around and saw him, towel around hips, walk out the door. In only a few second, he reappeared with her jeans and underwear and a long sleeved flannel shirt that belonged to him.

With a wicked grin on his face, he handed them to her. Danni felt heat rising up her body in embarrassment. "It'll bring up everything else." He disappeared again.

Danni vigorously dried her skin, then slipped on her panties. The slight soreness of her body reminded her of just what she'd been up to.

A shudder slid up her spine. Yesterday hadn't been as bad as it could have been. Seeing him in a drivers suit had almost made her come apart. Ashley had been supportive, understanding. It had been... sweet.

The day was not something she cared to repeat, but the flight, dinner and last night? That had been wonderful.

So wonderful she closed the door on that part of her brain that was busily sending warning signals.

Ashley wondered how he had let her talk him into this. Danni was a few feet ahead of him in the department store, her shopping cart, half filled with toys, donations for a local shelter, right behind her. There were a few things she'd gathered for family and friends. Now, the rack before her slowly spun on its axis, as she pushed it around.

"Oh, look at this." Danni looked back over her shoulder, a bright smile on her face.

Ashley moved up behind her. If there had been a hole in the floor, he would have gladly dropped into it. Several pictures of his own face, and his car, were plastered across the front cover of a calendar.

"I should buy it for myself," she said softly. "Look at it anytime I wanted to see you."

"Now, why would you do that?" He ran his hands up under her jacket, squeezed her waist. "You can have the original, all to yourself."

She leaned back into him. He didn't know if he was relieved or excited by her response. Maybe both?

Too bad they were standing in a very public place.

"I can?" she asked.

He breathed in the scent of her perfume, as he leaned a little closer. "Any time." He let go of her waist. She put the calendar back on the rack, then turned into the Christmas decoration department. Please, he thought, please be sold out.

No such luck.

Danni's brows lifted, a crooked smile teased him. "Ornaments?" she asked, holding up the glass replica of his car.

"Some of the other guys are there, too," he grumbled.

"I've never known anyone who was an ornament."

He'd like to ornament her. Hmm, interesting thought.

Trying to stave off further embarrassment, he said, "There are kids' toys, too."

"Royalties?"

Not insubstantial ones, paid for the use of his face and the depiction of his racecar. Part of the income went to his charitable foundation. He nodded. "Yeah."

"Come on." Her lips twitched in a suppressed smile. It made him want to kiss her. "You drive."

He chuckled. "I am not sure I'm qualified for a shopping cart."

She walked beside him, her hand looped around his elbow as they strolled through the store. They made several more stops, and then the worst happened. An official merchandise location. T-shirts, caps, coats, jackets, many of them with his name and or face, all over them.

Danni jabbed an elbow, rather gently. He sighed.

"At least let me look," she said, not entirely without sympathy for his uncomfortable predicament.

He stood feet away, looking at other things as she sifted through the stuff.

"Do you see an Ashley Jenkins T-shirt in a small?" a woman's voice, not Danni, asked.

Ashley looked up to see a forty-ish woman digging through the shelves next to Danni.

"I, uh, can't say I have," Danni answered.

For the second time, Ashley wished for a hole to appear in the floor.

The woman continued, oblivious to his presence,. "He's my daughter's favorite driver. She's fourteen. She thinks he's gorgeous." The woman chuckled, then, still digging through the shirts piled on the shelves, said, "So do I."

Danni leaned back, caught Ashley's eye, and winked. "So do I."

He could not ignore the gleam in her eyes, or stop his answering, embarrassed smile. A hole about twenty feet deep would do nicely.

Danni helped the lady look through the remaining shirts, while Ashley kept his distance.

"Here's one," Danni proclaimed, a note of triumph in her voice. She held it up by the shoulder seams.

"Oh, that's perfect. Thank you for helping me."

"It was no trouble." Danni smiled.

Ashley knew she meant it. It had only taken a couple of minutes to lend a hand and make someone else smile.

Danni did that to people. She took care of them, made them comfortable and seemed to enjoy every second of it. He had seen it with her friends, heard it, in the way she dealt with her parents.

Ashley took a step, then another, then walked toward them as he reached into his jacket pocket for the indelible ink marker he kept for the occasional odd autograph. "What's your daughter's name?"

The woman's mouth fell open, her eyes blinked, as if she were seeing a vision.

Danni smiled. Ashley would do a lot to make her smile.

"Ah, it's Carrie," the shopper answered.

Ashley uncapped the pen and took the shirt from her hands. "With a K or a C?"

He watched as she tried to make her mind and mouth work. She started twice before she finally said, "With a C. C-a-r-r-i-e."

Ashley signed the back, <u>Merry Christmas Carrie</u>, then his name, and handed it back to Carrie's mom.

"Merry Christmas," he said.

"Th--Thank you. I think my son may have to change his favorite driver."

Ashley smiled. He liked converts. "I'd be happy to sign something else, for him."

The lady laughed. "Serves him right. I think I will let him be jealous. But, would you sign one for me?"

"Sure."

She turned back to the shelves to find a shirt for herself.

Danni's whole face seemed to glow with approval.

He tried to remember the last time he'd offered to give an autograph somewhere other than at an arranged event.

He did them all the time, signed things for hospitals, charities, special events, or if someone asked him, politely. But simply to offer? It had been years. But this felt good. Danni's approval felt better.

"Here, here's one." The woman turned toward him.

"And your name?"

"Debbie."

He scribbled his name on the shoulder of the shirt. "Here you are, Debbie."

"Thank you, thank you. They are never, never going to believe this."

"You and your family have a wonderful holiday. Excuse us."

Pushing the cart, he felt Danni in his wake as he walked away. He let out a deep sigh, and relaxed.

"That was very sweet of you," she said as she gained his side.

"Sweet? That's hardly a flattering statement."

"All right then," she grinned up at him, "gentlemanly."

"That's better." Ashley enjoyed the feel of her hand as she wrapped her fingers around his arm. "Are you just about finished shopping?"

Her shoulders shook with her silent laugh. "You really do not like to shop do you?"

"Ah, no, I don't."

They checked out, loaded everything into the car and went to the next stop.

Danni wanted more presents for charity. Ashley donated to a number of worthy causes. He'd never thought to do the shopping himself.

There was a certain satisfaction in joining her, helping pick out things for various ages of children, practical things for adults, blankets and bedding. By the time they were done, the car was full.

"This was fun, for shopping," he glanced over at Danni where she sat in the passenger seat, humming along with the radio.

"I'm glad you enjoyed it."

"Do we need to wrap all this?"

"No, I just drop it off. That way they can give the stuff to the people who need it most."

Ashley looked at the clock on the dash. It was only four, though it would be dark soon. "Could we drop it off now? It'll save you a trip later."

"That's a great idea."

Danni gave him the address and he made it most of the way there without directions. The presents safely delivered, he turned toward home. Ashley felt more of the Christmas spirit than he had in years.

Danni offered to cook dinner, and, he accepted. After a quick stop at the grocery store, he drove to her house. It was fun to cook for someone again, just one someone.

And to make it even better, Ashley spent the night.

In the small hours of the morning, Danni lay awake. Guilt stabbed her. How could she have a lover in Colin's bed? She squeezed her eyes shut and bit her lip to stop the unexpected sob.

Suddenly, she was in Ashley's arms. His husky voice asked, "What's wrong?"

She opened her mouth, searching for the right words. Before she could manage a sound, he said, "I understand."

The warmth of him surrounded her. Still, it took a few minutes to get her emotions under control. She felt horribly awkward. Crying over one man while in bed with another.

Finally, she muttered against his chest, "I'm sorry."

"If you're not comfortable with me here, then I'll go."

"I don't want you to go. I want you here. It's just-- odd. I've never thought of anyone else being on that pillow."

"I could sleep on yours," he teased, then added, "Really, if you are uncomfortable..."

She burrowed closer to him. She needed to get over this. "No, Ashley, please stay."

Christmas morning. Cozy and warm, wrapped in the lofty comforter and most of Ashley's body, Danni woke slowly.

He was still asleep, and just as gorgeous as he was awake.

Why did men have longer eyelashes than women? Ashley's almost brushed his cheeks.

Lifting her head, she glanced over his shoulder at the alarm clock, almost eight. There was still time to luxuriate in bed. She put her head on the pillow and closed her eyes, but her brain refused to sleep. Instead, it insisted on drifting to the man beside her. He was intelligent, warm and thoughtful of her. She wanted to share time with him. But, soon he would be off. Testing, then more testing. In less than two months, the race season would begin.

Suppressing the chill that threatened to creep up her spine at the thought of race, she tried to relax. Ashley was a marvelous man. The last weeks had been wonderful. If she let her imagination run wild, she could imagine herself in love with him.

No, no, no, she wasn't and she wouldn't be. She would not relive the worry and fear.

Colin had loved her and she him, but she hated racing. It started with a deep sense of unease that grew each week during the race season and got worse each year. Eventually, she stopped watching, stayed in the motorhome or hotel and frequently had severe headaches. Intellectually, knowing a driver was safer on a track than on a freeway did not help. What had made her so frightened? She'd wracked her brain, and never thought of anything.

The bed beneath her shifted. Ashley had moved. Their relationship was a good diversion for Ashley during the off-season. And, a welcome change for her solitary life.

Nothing more.

A driver was the last person she wanted a serious relationship with.

It is already serious, her inner-self chided her.

Ashley shifted again, on the edge of wakefulness.

Stop worrying and enjoy what you have, the other half of her brain argued. Danni stifled a groan. Here she was, staring at this incredible, gorgeous, warm, man and doing everything to convince herself that it was nothing serious.

It was like a mantra, over and over in her mind, it's not serious. It's not serious. If she repeated it enough, maybe she'd believe it.

"Stop wiggling," Ashley's voice was husky and deep. His eyes were still closed.

"Did I wake you?"

He tugged her closer. "What do you think?"

She took the time to wallow in the warmth of his skin, naked and glorious beside her. "I think I did."

"Do we have time to go back to sleep, or do we need to get going?"

Moving her hand from his hip, down over the soft skin of his groin, she said, "I think we have to get going, but I don't think we need to get out of bed, yet."

Ashley's eyes were still closed, but his face held a new intensity.

Gently, she stroked his soft skin, enjoyed the feel of him under her fingers. In a quick move, she easily pushed him onto his back and straddled him, keeping contact with the growing evidence of his interest.

The covers slid down her back.

Ashley looked like a pampered sultan, his arms back, hands under his head, eyes closed, a very contented smirk on his face. "I could get used to waking up like this."

Danni ignored the warning that clanged at the back of her brain at his simple words, and focused on making love to him.

Nearly an hour after Danni had awakened him so deliciously,

Ashley got out of the shower, slipped on a pair of jeans and went to the kitchen, barefoot, to see if there was anything Danni needed help with.

He still felt uncomfortable here, especially in her bedroom, even after he'd helped her rearrange the furniture.

Last night, after church, they'd stayed here so they could prepare for Christmas brunch. Ashley wondered how he'd deal with the influx of people, somewhat intruding on his private life.

Neither of them had said much to anyone about seeing each other. People knew they had gone out, but he doubted anyone knew the depth of their affair. Today most folks would figure it out.

It was scary. He had no idea how to go forward, no clue if she wanted anything long term with him. But, he couldn't put her out of his mind for long.

They had spent hours last night doing prep work. He'd learned more about food than he'd ever thought to. And, he understood why she had a kitchen that would make a lot of chefs envious.

Now, two huge, whole rib roasts sat in glory on the counter top, seasoned and ready to put in one of the double ovens.

Danni, luscious even in jeans, a t-shirt, and slippers, stood by the refrigerator, leaning on the door, searching for something. Her hair was still damp.

"What did you lose?" he asked, teasing.

"My roasted garlic. It's in here somewhere."

"What can I do?"

She glanced up from the refrigerator. "Make some tea." She grinned. "And some coffee. I have a strudel thawed out and ready to heat. You could do that."

He lightly ran a hand down her back then kissed her cheek. In only a little while he had the teakettle on, coffee started and the pastry in the smaller of the ovens, the timer set.

The domesticity of it struck him somewhere in the middle of

his first cup of coffee. Danni hustled about the kitchen, making an occasional request of him. He did what she needed, then got out of her way. Somehow, it all felt comfortable, contented.

A month ago, he couldn't imagine helping a lover in the kitchen while she made Christmas dinner, much less enjoying it.

Last night he'd help set the table in the dining room with candelabra's, silver, crystal, and china. Ashley wouldn't have known where to start on a feast like this.

Danni was a unique combination. A woman who had grown up in a solid middle class American family, had married into a Scottish noble family, been left, he was sure, a rather sizable estate by her late husband, could set a table with thousands of dollars worth of china and silver, prepare dinner for twenty, and think nothing of it.

"Do you need anything else?" he asked, after he picked up the plates from their light breakfast.

"Not right now."

"Then, I am going to run home, change clothes and make the Christmas phone calls. I'll be back in an hour or so."

She stood on tiptoe, and kissed him softly. "Okay. Thanks for your help. Don't forget you have to watch Holiday Inn, Muppet's Christmas Carol and It's a Wonderful Life with me tonight."

If she would be next to him, he could manage. "I haven't forgotten."

"No argument?"

He shook his head. "Nope." In a weird way, he was looking forward to it. He slid his hands over her waist and kissed her. "Dress pants and shirt, right?"

She nodded, a sexy smile lit her face. "But bring a change for later."

Chapter Six

Ashley backed his car out of Danni's garage and down the driveway, feeling impossibly happy. Fresh snow glinted in the sun, the sky a crystalline blue. It was a beautiful day, making him even happier.

How had she turned his life upside down in three weeks? Would she want to travel with him, at least part of the time? Could she?

Unsure of her the depth of her feelings, for him, and her fear of racing, he thought it was too soon to press for any kind of future commitment, or even talk about it. It was obvious she liked him. Enjoyed being with him. He had met her family, her friends. Somehow, he had trouble envisioning next Christmas without her.

Hell, he had trouble imagining next week without her.

Last night, when she'd opened her gift, she'd smiled, said <u>thank you</u>, told him it was extravagant, but lovely. But that was all.

She was a mystery, one he wanted to solve.

He couldn't spend all his time ruminating. He got busy, did a twenty minute run on the treadmill, took another quick shower, shaved, sent an email off to his parents and to Cade. He would talk to everyone else later. He put clean clothes and his shaver in a bag. All the while, he tried to think of ways to ask Danni if she wanted to go with him, and of all the ways she might say yes, ignoring the thought of 'no'.

Wearing the knee length, butter soft, black leather coat Danni had given him last night, Ashley drove back to her house. There was a car in the drive when he pulled up. Positive it was Danni's parents, he used discretion, left his overnight bag in the car, and instead of using her garage door opener, he parked like a normal person and rang the doorbell.

Danni's dad, Tom, answered the door. "Merry Christmas, Ashley," he said as he held his hand out.

Ashley accepted the handshake. "Merry Christmas to you."

"The girls are in the kitchen. Danni said you'd be joining us. I'm surprised you aren't home with your parents."

Ashley shrugged. "They're on vacation." True enough, as far as it went.

The scent of the garlic and herbs on the slowly cooking prime rib teased his nostrils. The soft sounds of Christmas music underplayed the voices of the ladies.

He followed Tom into the kitchen, where Danni and her mom, Laurie, sat at the island. They both looked up and smiled at him.

Danni smiled often, but each one seemed to touch him a little deeper now.

"Coffee?" she asked.

With a shake of his head, he resisted the urge to go kiss her. "Water, please."

"It is a beautiful day, some nice fresh snow, then sunshine," Laurie commented, obviously making small talk.

They knew he and Danni were dating. He doubted they knew where they spent most of their nights.

"I almost walked over, but then I realized I was running late,"

Ashley said.

"Well, now that you're here, it's time to open presents," Danni's voice was excited and her eyes had a glimmer to them.

"You didn't have to wait for me," he said.

"Sure we did," Laurie answered, a bright smile on her face.

Ashley suppressed a grin. Danni hadn't been teasing last night when she'd said when it came to Christmas she was perpetually a seven year old. He followed Tom and Laurie out of the kitchen, and took a half a second to pat Danni's backside as they walked down the hall.

Settled in a chair with his bottle of water, he enjoyed watching all three of them open their packages. This was what Christmas was supposed to be.

Things had been strained with his parents for so long, he'd almost forgotten. Watching her and her parents enjoy each other, transported a part of him to a simpler place in his life, a time when his family gathered around a tree and laughed. A twinge of longing twisted through him. A desire for something this uncomplicated, this good.

Danni produced a small package and handed it to him. "I tried to think of something unique, thoughtful and inspired, and failed, completely." She grinned.

Slowly, he pulled at the tape, noticed that Laurie squirmed almost as much as Danni, willing him to hurry. Pushing their patience even further, he carefully unfolded the paper.

"Oh, hurry up," Laurie said with a laugh.

"She has actually taken presents out of my hands and ripped the paper open," Tom's voice held a note of complaint, but his smile said something very different.

Ashley chuckled, then opened the box. It was a gift card to a national bookstore chain.

"I figured you could use that anywhere."

"Thank you, it is thoughtful and useful. " Then he smiled at Danni. "But, it isn't unique."

There were a number of packages still under the tree, for the people who were coming this afternoon.

"I think I hid yours in the back," Ashley said.

Danni looked up at him, blinking. "You didn't need to give me anything else."

"I know. You didn't need to either," Ashley said as he got up and looked under the tree. After a half a minute he found the long, narrow box. He handed it to her, then resumed his seat.

Tom gave him a very interesting look that Ashley could not quite define. He must have caught the <u>anything else</u> comment.

Laurie said, "Well, open it, Danni."

With a little exaggerated sigh, Danni pulled off the bow, then ripped the paper.

He didn't know what she thought it might be, but her frown told him she was afraid it was something expensive.

"Oh," she said as she slipped one of the black leather gloves over her hand. "These are warm." A bright smile lit her face.

"I couldn't resist. The shop had extra smalls."

"I do have trouble finding gloves that fit." She got up from her seat on the floor and gave him a quick kiss. "Thank you."

Ridiculous, how good he felt over something as simple as pleasing her. "You're welcome."

"That should be everything," Tom's voice reminded Ashley there were two other people in the room.

"Now what?" Ashley asked, as Danni stepped away from him, and he stood.

"You and Dad can sit and watch TV, staying out of our way."

Tom shook his head, and winked at Ashley. "Sounds like a good plan to me. Especially since there's some football on."

Ashley leaned back in his chair, as Tom picked up the remote and flipped channels. The channel surfing stopped when the first game of the day filled the screen.

Tom, a wry smile on his face, looked at Ashley. He had the sinking feeling he was about to be interrogated. After all this was Danni's father.

"When do you start testing?"

Ashley had thought <u>what are you doing with my daughter</u>, would have been the first question.

"Second week of January at Daytona, then a team test in Kentucky, a tire test in Texas, a media tour, then another test at Las Vegas."

Tom nodded, listening while he watched the players on TV. Then, remained silent.

Ashley's attention drifted to the game.

"Not that it is any of my business..." Tom's voice cut into Ashley's concentration, "...but, you've known each other, what? Three weeks?"

Nodding, Ashley answered, "Yeah."

"I'm surprised she's seeing you." There was no rancor, not even a hint of dislike, just a plain statement of fact.

Ashley suppressed a chuckle. "So am I."

Tom's brows rose in surprise and then his shoulders shook slightly. A bit of a grin appeared. "So, she's not holding your profession against you."

Ashley wished he could say that was true, but he just wasn't sure. "I don't know. We don't really talk about it." He leaned forward, looked around, made sure no one else was in earshot, then rested his elbows on his knees. "I thought it was because of Colin."

Tom's lips twisted. "Only in part. I can't tell you why, but she..."

he barely moved his head, a tiny negative gesture. "It goes deeper than that. She was afraid even before the accident."

"You've no idea why?"

With a small shake of his head, Tom said, "I wished I did."

In the kitchen, Danni listened to her mother ask questions. Questions Danni did not want to hear, didn't want to think about, and certainly didn't want to answer.

"You seem to really like him."

Annoyance growing, Danni lifted her knife from the tomatoes she was cutting and watched Laurie tear some more lettuce and drop it in the salad bowl. "I do like him, and he likes me. But he'll be off testing soon, and we won't see each other much."

"Where is this relationship going?"

With a sigh, Danni turned back to her tomatoes. She sliced, enjoying the firm feel of the cutting board as the knife struck it. Deliberately, she misconstrued her mother's question, and answered, "It's going fine."

"But what about the future?"

Exasperated, she put the knife firmly down on the counter. "Mother, stop it." For distraction, Danni went to the refrigerator, got out the radishes, added them to the green onions and cucumbers already residing in the sink, ready to be rinsed.

"So, this is just a... fling?"

Danni rolled her eyes. "So what if it is? Am I not allowed to date someone without planning a permanent relationship?"

Only the sound of Danni's knife as it cut through salad makings, the muffled voices of the guys and the television interrupted her simmering temper.

She thought the inquisition had ended until she was half way through the green onions.

"Do you think he's serious about you?" The quiet question came from the general direction of the oven.

A deep breath, count to ten, backwards, keep your voice low. After all, the man sat not all that far away. "Mother, we have known each other for three weeks. He has his life and I have mine. Drop it."

A loud sigh. A sure sign Laurie's feelings were hurt.

In a new hush, they continued the preparations.

The silence stretched like a rubber band, until finally, Danni had to say something. "Mom, please, just let me enjoy what I have right now. I don't want to worry about what may or may not happen in a week or a month." She poured hot water into the waiting teapot, then managed to direct a small grin to her mom. "In case you haven't noticed, he is incredibly handsome. I am sure he has lots of female friends." He probably did. If she didn't care about a future, why did that thought bother her? "I hope we can stay friends, but he's not serious about me and I am not serious about him. Okay?"

A skeptical look crossed Laurie's face, and then was hidden behind a diminutive smile. "Okay, I'll let it go."

The doorbell rang, announcing the first of the guests. The activity of the day took over, erasing any uneasy thoughts about her relationship with Ashley from Danni's brain.

Late in the evening the group broke up. All of the dishes were stacked in the kitchen, but washing would still take a while.

Her parents were the last to leave.

Laurie opened the hall closet and got her coat.

Ashley took it from her and helped her. She asked Danni, "Sure you don't want some help?"

Danni shook her head.

"I, for some reason, maybe insanity, volunteered to help." Ashley said, and winked at Danni.

"Insanity is a good term for it. I'm glad our house won't hold this many people." Tom chuckled.

"Oh Dad!" Danni gave him a hug.

"Will you be at my Open House next week?" Ashley asked.

"We thought we'd drop by for a bit." Tom extended his hand and shook Ashley's.

Danni was pleased her parents liked Ashley. He walked out the door with her dad, their voices reached her as a low murmur.

"You know dear," Laurie gave her a gentle squeeze around the waist, "I think a man who gives a woman a full length mink coat is pretty serious."

Danni's mouth dropped open.

"I saw it in the closet. I know you didn't buy it for yourself."

"It's faux," Danni said.

Shaking her head, Laurie said, "Makes no difference. See you next weekend." With that she went down the stair and waved bye to Ashley as they crossed on the sidewalk.

Danni shook her head. Ashley stopped, stared at her. "What happened?"

She started for the kitchen. "Something Mom said. She is really good at gob-smacking me."

"What does that particular Scottish-ism mean?" Ashley asked, only a step behind her.

"Not Scots, English, but it means...speechless."

"Wonderful language, English."

That broke her earlier train of thought. She chortled, then took pity on him. "You don't have to help me clean up."

He put the stopper in the kitchen sink, and dug out the soap. "Sure I do. You're helping me next week. And besides, this way it will go quicker." He turned and smiled at her. "We still have old movies to watch."

"Okay, but it is your dishpan hands."

The minutes rolled by in a domestic state Danni had not experienced in a long time. The quiet left her time to think. Ashley's gift to her did seem extravagant. On the other hand, she knew he could afford it. It was thoughtful of him. Conclusion reached, she ignored the little voice in her head telling her it was a good rationalization.

She finished cleaning off the table, gathered up the table clothes and napkins and got them in the laundry, then put away as much as she could.

The dining room almost looked normal.

She peeked into the kitchen. Ashley still had a few pieces of crystal to go.

"Which movie?" she asked.

"I am ashamed to admit I have never seen <u>Holiday Inn</u>."

"<u>Holiday Inn</u> it is." She went into the great room, opened the cabinet and found the disc.

"How about a drink? For some reason a martini sounds great," Ashley called from the kitchen.

It did sound good. She loaded the movie, while giving Ashley the recipe for her favorite martini.

A few minutes later, he strolled in. He handed her a glass with a flourish. "Thank you, Danni. This has been the best Christmas I've had in years." He touched his glass to hers.

A day spent with people he had known for a few months, or weeks, and it was the best Christmas he had in years? How alone must he have been? Careful of her drink, she leaned over and kissed him. "Thank you, for being here."

On the couch, she settled into the curve of his arm, pushed the appropriate button on the remote. Homey, warm comfort oozed through her.

The music started over the brief credits. "Be prepared," she glanced at Ashley, "it's sort of--well-- corny."

The alcohol sloshed around in his glass as he laughed.

"But it's fun," she added. A diabolical idea popped into her head. "And you have to sing along with all the songs."

He raised one eyebrow and twisted his lips.

The comical expression made her chuckle.

With a shake of his head he said, "Oh, no. I do not sing. Not even for you."

"Coward." She returned her focus to the TV screen.

At least thirty seconds later, he said, "Be really nice to me though, and I might do my Kermit the Frog imitation."

Three movies, two martini's and several hours later, Ashley said, "This is the most fragrant bathroom I have ever been in. Good fragrant, not bad."

Danni chuckled. "It's the Earl Grey and rose candles, one of each. The rest are unscented. Two of my favorite smells, how could I possibly go wrong?"

She leaned back, in the full, deep, jetted tub, and rested her back against his chest. His legs were on the outside of hers. Her butt cradled closely against his crotch. The water came nearly to their shoulders. Softly scented, erotic. Like a swim in a tropical pool.

Too bad she was half drunk. Of course, that was Ashley's fault.

He wrapped one arm around her waist, keeping her snug against him.

Ashley handed her one of the long stemmed martini glasses, then picked up his.

"What did you call that drink?" he asked, a smile tinting his voice.

"A Parisian martini." She leaned over and craned her neck to one side to try to see his face. "You took me literally. Didn't you?"

"About what?"

"I said two to one. Two parts vodka, one part Chambord. You put in two jiggers of vodka and one of Chambord. Didn't you?"

"Yes, I did," he said proudly, then took a sip of his own plain, ordinary, very dry martini.

She plopped her head against his shoulder. "Too bad for you." She took another sip. "You know, I used to be a real lightweight. Then I married a Scot and learned the true meaning of party."

"What are the holidays like? In Scotland, I mean."

"Christmas is fairly quiet, befitting a religious holiday. Something we American's seem to miss entirely. But come Hogmany..."

"Hog-ma what?"

"Hogmany, Scot's for New Years. Now that is a party."

She turned a little in his arms. "Hogmany is a large party, family, friends, games and as much whisky, or what ever you fancy, all night long." Savoring the heat of the water and his body, with a sigh she settled more heavily against him. "I liked it." Carefully, she set her glass on the wide tile surround of the tub.

Warm lips touched her neck, then her shoulder. "I like this."

Danni giggled. "I can tell." Her head against his shoulder, she said, "Too bad for you, when I get inebriated I go to sleep."

"What? Don't think I could wait a while?"

"The way I'm feeling, you're gonna have to wait more than awhile."

Relaxed in the gentle strength of his arms, Danni drifted.

"Come on. Up you go," Ashley's voice seemed far away.

She heard the soft sucking sound of the water draining. A little unsteady, she stood. Ashley moved in a blur, and wrapped a big soft towel around her. Another quick movement and she was lifted in his arms.

"You fell asleep," he said quietly, as he carried her to the bedroom.

It was a rainy gray afternoon. The scent of the big bouquet of roses filled her nostrils. She'd put them on her desk so she could see and smell them while she worked.

The man was a wonder. Instead of giving her American Beauty roses, that have little scent, he'd bothered to find floribundas. Every few minutes the clicking of the keys on her keyboard stopped as she paused long enough to bury her nose in the fragrant red blossoms.

She inhaled, then leaned back in her chair, returned her fingers to the right places on the keys and watched the screen as the words flowed from her brain to her computer.

The sound of the doorbell drew her mind from the Nineteenth Century. Resigning herself to the interruption, Danni went to the door. She peeked through the peephole.

What in the world?

Quickly, she unlocked the door. Pulled it open. "Edward, why didn't you let me know you were coming from Scotland?"

"Danni, oh Danni. I'm so sorry. He's dead."

She opened her mouth to scream.

Her eyes opened. Her heart hammered in her chest. She heard it in her ears. She threw back the covers. Sat up. Took one deep breath, then another, and another, chasing the panic of the dream away.

A dream. Only a dream. But, she was alone. No one rested in the bed beside her. Hands shaking, she grabbed a robe, tied it around her waist and looked at the clock. Nine.

She hurried down the hall to the kitchen. Ashley, in jeans, un-tucked shirt and barefoot, sat at the breakfast bar, sipping a cup of coffee and watching TV on the small set she kept in the kitchen.

Relief engulfed her. The vise constricting her lungs loosened.

It had only been a nightmare.

Danni assured Ashley she was fine, no hangover. If he noticed she'd been trembling, he didn't say anything. He'd held her, gave her a kiss. They'd planned dinner for tonight, and then he'd left.

After a quick breakfast of Christmas leftovers she settled down to work. She had stacks of reference books, notes on articles and original source documents and electronic bibliography cards. It was time to make sense out of it.

Her fingers rested on the keyboard, and nothing came out of her brain. Nothing, but the specter of her dream. How long would it be before the frightful night visitor became a housemate? Never. They would not come back. Not like they used to.

The dreams, the headaches, the panic attacks.

It would not be like it was with Colin. She would not be at the tracks, and besides, she was not in love with Ashley. People don't fall in love in a matter of weeks.

Something twisted in her stomach. She and Colin had married a whole three months after they met. "Yeah, stupid. Would you have married him if you'd waited a year?" she asked herself, as she glanced at his picture on the wall. If she'd gone through the hell of a full racing season, would she have married him anyway?

She didn't know, but she was damn sure she didn't intend to go through it again.

It was a good thing Ashley would be leaving soon. Out of sight, out of mind, as good a cliché as she had ever heard.

He would be busy with his life, and she would be back to her usual habits. There would be distance between them. Enough space for clear thought instead of reasoning with her libido.

She had no intention of ever, ever falling in love again.

Ashley spent an hour and a half with his trainer, then took a shower. He and Doug were meeting at Mark's to finish putting the motor into Mark's MG B vintage racecar. They would have it running for a test and tune on Wednesday, at one of the local road course tracks. Ashley's brain itched to drive. He was almost ready to beg for a ride.

Getting to the speed limit on the freeway as fast as possible didn't substitute for a few good laps.

He parked in the Williams's driveway and rang the doorbell. Sally answered the door with a smile. "The master mechanic is in the garage. Beer? Soda?"

"Soda sounds good." Ashley got his cold drink and went into the garage.

Mark's feet, legs and half his torso were visible. The rest of him was beneath the right side of the car.

Ashley laughed, quietly. How many hours had he spent in that position? When he'd started, the crew was him and his grandpa, with his grandmother supplying food, drink and moral support.

"Find anything?"

Mark chortled. "Not much."

The engine hung from the hoist, ready to be lowered and stabbed into the empty engine compartment.

"You ready to put this beast together?"

"Almost. But it's just us. Doug called, he's not feeling well." Mark rolled out from under the car.

"Just as well." Ashley nodded at the tiny space under the hood. "There's not room for two, much less three."

Ashley pulled on a pair of surgical gloves to protect his hands from the solvents and grease, and the two of them set to work.

Two hours, bruised knuckles and only a few cuss words later, the engine was in.

"You still want to change the starter?" Ashley asked.

"Yeah. The old one got stuck one too many times last year."

"Let's get her done."

Mark glanced up at the clock hanging on the peg-board above the workbench. "Don't you have a date?" A very slight smile turned up one corner of his mouth.

Ashley nodded with a grin. "Yeah, later."

The smile was still there when Mark shook his head. "I've known Danni since she was in high school, when she bought her A and joined the Club."

Ashley had assumed the MG was something she'd gotten after her marriage. He knew where to tickle her, what spots on her body were particularly sensitive, but he didn't know that.

Mark took a long swig of the Guinness he'd opened fifteen minutes ago, then said, "It's none of my business, but... much as I like you, I'm not sure now that she's ready for you."

Ashley leaned one hip against the side of the workbench. "Despite you pushing me in her direction in the first place," he said, without rancor. "I'm not sure either." He stopped. "Let me rephrase. I'm sure about me. But, I bring up racing and she shuts down. I might as well be talking to myself." He pulled the gloves off, tossed them in the trash.

Mark set down his beer. "She never had trouble at vintage events. But that was before Colin was killed."

First Tom, now Mark. The warnings, even though somewhat subtle, were way too late, at least for him.

Mark drained the last of the beer, then dropped the empty into the glass recycle bin. "Gee, I think I need another beer. You can have one, too." He paused. "Do you have a suit, and stuff here?"

Ashley always had a drivers suit, shoes, helmet and Hans devise in a bag, wherever he was. "Yeah." He felt a smile coming on.

"Good, cause I am hoping you'll come with me Wednesday."

"You mean you'll let me drive your baby?" Ashley said without dancing for joy around the garage.

Mark grinned. "You bet. I'm hoping you can drive around and give me some ideas. Besides, there'll be a couple of guys there who think they're pretty hot stuff. I'm hoping you smoke 'em."

Chuckling, Ashley followed Mark. Sally waved from her position on the couch, a glass of wine on the table beside her, an open book in her lap.

Mark grabbed the beers, opened them, handed one to Ashley, then they clinked the bottles together. "Thanks for your help."

"You're welcome."

Test and tunes were fairly low key. A chance to fine tune the car and make sure it was working right. Would Danni come? It might be the right situation to see if she could handle racing again.

Maybe he could figure out what was going on in that beautiful head of hers, but Ashley hadn't a clue what it was.

Chapter Seven

$\mathcal{E}$verything for the overnight trip downtown was in a separate, much smaller bag sitting at the foot of Danni's bed. All these years living in Denver and she had never been to the New Year's Eve bash at the Brown Palace Hotel.

Carefully, she slid the zipper up the side of the formal bag, safely ensconcing her evening gown inside. She'd known she wanted it the second she slid the deep red moiré silk over her head and let it flow down her legs.

The sheath shaped dress had a sweetheart neckline that ended with slender off the shoulder sleeves, only an inch or so wide.

She'd debated about the jewelry. Pearls? Rubies? Garnets? Finally she'd settled on a pearl choker with a diamond enhancer, pearl drop earrings, a matching bracelet and her favorite pearl and diamond ring.

Her red evening gloves where not going with her. She wanted to feel Ashley's skin beneath her fingers.

The doorbell chimed. She bustled through the hall to the door and peered through the peephole. Ashley stood on the front porch, and waved at her.

With a laugh she opened the door. "You have a key."

He shrugged, the hint of a smile lighting his eyes. "I know, but

I'm here to take you on a date. Only seems right to ring the bell."

She swept her hand through the air, gesturing him in. "I'm packed."

"Good."

With one arm, he pulled her up against him. "You look wonderful."

When his lips touched hers, an almost overwhelming desire enveloped her to hold him as close as she could, and not let go. Relaxed in his arms, she absorbed the heat of him.

It was wondrous. And frightening.

Slowly, he drew back. It felt like losing a warm blanket on a cold morning.

"I'll get your bag," he said. His breath ruffled her hair.

Sometimes, Danni thought he was perfect. Then, she remembered what he did for most of the year. But that was in the future. Not now, not tonight.

Danni pushed the troubling thoughts out of her mind and waited for him.

He reappeared from her bedroom, her small suitcase in one hand, the formal bag draped over his arm. "Is this all?"

She nodded. Nightgown, cosmetics and casual clothes for tomorrow didn't take up much room. Her shoes and bag for tonight were in the bottom of the bag with her dress. She was looking forward to dressing up. It was one of her favorite things. More than once she had remembered how good Ashley looked in a tux.

"You sure?" he asked, a wicked grin on his face. "You seem to have a penchant for forgetting things."

Not at all offended, because it was true, Danni batted her lashes, and said, "I pack very carefully."

He gently deposited her things in the back of the Corvette. Her taste in cars had always run to imports, especially European, but the 'Vette was powerful looking and handled like a thoroughbred.

The afternoon was clear and blue. The winter sky held not even a hint of a cloud. It would be very cold tonight, but she wouldn't worry about that. She'd be warm and comfortable at the Brown Palace, wrapped in Ashley's presence and she hoped, arms.

The Brown was triangular, the center atrium open to the skylights above. Velvet swags and all sorts of Christmas décor hung from the pillars, filling the space with the holidays. It was beautiful.

After they checked in, and deposited their bags in the room, it was still early afternoon, so they repaired to the Ship's Tavern.

They agreed on an appetizer, and ordered champagne. "I'm not driving and I'm not racing, so I can have as much as I want," Ashley declared.

Then, they talked.

Danni loved it. They talked about everything. Except the thing she wouldn't talk about. Otherwise, religion, politics, movies, books--nothing was out of bounds. Even when they disagreed, they could talk. He respected her opinions, and she valued his.

Dark settled outside, the streetlights slowly overcame the light of the sun. Ashley glanced at his watch. "We have dinner reservations in three hours." His rich baritone voice rippled over her, caressing.

She suppressed a shiver. "You want to go up?"

One side of his mouth curled in a luscious smile. "Yeah."

She waited for him by the door to the bar, while he paid their tab. In the elevator, he wrapped his arms around her. The muscles of his legs and stomach pressed against her. She wanted to feel his hands, everywhere. But not here. For all she knew there were cameras in the elevators. That thought made her uncomfortable.

She touched her lips to his chin and pulled back. The elevator doors opened, Ashley seemed to sense her need to leave as quickly as she could from the enclosed space.

Their feet moved in step as Ashley guided them to their room.

Inside, he swiftly pulled her up against him. The movement caught her off guard and nearly squeezed the air from her lungs. He kissed her, not just with his mouth, but with his whole body. She thought she would simply melt into him.

Her fingers were in his hair, delighting in the silky strength of the dark strands. A scruff of beard lightly scratched her face. She felt her heartbeat, echoed by his.

A loud knock.

Danni jerked back. Ashley gave her a lopsided grin and set her away from him.

She stood like a statute as he opened the door, said, "Thank you," tipped the waiter and brought the bottle and two glasses into the room.

Fascinated as always with his movements, she watched as he uncorked the champagne, then poured a glass for each of them. He was graceful, like a big cat. Sometimes she couldn't stop watching him.

Deep inside, her muscles contracted as he brushed his fingers lightly over hers, handing her a glass.

"Thank you for a wonderful holiday, and Happy New Year." He touched the rim of his glass to hers.

"You're welcome, and thank you. It has been a wonderful few weeks."

Somehow, she managed to bury the troubling thoughts he brought to the surface. This was an amazing affair, and nothing more. No commitments, no promises, just company, friendship and a lover to be with.

Ashley took her hand, led her to the sofa, curled her into the curve of his arm, just holding her. She couldn't have asked for more.

They cuddled together, close, talking, watching television, just enjoying the others company. A football game was on the television, as they nestled together and sipped their champagne.

"I never get to watch much football. Always too busy," Ashley commented.

"Did you know... Danni started, thinking her observation insightful, "that your accent gets deeper, stronger when you've had a drink or two?"

A frown wrinkled the space between his brows. "Really?"

"Really." She'd noticed it the night they'd had martini's, and paid more attention ever since. "Have you tried to soften it?"

The frown deepened. He was thinking, hard.

"Not consciously," he said, a bit hesitantly.

"Too bad the stereotype is <u>Southern equals ignorant</u>."

Ashley's snort showed his disdain of those who thought so.

She rolled her head an inch and kissed his shoulder. "Who does the media interview?"

"The top drivers, the winners, the most popular..." The frown completely disappeared. "I get your point. Demographics. And it helps if you don't particularly sound southern. 'Course a lot of the drivers aren't from the south."

Nodding her head, she settled more firmly against him. She savored the warmth of being held. She dozed off.

Soft, cool air blew over her, waking her. Ashley chuckled, then blew on her neck again. "I need to run through the shower, then, I'll turn it over to you."

"Thanks, I think." She looked up, grinned at him. "We could just stay here." In demonstration, she ran her foot up his shin.

Dark brows rose high. "Tempting. But I'm going to dance with you till next year."

Ashley was out of the shower in no time. The sight of him, hair wet, towel wrapped around his waist, muscles rippling, made her mouth dry. He probably knew how good he looked.

"All yours," he said, waving his hand toward the bathroom.

Danni spent nearly an hour doing hair, makeup and getting dressed. She walked out of the bathroom completely ready, hoping she looked as good as she felt.

Rewarded with his slow smile, and a soft whistle, she smiled and twirled in a small circle to show off her dress.

"You are so beautiful," he said.

She stopped her turn and looked at him. Nope, she still didn't look as good as he did. Black tux, white shirt, black tie and studs, he was a vision of classic fashion wrapping a great body and a very handsome face.

A woman should never go out with someone better looking than she. "You look fantastic."

He grabbed her hand, lifted it, and looked straight at her, then kissed the back of her hand. Suddenly, she felt like a fairy-tale princess who'd met her handsome prince.

"Ready?" Ashley asked.

Where had she put her purse? "I need to change purses." She floated toward her overnight bag.

"Here it is." Ashley lifted it from the top of the desk.

It was nice that he didn't tease her too much about her inability to keep track of things, like her purse--keys--car. Quickly, she moved the absolute essentials from her purse to the tiny, beaded evening bag.

They dined superbly at Wellington's, inside the hotel. She felt so comfortable with him. Warm, intelligent, funny, self-deprecating, and attentive, he made her feel like the only woman in the world.

"Ready to dance?" his words held a smile. He offered his arm, and escorted her into the ballroom. The rest of the night, they drank champagne and sat down only two or three times before midnight.

The brush of his lips was gentle as he kissed her after the cheers of <u>Happy New Year</u>.

"Do you know the words?" he asked, just as the strains of Auld Lang Syne began.

She sang them softly, his arms around her, as they slowly moved together. He didn't sing, claimed he couldn't, but she could feel the rumble in his chest as he hummed along.

The song over, she stretched up, kissed him, just as gently as he had her. "I know the words and what they mean." There were five verses. "Burns's tribute to old times, old friends, old lovers, and a happy remembrance."

Ashley took the champagne glass from her fingers, set it on the table next to his. Opalescent eyes shimmered with heat. "One more dance?"

Too astounded by the way he looked at her, all she could manage was a nod. Artfully, he moved her across the floor. The music floated by, the world narrowed to the familiar <u>slow, slow, quick, quick,</u> rhythm of the steps and his face.

In their room, he twirled her, without music, into a chair, served her a glass of ice water, and then stood before her. His eyes never left her face as he slipped off his jacket, slowly unbuttoned the vest, starting a very private strip tease.

With a pull, he untied the black silk, bow tie. It flashed through Danni's mind that he actually knew how to tie one.

Was the room was getting warmer, or was it caused by the look on Ashley's face?

The green malachite of his shirt studs and cuff links flashed through his fingers. With a slim smile, he put them on the table. The crisp white of his shirt gapped open, then he slipped it down, off his shoulders. It joined the pile of clothes on the floor beside her.

She admired the view. There wasn't any fat on him. His body was lean, well defined, without the bulk of body builders, more like a well-muscled runner.

His pants were still on when he dropped to one knee and took off her shoes. He skimmed his hands along her calves, then cupped her left heel in one hand, and massaged her foot with the other.

"Oh," she sighed, then leaned back in the chair and let the pleasure sweep up her body. "Hmmmm," was the most cogent thought she could come up with, and she watched Ashley's shoulders shudder with suppressed laughter.

As he lavished similar attention on her right foot, Danni wondered what he would do next.

His warm fingers stopped in surprise at the tops of her thigh-high hose, held in place by the silky garters. Danni opened her eyes in time to see one dark brow lift in unison with one corner of his mouth.

"Interesting," he said.

Wait till he found what else she was wearing.

Deftly, he slid his thumbs under the garters and the tops of her hose, then, like a magician with a silk scarf, slid them down and off. The slight fresh aroma of soap and Ashley's own, earthy, smell teased her wits. What little of them she had left.

He pulled on both her hands, urging her up, where he held her close, kissed her and simultaneously touched her neck, searching.

She broke the kiss, and appreciated the little frown he wore.

Draping her left arm over his shoulder, and pointing down with her head she said, "Under there."

"Very clever." With one hand he pulled down on the little metal tab.

Immediately, Danni felt a touch of heat in her skin. She waited. Careful of the silk, he gathered the fabric in his hands and swept the gown up and over her head. She heard it land with a shushing sound on the chair behind her.

His mouth dropped open, brows rose. "What is that?" he asked, staring at her body with a wicked look in his eyes.

Danni managed to smile only a little. "It's a slip."

"With no straps and sticking to your body like--"

"Lycra?"

She was rewarded with a sexy, humorous smile.

God, he was gorgeous.

"How do you get it off?"

"Well, you sort of --peel it."

His mouth twitched.

Danni had not felt this sexy in years. She drew in as deep a breath as she dared, as the tips of his fingers dusted the tops of her breasts. He hooked his thumbs at either side of the cups and very gently pulled down. She had to exhale.

Cool air touched her skin, immediately covered by the warmth of his hands. "Beautiful. So beautiful."

Her breasts were cradled in his palms as if they were precious. He made her feel that way.

If only he didn't... Tired of the debate with the logical part of her brain, she quashed the thought and let him take her away.

He made love to her with exquisite slowness. He soothed away every frustration with his hands, met every demand with his mouth, and held her to his pace.

When she thought she would explode in want, he stroked her with his fingers. The fuse he had lit detonated. Spasm after spasm shook her.

Finally, when she regained a sense of something other than her body, Ashley was above her, his fingers woven through her hair.

"Come for me," she said. Lightly, she grazed her fingernails along the outside of his hips. His eyes closed, he sucked in a jerky breath, and did what she asked.

His instant reaction was all she could hope for. She loved this, this ability to break him into the shattered pieces he commanded from her.

The warm rush filled her, then she pulled him down, closer, on top of her. She loved the weight of him, pressed against her like a heavy blanket.

After the incredible rush of his orgasm, Ashley rolled onto his side and curled against her. The back of her body pressed close to his.

The change in her breathing told him she had slipped into sleep, still cuddled in the curve of his body.

He'd nearly blown it several times tonight. Almost let the words escape.

I love you.

What would she say or do?

He had to convince her to come with him, maybe to testing in Daytona. At least to his place in Richmond. He had to.

He'd tried to think like her. What would he feel? Would he be afraid? Not just of racing but, to care for someone again?

There were people he knew who'd lost loved ones in track accidents. Most of them were racing families. They accepted it, often with an incredible amount of dignity and grace. But that didn't change what had happened.

Ashley was ready to tell her how he felt, but something in his gut told him she wasn't ready to hear it.

People who didn't know him well might accuse him of not having feelings. He was just good at hiding them. He'd revealed more of himself to Danni than anyone else in his life.

Something woke him. The bed shifted. Danni pulled the covers back over the top of them. With a groan, he lifted his head, squinted at the clock and groaned again. It was only six.

How the hell did she wake up so early every morning? And so damned cheerfully?

He let his head fall back on the pillow, eyes closed.

Slightly cool fingers touched him, her chilled body pressed up against his. He pulled her closer and the deep tug of desire rose. Her breath tickled his neck. Soft lips touched the hollow of his throat.

"Hmm?" she inquired, moving her hips against him.

His brain was half asleep, but the rest of him was wide-awake. "Hmm," was the only reply he could manage. In only a few seconds, she lay on top of him, driving him crazy.

He let her.

Much later, relaxed, sated, he heard, "You asleep?" her voice as soft as down.

"Almost."

A chuckle rippled through her body. Then, she got out of bed, waking him fully.

"It's nearly eight. If we're going to get a shower, breakfast and still get to your house before the party, at two," she stressed the number, "we have to get moving."

"I suppose."

"Reveille." She smiled, then pulled the covers off him leaving him suddenly naked.

She must have turned down the thermostat in the night. For someone who sat around her house wearing a fleece jacket, or flannel over-shirts, she loved cold bedrooms, at least to sleep in.

He watched her turn, and admired the finest rear-end of any woman he'd ever known.

Dragging himself out bed, he followed behind her. He'd love to make love to her in the shower, but that was out of the question.

She hurried them out of the nice, hot water and into the now much warmer bedroom.

They were at brunch downstairs in the restaurant by nine.

Afterward, Ashley opened the door of the 'Vette for her, barely beating the valet to it. Settled inside, he looked at her, watched as she snicked the seatbelt into place. His stomach tightened again. He blinked as fast as he could, made sure his eyes were clear, then touched her cheek, turning her face toward him. He stopped the words he wanted to say, and instead asked, "We do this again some-time?"

The corners of her delectable mouth turned up. "Maybe next New Year's."

He smiled to himself. Maybe she was coming around? He shift-ed into first and squeaked the tires as he turned onto Broadway. "I don't want to wait that long."

"I'd dance with you anytime."

The word dance had a special note to it. As he glanced over, her blue eyes sparkled with mischief and double entendre.

"I could put a note on the door, canceling the party," he said.

"Oh, no you don't. We've worked too hard to make this a smashing success."

"Then I guess," he slowed to a stop at the light on Park Avenue, "I'll just have to dance with you tonight, and maybe all day tomor-row."

Her honey blond brows rose.

"You doubting my ability?" he asked.

Her facial expression was lost, as the car behind him honked. He looked forward. The light had turned green.

Green, green, green, Cade's baritone voice, filled Ashley's mind, a sure sign he was ready to get back to racing.

"Your ability? Oh no, not really." Danni's feminine tone was almost a shock after hearing someone else's voice in his head. "More like questioning mine," she added.

He put his hand on her thigh. "Baby, you're indefatigable."

She threw back her head and laughed.

They had plenty of time to get the food and drinks out, with Ashley helping, it didn't take long at all.

He'd gotten nearly a hundred RSVPs, members of the MG Club and the vintage race group. He'd said he'd hire a caterer, but she'd told him no. She actually enjoyed arranging this sort of thing.

As they both hurried around, she nearly ran into him coming out of the kitchen. He grabbed her upper arms, just enough to keep her from stumbling. Danni glanced up.

The look in his eyes, soft, something there, a gentle smile.

She recognized the look, that touch, had seen it before, but not on Ashley's face. Her heart stumbled. It wasn't possible. They'd known each other a month. No, it just couldn't be.

Danni blinked, Ashley winked at her, then disappeared into the dining room.

Chapter Eight

The doorbell rang, startling Danni and taking her mind from the disturbing direction her thoughts had taken. Mark, Sally, Bryan, Ann, Doug and Liz, as usual, were the first to arrive. The same people who had so neatly arranged for Ashley to meet her at the MG Christmas party. It pleased her that they liked him, and at the same time gave her an odd sense of déjà vu.

In moments, the discomfort was swept away, because rather than relaxing, they asked what they could do to help. Where would the coats go? Was it okay to tell guests to take themselves on the grand tour of the house? Could they touch the trophies?

Ashley answered the last question with a grin. "Everything but the Championship trophies."

By two-thirty, there were people everywhere. Danni made sure every thing worked smoothly, checking drinks and food as she moved easily from group to group and room to room, leaving Ashley free to play congenial host.

For anyone who wanted to see the house, the bedrooms were on the third floor. On the second floor, the door to the part office, part trophy room was open and the media room's big screen TV was on, tuned to the New Years Day games. Music played softly on the first floor. The lights blinked on the Christmas tree and through the garland Danni had swaged along the stair rails and banisters. The basement had all the work out equipment. It looked a lot like a professional gym.

In the dining room, Danni checked the contents of the dining room table that nearly groaned with the weight of the finger foods laid out.

The air smelled of cinnamon, hot cider and mulled wine.

Ashley came up to her in the kitchen, touched his glass to hers. Danni winked at him. "See, I told you it would be a smashing success."

He straightened his shoulders, and smiled back. "Why, thank you. My staff has been most helpful. Maybe she should demand a raise."

"I'm glad to help." Danni glanced away, felt heat flush her face, embarrassed. Searching for an excuse, she said, "I need to check on the food."

Her brain was at war with her heart, and her brain was losing.

By five-thirty, the crowd had thinned down to the six people who'd been the first to arrive. Mark, Sally, Doug, Liz, Bryan and Anne.

They sat around the big screen TV, talking and watching a college football game that quickly became a blow out.

"Something better is on," Mark said, as he grabbed the remote. Channels flipped by. Suddenly, pictures of the past stock car season lit the screen.

Danni glanced at him, as she took a very deep breath.

"Oh, please. I was there, I know what happened," Ashley complained, though with a grin.

Her stomach did a slow roll. Could she watch this? Her feet felt glued to the floor. The glass of wine in her hand was the only thing keeping her from wringing them together. She stared at the television.

Ashley lightly touched her thigh, leaned close and whispered, "It's okay. I finished in one piece."

"What <u>were</u> you thinking?" Doug's voice rang out.

Danni watched the image of his car as it spun, once, twice and a third time before he straightened it and continued.

"Before, during or after?" Ashley asked.

Doug laughed. "In that order, please."

"I thought, <u>this thing is wicked, evil loose</u>, then, <u>yep, out of control, pushed it too hard</u> followed by <u>great save</u>. And it was, if I do say so myself."

Everyone else chuckled, but the roar in her ears made the sound distant, an echo of reality. It broke her odd paralysis.

She knew this, knew the care that lay beneath the fear. Oh, god, she was in love with Ashley. The reality slammed into her. She couldn't do this. She couldn't love him.

"Excuse me." She felt him watch her as she fled down the stairs. At the bottom, she leaned against the wall, took a few seconds to try to calm down.

Damn it. How could she have been so reckless? A casual affair? Just someone to be with for a while? How dumb!

He'll be leaving soon, she told herself. It will be easier then. He'd be half way across the country, busy racing, his life back at full speed. And she could slow down.

She could do it. She had to. Love was too risky, it cost too much, hurt too much when...

<u>Stop thinking</u>!

Decision made, hands still shaking, she went into the dining room, kicked off her high heels with a bit too much force and stared at the food.

"What's up?" Ashley's voice was soft.

He looked the same, but now she understood her heart, and could not see him as he'd been only an hour ago. She loved him, but all that would bring was pain.

She tried to smile, and knew she'd failed. "Trying to figure out what to do with the leftovers."

A lopsided grin appeared. "Send them home with everyone?"

This time she did manage a little grin. "Not a bad plan."

She didn't resist as he lifted, then kissed her fingers. He shook his head. "It's only TV. Nothing bad happened. Promise."

"I know."

The strength of his arms surrounded her, the warmth of his body threatened to melt her resolve. His touch gentle against her, he stroked her back. "It's okay. I'd like you to get a bit more comfortable with it, that's all," he said.

She nodded, her head against chest. The sound of his heart drowning out the pounding of hers in her ears.

Still holding her, he asked, "What can I help you with?"

Thank goodness, he'd changed the topic. She tipped her head back and looked at him. "You go back and play host."

"Sure?"

"Yep."

He hesitated, then let her go. She had to find a way to let him go.

Danni heard Sally, Liz and Anne before they got anywhere near the dining room. Multiple large zip lock bags of food sat in piles of four on the table.

"What? You think we're taking this home?"

Smiling at Anne, Danni answered, "Yes, you are. Hold on a second." She dashed up the stairs to the bedroom, came back with a grocery store sack, then laid out three pairs of slippers.

After a good laugh, her friends slipped off their heels and slid on the comfy footwear.

"Maybe we should start keeping a pair at each others houses," Anne said.

"Speaking of clothes..." Sally let the comment drop into silence then added, "while on the house tour, did I spot some feminine apparel in Ashley's closet?"

"Ooohhh," Anne cooed, her dark brows rose to her hairline.

Danni wasn't sure if she was more surprised by the question, or by Sally peeking. "You looked in his closet?"

"She always does. Nosiest person I know." Liz smiled. "But only in the best ways."

"So," Sally wiggled her fingers. "Give us the scoop."

Determined to try to maintain some semblance of dignity, and the shreds of her heart, Danni continued packing up food. "We've been seeing each other."

"Looks like sleep-overs to me," Anne quipped.

Heat swept up Danni's face. "Anne!"

"Can't say I blame you."

"He's intelligent, funny, warm, and he is drop--dead--gorgeous," Liz added.

Despite embarrassment at being caught so blatantly, Danni smiled. "Well, yeah." She finished zipping together the bag of food she held. "You should see him with his shirt off."

Three appreciative oohs and ahh's made her smile.

"What about racing?" Sally asked

Danni's stomach unpleasantly churned. Leave it to Sally to cut through the preliminaries.

"It's what he does, but that doesn't mean I have to watch it. And I won't."

"So, this is short term?" Liz asked, not unkindly.

Danni shrugged. "Maybe, maybe not."

"So when he leaves for the season, you'll just wave bye?" Sally persisted.

Danni closed her eyes. Then lied, "Until he's back." Once he'd left, she would not see him again.

"I'm going with Mark out to the test and tune Wednesday, want to come with us?"

The question had sounded tentative and hopeful. Danni's stomach did a slow roil. She risked a look at Ashley. His expression matched his tone. He wanted her to go.

She couldn't, simply couldn't.

Trying to muster a smile, she said, "No, but thanks for the invitation."

"How about a fast trip to Richmond on Friday? I need to go to the shop."

The bright light of the kitchen faded. The edges of her vision filled with darkness. She shook her head. "No, I have some things to do."

"Okay," he said, with a wistful smile, then leaned in and kissed her cheek. He didn't press and she was thankful for it.

All day Wednesday she wondered how he was. It was idiotic, in a way. She wasn't worried about Mark, Doug or Anne or anyone else she knew who did the vintage race thing. Just Ashley.

Logic asked why? Was he somehow more vulnerable than anyone else?

His driving skills were unquestionably sharper than theirs.

More than likely, he was having a great time. So, she should relax and enjoy the day, too. Working seemed a good answer, until she spent the better part of a half hour staring at the same paragraph, brain whirling in circles.

A quick call confirmed her dad was home, mom out shopping, but that was okay. She just needed someone to be with, talk to, preferably about nothing important.

The big hug her father gave her after she came in the door settled a bit of her nerves.

Grinning, he took her coat. "I was surprised when you called. I figured you'd be busy with that good looking guy you've taken up with."

Danni rolled her eyes at his gentle teasing. "He's at a test and tune."

"So you're at loose ends, and decided to come visit your dear old dad." He led the way into the kitchen.

"You're not old." She popped open the door to the refrigerator and grabbed a soda. "How about a game of cribbage?"

"Deal."

Cards, matches, and board on the kitchen table, she settled in and did her best to keep focused on the game.

Twenty minutes later, she barely heard, "Fifteen two, fifteen four..." he stopped. "Danni, just where are you?"

Her thoughts had meandered. Game. Ashley. Concern. Fear. Ashley. Game.

"Oh, Dad, I don't know." Frustrated with herself and her life, she had no idea what she was thinking.

His warm hand engulfed hers, where it rested on the table. "You know I love you. I wish I could keep the pain you've suffered away from you. Protect you from it..." He squeezed her fingers almost to the point where it was painful. "But I can't. I can only be there to catch you if something goes wrong."

"Dad--"

"Sweetheart, you have to stop running."

She pulled her hand away from his. "Running? From what?"

"Life."

"I'm not..."

"I'm going to say this, no matter what." He captured her hand again, tugging it toward him. "Ever since Colin's death, you won't open to anyone. You withdraw, from your friends, even us to an extent. Hiding, whenever life gets too complicated or too emotional.

Think about it. When was the last time you actually volunteered at any of the places you used to? The Action Center, the Rescue Mission, the women's shelter? You avoid them. You still give financial support, but your time?" He shook his head, then continued, "Same thing with the people in your life. If things get too close, you high tail it."

Danni stared at the cribbage board, and wished she could sprout wings and fly away. But she was pinned to the surface, by her father's strong hands and deep voice.

"I don't know if Ashley has said anything. It's not my business, except I care what happens to you." He gave her hands an extra pull. She looked up into his eyes, so like hers. "But in my opinion, that man is crazy about you."

Not sure what to think, Danni just stared. What was she supposed to do?

For several days she'd known she was in love, and had stubbornly shut it away. She repeated what she was still trying to convince herself of, "I'm not in love with him. We enjoy each other's company. That's all."

Her father let out a long, deep sigh. She knew what that meant. He didn't agree, but he wouldn't argue, either.

"Fine." He let go of her hands. She missed his strength. "Let's finish the game."

They finished two more games before she decided she needed to go home.

The azure blue sky was alight with salmon pink streaks of

clouds, as the sun dipped behind the mountains. With a beep, the doors of her Audi unlocked. Her father put both hands on her shoulders, something he'd always done when he wanted her undivided attention. He said, "Not every man you love will leave you, you know?"

"What?"

Strong arms circled her. His voice rumbled against her ear. He hugged her tight. "I spent a good deal of your life leaving you behind, then little Struan died, then Colin. You've had more than your share, but that doesn't mean it will always be that way. At some point, you have to realize not every man you love will leave you."

Wrapped in his arms, her head against his shoulder, she choked out, "You've never left me."

She drove toward home, numb. A block from her house her cell phone rang. Ashley. Did she want to get together with everyone for dinner?

Shaken, she thought of declining, but a different answer popped from her mouth. "Sure. Where?"

A half hour later she sat with Sally, Liz and Anne, facing Mark, Doug, Bryan and Ashley as they talked about the day.

"We were freaking freezing, but it was a good day. Ashley looked pretty much like the rest of us. Plain old driving suit, then he slapped on a Hans and a helmet that probably cost more than my car," Mark laughed.

"It didn't cost that much," Ashley said, a grin on his face.

"We took him on a van ride, like a rookie," Doug jokingly complained, rolling his eyes.

"Hey, I had to get familiar with the track."

Despite the twist in her stomach, Danni listened as they told the stories of the day. They'd had a great time.

After a couple of slow laps to get used to Mark's car, Ashley's times got faster and faster, until he was just about the fastest thing on the track. He'd been the highlight of the day.

"It was fun," Ashley's smile told Danni just how much fun. His eyes flashed with excitement and joy.

Anne nearly bubbled over. She was going to driver's school in April. Her MGB had a second seat. "Ashley rode around with me for a while, giving me pointers, and I ended up taking almost <u>ten</u> seconds off my lap times! I wasn't scared anymore. I felt like I knew what I was doing."

"You do," Ashley said, his voice and smile full of conviction. "You did good."

"Before we were done, he'd had offers to ride in... I don't know how many cars," Doug said. "He turned down a ride in Kevin's '67 'Vette."

"Pardon my language ladies, but as a friend of mine once said, <u>my balls aren't that big</u>."

Danni watched everyone else laugh. Ashley continued, "That much power, I'd be too tempted to open that baby up. Someone else's car? No thanks, not that crazy."

"You turned down a Cobra, too," Mark chimed in.

"Oh yeah, my sponsors would love that, a shot of me driving a Ford, posted on the Internet."

"You were in an MGB, two of them," Liz teased.

"Big difference. One, they don't make them anymore, at least right now, and two, they are not in competition with GM."

Danni allowed their laughter, talk and joking to wash over her, just as she had for years.

Damn it.

Ashley and Colin were similar, not identical. Colin loved being the center of attention. Ashley accepted it, reluctantly. He used his sense of self-deprecation to deflect attention away.

The differences between Colin and Ashley were significant, but what she felt for Ashley was just as strong, if not stronger, and that scared the hell out of her.

But, so far, she had not faced the inevitable. It would just be easier to break it off once the season started. He wouldn't be in Denver much, and there was no way she would travel with him. Been there, done that, and had no desire to do it again.

They left the restaurant, his hand warm and wonderful in the small of her back, chasing the chill from around her spine.

"Danni?" he asked quietly as he walked her to her car. "You okay?"

She nodded. She felt far from okay, but without a better idea of what to do, or say, she'd just let events take her where they may.

Ashley's breath warmed the side of her neck as he whispered, "My house?"

Nodding, she knew she'd just dug the hole a little deeper. She couldn't let go of him, not yet. After all, the only one she was hurting, really, was her.

Ashley was out of ideas. It was the tenth of January. Since New Years Eve, he'd gently prodded, talked about his schedule, where he'd be going, what he'd be doing and when. Instead of encouraging her, it seemed to have the opposite effect.

As if she was pushing him away.

They sat on couch at his house, and he was out of options. It was time to go at it head on. "Testing starts Monday at Daytona. Come with me. Please, I want you to be there." He watched her face, scrutinized her expression. It was blank. Not good.

She blinked. Her shoulders dropped, then she took a deep

breath, and said, "No, Ashley, I can't."

"Why? It's just testing."

If he had to push to get an answer, he would. He had fallen in love with her. He wanted her with him.

She stared into space, not at him, not through him, but at something not in this room, or maybe, in this time. It was a look he'd started calling the ghost. How could he fight a dead man? He almost hated him.

"Danni?"

The present leaked back into her gaze. She shook her head, very slowly. "No."

"I asked why, will you answer me?"

"I will not go through that again." She leaned back, farther into the deep cushion of the sofa, away from him.

He reached out, tried to take her hand. She crossed her arms over her stomach, hands tucked away.

"The chances of something happening to me are very remote. I'm a lot safer than you are on the highway or on a plane. You know that."

She looked down. The small distance that separated them might as well have been a planet.

"This has been a mistake," she whispered.

Anger tickled his senses. "It's nice to know you think so."

"I thought I could enjoy you and your company and not worry about--anything else." She did not look at him.

Truth was his only choice. "I want you in my life, Danni. I love you."

Her head jerked up. "No! No! You cannot love me. You can't."

Confused by the hysteria he heard, he said, "I do."

She stood as if a puppeteer had jerked unseen strings. "No." She turned away. Grabbed her coat. Flew through the door.

"Danni," he called.

She ran.

"Danni!" He took off after her. And caught her. By the shoulders, he turned her toward him and gave her a little shake. "If something happened to me, tomorrow or next month, or a year from now, would not being with me somehow make it easier?"

"Yes!"

The word hit like a punch in the gut.

"Danni, please. I love you. We can work through this. You are a lot stronger than you think."

She straightened. "No, Ashley. I am not as strong as you think. And for once, I want someone stronger than me!" A film of tears covered her eyes. "Let me go."

Feeling more bereft than he ever had in his life, he took a breath. And let her go.

She turned her back and walked away.

It took minutes for him to move. Finally, he turned and went inside. A fist squeezed his heart. His stomach tied in a knot. The door closed behind him, with a nearly silent swish. He swept the back of his hand against the porcelain vase Danni had so carefully placed on a pedestal table, then watched it shatter into a thousand pieces against the wall.

Chapter Nine

Danni watched her feet as she took step after step. With each step, she hoped he would not follow her.

He would forget her. He would. He would quickly find someone else. He only thought he was in love with her.

At least she hadn't lied, again. This--they--had been a mistake. That didn't stop her heart from breaking. She rubbed her eyes with the back of her hand, flipping the tears away.

It seemed an eternity before she was on the walk in front of her house.

A sound stopped her progress. A car motor. She looked up. Ashley's car screeched to a stop just past her.

He leaped out. "You forgot your purse." The small strap of the black leather bag dangled from one finger as if he couldn't stand to touch it.

If he touched her, she would fall into a million pieces. "Thank you." With one hand she reached out, took the bag from him. She couldn't meet his eyes.

"You have my address in Richmond, in case you feel the need of a good fuck."

With nothing better to do, Ashley left for Richmond before he had to, before the Daytona tests. The one person he confided in was Mark. Ashley had needed to talk to someone. Mark knew both of them and he tried to lend some perspective.

He'd promised to let Ashley know what Danni was up to, how she was doing. Though, just why Ashley should care was beyond him.

He went to the shop and tried to behave normally, whatever that was.

Cade was Ashley's spotter, one of the team engineers and Ashley's best friend since seventh grade.

After on one look at Ashley, Cade had said, "What's up? I thought maybe someone might be with you."

Ashley had been tempted to tell him just how bad it was. With Cade, Ashley would have gotten the blame the girl speech. For the first time, he didn't tell Cade the whole truth. "It didn't work out."

"Sorry man." Then, he'd grinned and added, "You should find a replacement pretty quick."

A week before Daytona, Ashley was at Cade and Pam's for dinner, when their three year old had padded into the living room, Ashley volunteered to read Erin a story, and hopefully put her back to sleep. It worked.

As he'd walked out of the sleeping girl's bedroom toward the kitchen, Pam's voice reached him. "...probably deserves it, as many hearts as he's broken."

"Come on babe, be fair, he's never been with anyone for very long."

"Yeah," her voice dripped with sarcasm, "Except you."

The words slammed into him. Ashley backed up several steps.

Leaning against the wall, he wondered how many things in his life had he screwed up?

He wanted to talk to Danni.

He had tried, called, but only got to leave messages. Last week he'd apologized on her voice mail for his cruel words. He hadn't meant them. But there had been no response.

Maybe a good fuck <u>was</u> all he was good for.

He rubbed his eyes until small stars appeared. Introspection had never been his strong point, but he had to try, had to think.

Danni's brother in law, Edward and his wife, Jane, picked Danni up at the small airport in Inverness. With out much discussion they drove her to the snug cottage she had shared with Colin. If they thought it strange that Danni had come to Scotland in February, they didn't say anything, until they rolled into her drive.

"Here you are." Edward sounded almost chipper as he opened his door and got out. Jane turned about in the seat and stared as if she could see Danni's feelings roiling over her head.

"You going to tell us what this is all about?" She asked.

Danni tried her best <u>I don't know what you're talking about</u> look, and escaped as Edward opened her door for her.

Jane still stared, a deep frown narrowing her eyes. "I suppose you'll tell us when you're ready."

"Nothing to tell. Just felt the need for some solitude and quiet. Thanks for fetching me from the airport. I'll talk to you soon."

Before she'd left Denver, her dad had told her how unfair she was being. Her mom seemed very disappointed.

Danni's life had been nothing but confusion since she'd shoved Ashley out of her life.

Yeah, he was out of her life as long as she hadn't turned on the television. It was everywhere, one of the sports networks carried testing, in Daytona, Las Vegas, then Daytona practices, just about everything leading up to the Daytona 500. And she watched it, nerve wracking, confusing, frightening, but she didn't want to miss a chance to see Ashley's face, listen to his voice. She missed him. More than she thought possible.

He'd left messages for her, just to talk. He'd sweetly apologized for his bitter words. Every part of her ached to call him back. She couldn't, wouldn't. It would only make things worse. That's why she'd left.

She took a deep breath in a vain attempt to stop the heart thumping pain. Maybe the quiet solitude of Scotland would bring her some peace.

Danni pulled the big, old-fashioned key from her bag, carefully placed it in the lock. The tumblers turned, the small, heavy, wooden door swung inward without a sound.

Unexpectedly, the pale light of the winter sun shown in on a spanking clean house.

The nostalgic sadness Danni felt whenever she walked in after an absence briefly touched her. It had gotten easier with time. She no longer imagined Colin's figure getting out of a chair, or surprising her from behind a door.

She was alone in her well-appointed cottage. She glanced at her watch, and gave a second's thought to what time it was in Florida. It took a second for her jet-lagged mind to catch up. It was about nine in the morning. The--what were they called? The Duel...150's? The outcome of the two races, with half the field in each, set the starting order for the Daytona 500, except for the first--how many positions? She didn't remember. She'd not paid as much attention to the details as she'd thought.

"You're here to get away, remember," she said to the empty house.

She spent the next hour bustling around, doing little things, called her parents, then Colin's mom and dad, Augusta and Jared, thanking them for the services of their head housekeeper, who Augusta had sent to open up the cottage, and told them she'd drop by in a couple of days.

The familiar feeling of desolation filled her. Today and tomorrow would be the worst.

Tired, she stripped off her clothes, took a quick shower, set the alarm for an hour away then turned back the crisp, cream-colored lines that smelled faintly of lemon and sunk down onto the mattress. She still slept on one side of the bed. She touched the other pillow, Colin's pillow, and took a deep breath. A tear leaked out. She closed her eyes, tight. "Oh stop it," she commanded. Finally, exhaustion overcame everything else and she fell asleep.

The sound of her old-fashioned clock radio woke her. She wiggled further down into the bed as for a fleeting moment, a phantom arm draped over her waist. A masculine scent drifted through her imagination.

Ashley.

She sat up, shook the strange feeling away, as a wave of guilt jolted her, like being doused in cold water.

This was Colin's house, and hers.

Ashley had never been here. She wasn't supposed to feel him here.

What the hell was wrong with her?

She'd fallen in love with a man in a few weeks. No way that was supposed to happen. But, she'd done exactly that before.

She might as well beat her head against a wall. It would make as much sense and do as much good.

How could she have been so--stupid?

In the end, she'd hurt Ashley just as much as she'd hurt herself. Guilt, even more of it.

She'd fallen for the wrong man, in the wrong profession, and felt even more desolate than she had a few minutes ago.

The bleakness of Ashley's mood seemed to permeate his life, unless he was in the shop or on a track.

In the middle of February, the two days before the Daytona 500, the cell phone in his pocket buzzed. Aggravated by the interruption, Ashley picked up the offending piece of equipment and said, "Yes", he sounding surly, even to himself.

"I <u>think</u> I should say good morning," Mark's voice answered.

"Sorry, not in a good humor."

Mark sighed. "Car trouble?"

"No. We've been great."

"Danni flew to Scotland yesterday," Mark said without preamble.

Ashley's stomach dropped to his toes. A humorless, dry laugh escaped.

Mark said, "I know she's been watching you on TV. Sally says Danni may not be capable of facing what she feels."

In his most ungenerous moods, Ashley had wondered if she was capable of any emotion. But, he'd done a lot of thinking in the last month, about himself and what went wrong.

"Hey, maybe she'll change her mind and come back," Mark said.

"Yeah, and maybe I'll win every race this year."

Silence lingered.

"We're having a Daytona 500 party." Mark's voice was suddenly cheerful. "Everybody is required to cheer for you."

Ashley appreciated the change in topic. "Want me to send you t-shirts and crap?"

Mark laughed. "Freebies are a good bribe." The laugh died away. "You got a bunch of friends here Ashley, not just fans."

Despite the disaster with Danni, Ashley was glad he'd moved to Denver.

"I'll call you after the 500," Ashley said.

"Good luck."

"Thanks." Ashley pushed the off button.

"Scotland," he muttered. As long as she stayed in Denver, he held some hope she would change her mind and try. Through the weeks, that hope had dwindled, and the infinitesimal amount left had just dissipated into vapor.

It hurt. A dull ache in the pit of his stomach that wound its way through every part of him. "Damn." He sank farther into the cushions of the black leather recliner in his motor home, and stared out the window.

He'd had a secret dream. That he'd sit where he was now, his mind clear and ready, and Danni near, her hand in his.

So much for dreams.

Hectic was the only word for it, typical for Speed Weeks at Daytona. Appearances, so many Ashley's publicist, Terri, had to remind him where he was and who he was talking to. Sponsor parties. Autograph sessions. Television shows. Fund raisers for other drivers and teams and his charity foundation.

The same routine, but this time it was different. This time, he wasn't alone by choice.

He had a reputation for being aloof, but lately he'd had to work at even being polite.

Ashley went through all the appropriate motions. Smiled, waved, signed, talked.

The morning of the race he woke late, and like most mornings, missed Danni, then got angry.

He met with Kenny, Cade and the rest of his team. He checked and rechecked. Then it was time. He went to the hauler, changed into his drivers suit. Sat through the meeting, Kenny beside him, taking notes.

Then came the driver introductions. They milled around behind the stage, talking to each other, the official guests, reporters and TV crews.

Ashley had hoped that this time it would have been different. He looked at colleagues, competitors, friends and a new wave of anger and hurt hit him. Most of them had people with them, wives, fiancées, girlfriends.

Danni.

He had to get her out of his head. She lurked there, in unanticipated and unexpected places.

He'd failed to keep her at arms length. He'd let her get close. That was his first mistake, the one that made him angry with himself, then at her. Concentrate. Concentrate. If she intrudes, fine, use it. Use it. Just like she used you.

Evan Murphy, the man who gave Ashley his start, and owned the team he still ran for, walked up, chucked him on the shoulder and smiled. "Ready?"

Ashley nodded. "Yeah, I'm ready. How 'bout you?"

"Oh, hell yes. I'm looking forward to victory lane."

Ashley smiled at the optimism and enthusiasm. Evan shook his hand, then Ashley went up the stairs to the flat bed trailer, magically transformed into a stage, and waited the few minutes until his name was called then announced to the crowd.

As he went through introductions, waving at the fans, he knew what he'd do. Just what he'd always done, from the time his parents kicked him out of the house when he refused to quit racing, he'd take anger, rejection, fear and use it, to sharpen his mind, his reflexes. Make him better.

The fans in the stands booed him as much as they cheered. As Dale Earnhardt had once said, <u>as long as they're making noise</u>. Any reaction meant the fans knew who he was.

He used that, too.

As the teams lined up at their pit boxes in straight lines, filling the pit road with vibrant color, he pushed Danni out of his mind and focused on what he needed now.

Finally, after what seemed like hours of pre-race activity, he slid into the car.

The routine soothed him. He took his helmet off the hook, put it on, then his gloves, while one of the crew made sure all the belts were secure, then fastened the window net.

One deep breath, two, three.

"Drivers, start your engines," were the words on the PA. What he heard was Cade's voice, "Start her up."

His fingers, resting quietly on the switches, flicked as the last syllable sounded in his ears.

The engine roared, along with forty-two others. The thunder reverberated through the ground.

He followed the car ahead of him off pit lane and onto the Daytona International Speedway.

Finally, Cade's calm voice filled his ears. "Green. Green. Green."

Two days after her arrival in Scotland, like the idiot she knew she sometimes was, she watched the start of the Daytona 500, on the national network feed from the States.

Blood pulsed, made her head throb, but she made it through driver introductions. Ashley appeared. Her heart stumbled. He smiled and waved at the huge crowds.

Was there a touch of sadness at the corners of his eyes?

No. She imagined it. He was happy, doing what he loved without the encumbrance of a woman who hated it.

She poured a very large whisky and sipped it as somehow, without a panic attack, she watched the cars go round and round the big track. He was doing well.

A commercial break cut into the action, it was a familiar one, featuring a driver hawking jeans, Ashley.

Satellite television had to be the best thing since sliced bread. What had been the best thing before there had been sliced bread? she wondered idly.

The commercial cut off. Cars spinning and sheet metal in the air filled the TV screen.

She gulped, strained to see Ashley's silvery blue, yellow and black paint scheme in the melee. Off her chair, she moved closer to the screen. Hoping, praying his car was not there.

The pile-up stopped in what seemed slow motion. The cameras focused on the mangled pieces of metal which only moments before had been hundred thousand dollar speed machines.

The pressure in her brain, twisting her stomach, eased. He was not among them. The caution flag had slowed the cars that were still in one piece, to sixty miles per hour, and they slowly made their way to the pit road. The red flag came out, stopping all of them. She watched the trailer at the top of the screen, showing who was in what position. Ashley was third. There was a long way to go.

Hands shaking, she took a long pull on her drink, set it down, then lifted the remote and changed the channel.

The television blabbered on, as she watched mindlessly, slowly sipping her whisky and trying to relax. Eventually, the power of the Highland Malt took effect.

Her eyes closed, and she drifted away.

A rear wing flew off a racecar. Spinning, it hit the wall. The entire front wheel assembly broke, breaking the wheel tether, and then the tire and wheel bounced high into the air. Then, with a slowness only the mind can see, gravity pulled it down.

Pulled it down onto the car behind, and the blue and white helmet protecting Colin's head.

"Noooooo!"

Danni woke, breathing hard, every muscle, tense. To stop the sobs, she bit her lip. The dream hadn't come to her in a long time.

It was only by chance she'd ever seen the accident. At home, alone, the night after the funeral, the news was on. She'd heard her name, and turned in time to see the image of the family leaving the church. Then, the picture changed, and showed the last few seconds of Colin's life.

His helmet had protected his head, but the force of the impact with the wheel had broken his neck.

He'd died instantly.

If she hadn't told him she was leaving him, would he have done something different? If she'd handled her grief from the loss of their child better, or managed the fear she felt when he was on a track, would she have ever thought to leave him?

Danni blinked, cleared the tears.

She'd never know.

No one knew of her last words to Colin. Everyone told her it was a freak accident. But the guilt never left.

She couldn't possibly endanger another man's life by being so afraid of what he did that her actions affected his.

No matter how much she loved him.

Ashley's brain only allowed him to think of the feel of the car, strategy and the hundreds of little things that went into winning.

White Flag. Lap one ninety-nine of two hundred.

Turn one. He spent more time looking in his mirrors than he did looking ahead.

Corner two, the car behind him was closing, but not close enough to pass, just close enough to push.

Backstraight.

Cade on the radio, "Almost there... watch your mirrors."

They always said stuff to remind him to do stuff he was doing.

Thanks to the aero push coming from the car behind him, Ashley went faster, passed the car on his right.

No tires going down. Fuel, fine.

Through turn four.

"Clear. Clear. Clear," Cade said.

Nearly there. Nearly there.

"You are the man!" Evan's voice crackled in Ashley's ears.

Front stretch. Two hundred thousand people on their feet, as Ashley, going two hundred miles an hour, flew past the start finish line, under the waving checkered flag. First.

"YEESSS"! The best. You guys are the best." Ashley pumped a fist in the air.

"How does your fourth Daytona championship feel?" Kenny shouted.

Ashley shouted back, "I love it! Maybe it's an omen!"

That was the plan--win his fourth Championship, after only thirty-five more races.

"Burn those tires down," Kenny said.

The smoke from the burn out nearly choked him. Then he did a victory lap, going the wrong way. Elated, he waved at the fans and tried to soak it in.

He steered into victory lane. He wanted him to climb out of the car, but he had to wait for the TV guys to give him the go ahead. In isolation for a few fleeting seconds he felt the awesome, incredible, rush of winning.

Swiftly, the appropriate sponsor/race team baseball hat was shoved into the car. He put it on. Then he reached up, grabbed the outside of the window opening, pulled himself out, stood on the door and shouted in joy.

He managed one deep breath before a microphone was in his face. Answer questions, thank his team, thank his sponsors.

Then the magic act, as he silently called it, continued. He was sprayed with Gatorade and champagne. A towel with one of his sponsors name emblazoned on it appeared, was placed over his shoulder. He used a corner of it to wipe his face.

Then it was his turn. Laughing, he sprayed champagne over Kenny, Evan and the crew. Cade stood at the edge of the chaos, hoping to stay out of the way. No way. Ashley ran toward him, covering Cade in a sticky shower. His teammates came by, hugged him, congratulated all of them.

When Ashley hefted the trophy he smiled till his face hurt.

But it was all-hollow. The woman he wanted to share it with, talk to, kiss, was thousands of miles away.

Ashley's car, still covered in confetti, was pushed into the garage by race officials.

He went to interviews. A quick one with the network covering

the race, a long one at the media center with print and TV reporters. Another one with Fox, NBC then another one with ESPN.

There was a party to go to with the sponsors. Those people he
kept happy so the dollars flowed in for racing. He genuinely liked
many of them, but after a big victory, he wanted to be with the
people who did the dirty work. Building engines, chassis, cranking
wrenches, changing tires...

Ashley knew Evan would have another party, just for the team,
the guys and the women who helped get him where he was.

Tonight he'd stay in Daytona, when he finally got to bed.

Tomorrow, there were more things to do. Sign the car and put
in on display in the museum, where it would stay until next year
then more interviews, TV appearances. By Wednesday he should
be back in Richmond.

The elation of winning faded, and reality and hurt returned.

Danni wasn't a mile away, ignoring his calls. He slammed his
closed fist into the side of the hauler.

It's over. She's done with you. He leaned his head against the
cool metal.

"Come on, I'll walk you to your limo," Kenny said, then slapped
him on the back. "You've been great all month but today, you blew
me away. You did a hell of a job."

"So did you."

"Why, thank you for noticing." Kenny smiled.

They walked side by side. "You had me going for awhile."

"What?" Ashley asked.

"Something's been on your mind. You've been different, quieter."

Ashley raised a brow and tried to turn it into a joke. "Here I
thought I was being less of a bastard than usual."

"Naw, you've been about the same." Kenny's quirky smile faded. "It's like, well...like you're someplace else, until you hit the track.
You haven't explained, and I haven't asked. But, it has something to

do with the woman you were seeing, doesn't it?"

Ashley turned toward his long time crew chief.

"So, you ready to tell me about it?" Kenny asked.

Ashley shook his head. "No. At least not without being drunk."

Kenny slapped him on the shoulder. "That might prove interesting, Ashley Jenkins drunk."

Suddenly, Danni had to know. Had to know what had happened today. Fingers fumbling, she changed the channels until she found the post-race coverage.

The reporter stood in the garage area, the dark night sky visible beyond the halos made from the large overhead streetlights. He said, "We hope to have him here soon, meanwhile, back to you".

Him who? Danni shouted at the TV.

Three guys sat on a stage by the track, and started talking about the race, recapping it by cautions, restarts, great moves and wrecks.

She just wanted to know what happened to Ashley. Surely, there was a rundown somewhere? ESPN would have a trailer if nothing else. She reached for the remote again.

"Bob has our winner, so let's go to him."

Danni snatched her hand back and watched intently, as the garage reporter said, "So, Ashley..." that was all she heard as the camera focused sharply. A dark trace of beard covered his face. His baseball cap, with his sponsors name proclaimed across the front, was pushed back just a little, she could see his eyes. He looked tired, dirty and happy.

The winner. Her tired brain put two and two together. He'd won? Danni giggled, her heart felt lighter than it had in weeks.

He'd won!

She watched, soaked in every word, as he complimented his

crew, crew chief, thanked all his sponsors, did all the things a driver needed to do. Then they talked about the race. Even did highlights with him commenting for a couple of minutes.

Then, the reporter said, "I know you have to get to the media center, so we'll let you go. Congratulations."

Ashley answered, "Thanks." Then disappeared off camera.

Chapter Ten

An incessant sound woke him from a deep sleep. Ashley fumbled for his cell phone, then mumbled, "Hello."

"I'm sorry, I didn't mean to wake you." Danni's voice was soft, tentative. "I wanted to congratulate you."

Ashley shook his sleep fogged head, and hoped it woke his brain. "Thanks. Did you watch it?"

"No. Not live. I saw some on the replay."

He sat up, swung his legs over the edge of the bed in his luxurious hotel suite. "Why did you go to Scotland?"

There was a long pause. "I need to be here."

The anger and hurt simmering inside for the last month bubbled over. "Is it easier for you, now? Are you far enough away from me, or do you need to move again?"

Silence. He couldn't even hear her breathe. Then, she said, "Yes, it is easier and no..." There was a catch in her voice. "...this is far enough."

Being punched in the gut would have felt better.

"I shouldn't have bothered you. I--I. Good luck."

The line went dead.

Throat closing, he shut his eyes, focused on breathing, slowly. Tried to push down the pain.

She'd finally called and he had lost control of his temper. But, damn it! He had the right to be angry.

He glanced at the clock. He'd been asleep for a whole three hours. Another two before he was expected at the museum.

Now, his good mood had been shot to hell.

So, why did he want to pick up the phone and call her back?

Tuesday afternoon, Danni went to the carriage house, no longer containing carriages, but cars, including hers. The Aston Martin convertible sat like a sleeping cat. With more than a touch of irony, she noted it was a deep, silvery blue, just like Ashley's racecar.

She shook her head at her own stupidity, crawled in, and drove through the freezing rain and snow.

What had possessed her? Why had she called Ashley? He'd been so...angry. She supposed he had a right to be.

The tires crunched on the gravel of the drive. She drove over the hills toward the keep that rose slowly from the floor of the valley. Misted in fog, it reminded her of the site of a Gothic novel. For all she knew, it had been.

All these years and she still felt strange, knowing people who lived in an eight hundred year old building that had it's own name.

She parked in the small car park by the family entrance. Most of the public, who paid fifteen Pounds for a tour of the house, gardens and grounds, never saw this part.

She stepped out, then took a deep breath of air that smelled of pine and peat smoke.

Jared, who must have been watching for her, opened the door and waved her in. That was something else she still found strange. The Duke and Duchess had servants of all kinds, but most of the time, answered this door themselves.

Wearing his customary jeans, tennis shoes, a shirt and heavy sweater, Jared was an older, slightly shorter version of both his sons. Augusta, nearly as tall as her husband, was an athletically built lady, her brown hair streaked with gray.

Danni hurried through the door, wiped her feet as Jared helped her out of her coat, then she was hugged and kissed by the two of the people she loved most in this world.

For the love of their son, who'd managed to fall for a middle class American girl, they had taken her to their hearts, taught her what she needed to know, guided, coached, supported and loved her. When Colin died, they had made it very clear she would always be their daughter. They treated her like one.

"All right Miss Mysterious, what has brought you here at this bleak time of the year?" Augusta asked as she led the way to the little parlor they used in the winter. Castles were impressive. They were also damned cold.

Danni sat in a big, overstuffed chair, and sighed.

Jared raised his brows, asking the same thing Augusta had, only silently.

"I... well, I met someone, and... things were moving too fast, and... he's just not right for me. Much as I like him."

"So, you flew all the way here, to get away from him?" Jared's question was filled with incredulity.

Deflated, because it was true, Danni nodded. "Yeah, sounds pretty dumb, huh?"

She stared at the smoke rising from the blocks of peat burning hotly in the fireplace.

"I'd say it depends on the strength of the attraction," Augusta said. "And the reasons for your objections." There was a smile in her voice.

Danni looked up. Augusta lifted the cozy off the teapot, and raised her brows in question.

"Please," Danni answered.

Her in-laws would wait all day for Danni to answer, and she needed a moment to come up with something intelligible. "We are very attracted to each other. We both know it just won't work. And I am so bright I came all the way here to put some space between us, then, I called him." One of her less intelligent moves.

"What did he say?" Jared asked, from his chair.

Ashley's words rang in her mind. He was right. She had run away, and she was just as worried, but at least she didn't argue with him before a race.

It hurt. And it hurt that she had hurt him.

Crap. She blinked furiously, trying to hold back the tears, then gave up and wiped her eyes with her fingertips.

"This is serious," Augusta said. "Surely the problems are not insurmountable, if he feels as you do?"

"Why wouldn't he be right for you? You're one of the most amiable people I know." Jared chuckled, trying to put her at ease, with a lopsided grin that reminded her of Colin. "Unless of course, you've found another driver."

It did seem too impossibly coincidental to be true.

"Oh, my goodness."

"What were the odds of that?"

Augusta and Jared spoke together.

They knew Danni too well. She hadn't said a word, so the look on her face must have spoken for her. Sometimes it bothered her that people could read her so well.

"Well?" Augusta prompted.

"We met at the MG Car Club Christmas Party. I didn't know who he was."

"None of your friends said anything?"

Danni shook her head. "Everyone seemed to think our dating a good idea. I haven't exactly gone around telling people I had had panic attacks.

"When he asked me to go with him, to testing, I fell apart. I can't do it. I should have broken it off after the first date."

"Do you intend to do anything more about the relationship?" Augusta asked.

Danni put her face in her hands and rubbed her forehead. Despite all logic, she missed him, wanted to talk to him, tell him what she was doing. How could she? "I don't know."

"You're not feeling guilty about caring for someone else are you?" Jared asked, his voice calm. "Colin would not want that. It sounds cliché, but it is true. He would want you to be happy."

How could she be happy if she was in a panic? And Ashley's season was twice the number of races as Colin's had been in Formula One.

She put her hands down, and looked at her in-laws. They were right, but the truth was, she had no idea what she would do.

An hour later she left with their good wishes and an invitation to dinner in two nights. The pale light of the sun did little to brighten the day. The wind had picked up, skittering dark gray clouds across the sky. It was bitterly cold.

A mile from the keep, she turned off the gravel drive onto a narrow side road. Though seldom used, it was perfectly maintained. A half-mile later, the outside of the church appeared in the watery light. The church where she'd been married, had the funeral for her son, and her husband.

She turned off the ignition, got out, zipped up her coat and walked to the churchyard. The metal gate had snow stuck on it, as if someone had started spray-painting it white, and only finished one side.

With a flick of her fingers, the latch opened and she walked in. Generations of villagers, the Scott's and their relatives lay peacefully, surrounded by high stone walls that in summer were covered with wisteria, the ground with carpets of blue bells and heather. Now, all was dark, the plants only sticks, the flowers hidden under a mantle of snow.

Shivering, only partly from the cold, she walked to the marker. The marble glowed brighter white in comparison with its older, more ornate compatriots.

Colin's name, date of birth and death, and inscribed beneath it, the name Struan Scott, the day of his birth and death. Her husband and son, in the grave, together.

She sank to her knees, then lightly traced her fingers over the markings.

Everything collided inside her. The grief of losing both of them so close together hit her again, and with it, the guilt that their deaths had been her fault. While aching in the grip of her tears, new pain came. She, who hated feeling abandoned, had left Ashley. Left any hope of love, and tore both their lives apart.

She knelt in the snow, and cried.

"What are you doing out here?" The softly Scot's accented voice burned into Danni's brain.

Hiccupping, she dragged her head up and looked around. Snow swirled through the now dark sky.

She attempted to speak, but nothing came out.

Shaking, scared, she tried to stand, but her muscles, stiff from cold, didn't seem to work right.

"Don't you think it's time to go home?" the gentle voice urged. It sounded so close.

Danni looked around, frantic. There wasn't anyone there.

Hallucinating, that must be it. She had to get a grip. With effort, she levered her aching body into a standing position. Then, haltingly, forced her legs to carry her away.

She shivered, so hard her fingers fumbled with the latch of the gate of the deserted churchyard.

Barely managing to turn the heater in the car to full blast, her teeth chattered for several minutes. With some control on her shattered emotions, she pushed in the clutch, put the car in gear and moved.

She still shivered but managed to drive home.

Her face tingled from blood flowing into it. Her hands felt hot. She'd be lucky if she didn't have frost bite.

At home, she stoked up the fire in the bedroom, then drew a hot bath. She eased down into the water, her eyes burned, her head ached, the wounds in her heart fresher than ever.

She didn't know what she wanted anymore.

No, that was not true.

At this moment, this very second, she wanted Ashley. Wanted his strong, yet gentle arms, his accented melodic voice, his common sense, his intelligence.

Danni wrapped her arms around her waist, pulled her knees up through the deep, warm water and shivered again.

Augusta called. What did Danni want for dinner? Danni coughed, then said, "I'm not sure I'm up to it. I don't feel well at all." That was perhaps one of the biggest understatements of her life. "I think I have a cold, or maybe the flu."

Twenty minutes later, Augusta and Jared walked in the door of the cottage, took one look at Danni and pronounced they were going to the urgent care center.

Danni had an IV. Dehydrated, they said. Antibiotics were pumped in, along with who knew what else. The x-rays ended all doubt. She had double pneumonia and could look forward to a nice long stay in hospital.

Served her right for camping out in a graveyard.

A week later, the doctors pronounced her fit enough to go home. She had assured her parents on a daily basis that she would be fine, there was no need for them to fly over.

She had strict orders about eating right, doing breathing exercises, taking her medication and getting rest. A lot of rest.

Jared and Augusta took her to her home. Though they had threatened to take her home with them.

As they drove through Fort William, the thought of not-hospital food made Danni hungry. "Could we stop for tea?"

Ignoring the we should get Danni home look from Augusta, Jared wheeled the car into the parking lot of Danni's favorite teashop.

The smell of fresh baked scones, pastries, and cakes, mingling with the scent of good tea, filled her now functional nose, and made her mouth water.

The teapot arrived. Danni almost touched the tip of her nose to the steaming brew, and inhaled, as deeply as she could without coughing.

Heaven.

"I know you said you came here to get away, but I doubt the object was to catch pneumonia. Why Danni? What's the real reason you came here?" Augusta's innocently phrased question caught Danni off guard.

She almost blurted the truth, <u>because I'm a coward.</u> Instead, she bit into a red currant scone, the perfect excuse to ignore Augusta's question.

She should have known better.

Around a bite of Scottish butter toffee, Augusta said, "You didn't answer my question."

Danni swallowed, and before she could say anything, Jared went on, "You are important to us. In December you sounded happier than I've heard you in years. Now..."

"You can't run from your feelings forever," Augusta said.

The statement set Danni back on her heels, mentally. "What do you mean?"

"Think about it. You not only gave gifts to charity, you did the work. You know nearly everyone in the village, because every time you heard of an illness, a birth, a death, you were on their doorstep, offering help, gifts, food. But, you don't do that anymore. You don't let anyone close anymore."

Indignant, Danni snapped, "That's not true." She looked at Augusta, then turned to Jared, and expected him to disagree with his wife.

His face, so like Colin's, showed how completely he agreed with Augusta. "You had a hell of a bad turn. I expected you to feel, well, isolated. I did not anticipate that those feelings would last this long."

Augusta touched the back of Danni's hand. "I think you are very much in love. Why is it so hard for you to admit it?"

They were mirroring what her mom and dad, and Colin's brother, Edward, and his wife, Jane had told her.

"Danni, if you had a magic wand, would you do it again? Knowing Colin would not always be with you, would you still go back and marry him?"

"Yes."

"Why?" Jared's tone challenged her.

"Because, I would not trade the years we had for anything."
She sniffed, her nose and eyes filling at the same precise moment.
"I loved him."

Jared handed her his handkerchief. "I know."

"Life is full of risk, Danni. If you don't risk anything, you don't
really live," Augusta said.

Danni knew that, too

Jared touched her cheek, wiped away a tear, his touch as gentle
as the look on his face. The gesture wiped away her rising anger.
"You lost your son, then your husband. We lost our son. We all
grieved. You raced away from life, just to stay safe.

"But you are not safe, Danni, none of us are. We have to grasp
each day and love everyone in it for all we are worth." His face held
an intensity she had never seen.

He was right. She'd known it for a long time, through all the
days she convinced herself not to call Ashley when he called her,
through the nights of missing him, as she wondered what he was
doing. She was not safe.

Her luck had run out.

"Do you love Ashley?" Augusta asked quietly.

Danni bit her lower lip. Oh, yes. And, she had never told him.
Never had the courage. New tears rose. She'd done everything but
slam the door in his face. She nodded.

"Another race driver. You always have liked irony," Jared said,
his grin easing the tension.

Augusta touched her hand. "So, you love him. When you got
here you didn't know what you wanted. What about now?"

Danni stared into the burnt orange depth of her tea, filled with
regret and fear. "What if it's too late?"

Augusta's eyes were bright, with sympathy and understanding.
"Then, you will hurt, but at least you will have tried."

"You're going to have to fight for him Danni, and not just to get him back," Jared said.

Danni nodded. "I'm afraid every time he's on a track."

"Of course you are," Augusta said with complete logic. "You don't want anything to happen to him. I daresay he feels the same about you."

Danni could not stop the weak smile. "But, I'm not getting in a race car."

"No, you're not, you are driving on an M somewhere in the West, with a group of wild cowboys in pickup trucks." Augusta grinned. She'd probably said it just to get Danni to relax. It worked.

Danni grinned back. "It's an interstate, and they are not all cowboys."

Augusta's smile dimmed only a little. "I'd say your fear is natural, but the actual chances of a death in a race are remote. Colin's was a freak accident."

"I know." Danni twisted Jared's handkerchief between her fingers, then balled it up in one fist, while she took a sip of her tea, then another, trying to get the dry feeling out of her mouth.

"Is he worth it?" Jared's blue eyes seemed to look straight through Danni's heart.

Danni closed her eyes, quelled the rising tide of panic, and thought. Really thought. What would she give to be with him, for another day? For whatever remained of either of their lives?

Everything.

"Yes, he is worth it."

"Then, my dear, we need a plan. Time to ring up Edward."

Edward, the family race fan, knew every statistic from every kind of motor racing in the world. And Jane, who enabled him, would be just as excited to help.

A big bag appeared on the table. Mrs. Ross, the owner of the teashop, stood, hands on hips. "There you go Lady Danni, no need to be cooking your own scones and cakes. That should keep you a few days. You ring me up if you need anything now."

Somewhere in the world it was warm, Danni thought. Somewhere like Las Vegas. That's where Ashley was this week. It had been a long couple of weeks.

She'd been too tired to accomplish all she wanted as fast as she wanted. A nap every afternoon was a necessity. Today's had been two hours. While her bed was warm, the wind outside howled, making her want to snuggle farther down under the covers.

Winter in Scotland could be bitter, and this year it was. With a deep breath, pleased that it didn't make her cough, she flipped back the covers and went back to work.

His fantasies were more elaborate.

Danni, naked, in his motorhome. In the garage to surprise him. Cooking him dinner at his home in Denver. The phantom Danni even appeared at his door in Richmond.

Stupid. Just plain stupid.

When he wasn't fantasizing, he tried to keep busy.

He'd done more socializing in the past month than he could remember. And, he read, played X Box, watched all kinds of TV and movies, played poker, anything keep from thinking of her.

And he drove his butt off. He was having the best season of his career.

Part of his new routine was a party, every Tuesday, at his house in Richmond.

The team, including girlfriends, spouses, significant others and children were all here. He provided meat and drinks. They did the rest. It was part of his new plan, devised to boost camaraderie among the team members and to keep him from going nuts.

Ashley drove the grille, and silently wondered what had possessed Cade to invite Jen.

"I'm surprised Pam would let you anywhere near me," Ashley said to the dark haired, statuesque lady. "She may be my best friend's wife and your best friend, but I think she hates my guts."

"Hey, our little affair was six years ago." Jen grinned, then took a sip of her beer. "And, she doesn't hate you. She just doesn't understand you."

"Sometimes, I don't understand myself," he muttered. "I don't suppose you've told her that we talk every few months, have you?"

"Oh no, I prefer to let her stew." Jen grinned.

"Gee, thanks. But, I think it's me in the stew." He lifted his voice, and called, "Steaks are ready."

"Not that I mind, but why did Cade invite you?" Ashley asked. Cade must've thought he needed some feminine companionship. It was the last thing Ashley wanted.

"I'm spending the week. Pam had to ask me."

Ashley chuckled at her frankness. It was one of the things he really liked about her.

They took their steaks to a small table near the gazebo.

Jen's brows rose, a humorous glint in her eyes. "So, how you been? Still the selfish bastard you told me you were?"

He smiled at the memory. He'd told her that the night they had met. The same night Cade met Pam. "To your first question," he answered, "I'm ok and to the second, of course."

"Pammy seems to think you've got a broken heart."

Fuck.

He slammed his fork down. "I wasn't aware it was any of her business."

The humor in her face disappeared.

Damn it. The grip he'd held on his emotions had given out. He stood and strode toward the house.

"Hey!" Pam caught his elbow.

Ashley jerked his arm out of her grasp. "Leave me the hell alone," he hissed.

Her eyes sparked fire. "Then don't be such an asshole. We're trying to help you." Her voice was soft, the tone, stone cold.

"How Pam? By reminding me what a shit I am?"

Without another thought he went into his well-appointed, perfectly decorated, empty house. He wanted to yell, throw something, take a long run, anything, to stop from thinking of how lost he was.

How lonely.

It was an ache, a deep hole that unexpectedly opened beneath him, sucking him down. The only thing that could possibly fill it was three thousand miles away in Scotland.

Chapter Eleven

What the hell was wrong with him? Ashley wondered.

Here he was, still hoping for Danni to show up? Why? She'd walked out, left him, literally, standing in the cold. He loved her. And what she felt for him was...nothing.

He leaned back into the chair in his bedroom. Eyes closed, he thought of the night he'd met Jen and Pam. He'd jokingly told them he was a selfish bastard. Pam probably still believed him.

It seemed like every relationship in his life was in disarray. His parents. Pam. Cade.

The thoughts stopped. It hit him. Like a wall at full speed. It <u>was</u> true. He was a selfish bastard. He'd pushed Danni too hard, thinking only of what he wanted, not what she could give.

If he'd done what he should, told her he loved her, maybe even at New Year's, she might still be in the country. At least he could have given her time, instead of shoving her into panic.

Eyes closed, he pushed down the pain.

"Ashley?"

He opened his eyes.

"Ash?" Cade's voice called softly from the hall.

"In here."

Cade leaned one shoulder of his six-foot-two body against the doorframe, looking completely relaxed. "You okay?" He took a swig of beer, waiting.

Ashley shrugged. Hell if he knew. "Yeah, just needed a minute of quiet. Not used to this much noise."

"Dude, the windows are open. It's not much quieter in here."

"But they are out there," Ashley pointed with his head, "and I am in here. Does make a difference."

"If you say so."

Ashley hoped Cade would move, signaling an end to this particular conversation. No such luck.

"Hope you don't mind we had Jen come with us?" Cade asked.

Better to ask forgiveness afterward, Ashley thought. "No, I don't mind."

Cade grinned. "For some strange reason, she says you're friends." He tucked his fingers into the front pocket of his jeans. "Pam figured that part out awhile back."

"Jen and I are friends, or at least we used to be."

Pam. Cade and Pam.

Ashley's gut tightened. How many relationships had he screwed up? "You know," he said, his voice sounding like a croak around the lump in his throat, "...if you want, if it would make things easier, I'll buy out your contract. Pay you the balance. Let you find something else."

Cade frowned. "What the hell you talking about?"

"If it would work better for you and Pam to go somewhere else. It's not that I don't want you, it's just, I'd understand if you wanted to move on."

Moving away from the doorframe, Cade sat on the foot of Ashley's bed. "You think working with you is hard on my marriage?"

He nodded.

Cade frowned. "Where did you get that idea?"

Ashley shrugged again. "Just put some things together."

"Well, you're wrong." Cade took another drink. "She just likes needling you."

Ashley could believe that. Cade was the only person who could get away with calling him Ash, and Pam had joined Cade as one of the few people who told him exactly what she thought.

And Danni.

He had to stop, close his eyes, before the loss over took him.

"Ashley?"

He opened his eyes.

Cade stood in front of him, his expression strained. "Damn," he muttered.

Ignoring the look, the word and everything it invited, Ashley levered himself out of his chair. "Come on. Let's go party."

Danni rubbed her hands, for the ninetieth time, against her jean encased thighs. Ashley had just gone by in the open topped car, waving at the fans.

The short track at Martinsville, Virginia was surrounded by stands, like a football stadium with a racetrack inside it.

Edward led Danni and Jane from the comfort and relative quiet of the luxury box and sat outside.

They had come along with her. Moral support, they'd said.

F1 races were noisy, full of crazy fans, but Danni had never really watched them. This time, she did watch the crowd and tried to pay attention to the incredible pace and excitement of the sixty-five thousand people filling the stands.

She might have enjoyed it if she wasn't scared half to death.

They had headphones and receivers. They could tune to the drivers' frequencies, to race radio or track officials. Determined to listen to Ashley through the race, Danni had programmed his frequencies into the unit.

By the time the honorary marshal had done the traditional, "Drivers, start your engines," her stomach fluttered with nervous energy.

She <u>would</u> <u>not</u> be sick.

"Relax, Danni," Edward shouted over the pounding roar of forty-three race engines. "He's damned good. And, we're here." He squeezed her hand.

She clamped the headphones back down over both her ears. Her world shrank back into the voices of Ashley's team on the radio.

The racecars swerved from side to side, scuffing the tires, making sure they were clean and checking their grip on the track. It was the chaos theory incarnate. It looked random, but order evolved.

"Going green this lap. Tighten the belts one more time," the calm voice with the soft southern drawl belonged to Cade Smith, Ashley's spotter.

"Roger," Ashley answered.

Side-by-side, row after row, the cars rounded the fourth turn of the paper clipped shaped track. The pace car turned off. The sound of the engines reverberated in her chest, like rolling thunder.

"Green, green, green," Cade said.

She could do this. She had to.

After two laps, Ashley was fifth.

Eight laps later, Kenny Morgan, Ashley's crew chief, said, "Talk to me."

More evidence that watching TV wasn't bad. She'd heard the voices enough to recognized them.

"She's handling good, a little tight off the exit. But okay." Ashley answered.

"Let me know if it changes."

Silence. She pulled up one ear of the headphones and turned to Edward, who repeated her motion. She yelled, "Have you listened to him before?"

Edward nodded. "He's usually fairly quiet."

Headphones back on, the silence continued. Only Cade's voice, issuing instructions as Ashley traded a couple of positions.

"Yellow, full yellow," Cade's voice rang in her ears.

Danni stared at the back straight. Two cars slid down toward the inside wall. Ashley was ahead of it, on the front straight.

Silence again. Then, "Pit road open next time around," Kenny said.

"Next time by," Ashley acknowledged. They got real technical about the changes they'd make to the car. Danni just wanted him to get on and off pit road without getting hit. He did. It was a quick stop.

This was nerve wracking, spine tingling.

"Going green this lap," Cade said.

Danni's nerves stretched thin.

The growl of forty-three monstrous engines circling the half-mile track every fifteen seconds filled the air to the point where it felt as if she were breathing the sound.

Just as Ashley entered turn four, Cade radioed, "Green, green, green."

The cars surged forward and roared past her.

"Good restart," Cade said. Then, "Clear low. Clear low. Clear low."

Ashley swept past two cars.

"Clear, clear, clear."

Edward turned to Danni. She lifted the headset to hear him. "That was smooth," he shouted.

Danni let out the breath she hadn't realized she'd been holding.

Her stomach still had a butterfly farm in it. Not just from nerves.

Excitement. She was excited. Not just scared, excited!

The realization made her grin. But there was a long way to go.

There were more cautions, bumps and spins. She watched, listened, as Ashley worked his way to the lead. Thrill mingled with her fear.

This was different from before, with Colin. She was more in control, still scared, but not to the point of panic.

There were knots in her stomach, but she was doing better than she thought she would.

"Yellow. Yellow."

Two hours later, the race less than ten laps from the end, there was another caution. This time as she watched Ashley go around the track behind the pace car, there was no talk of making a pit stop. They would stay out, and try to win.

"This is a piece of cake," Kenny commented.

Ashley was silent.

"Ash, you've been running faster than these guys all day. This is a gimme," Cade said.

Danni bit her lip.

The pace car led the way. She rubbed her hands on her jeans again, her heart hammered in tempo to the beat of the engines.

"Get the tires clean. Let's have a good restart. How does it feel?" Kenny asked.

"She's good," Ashley answered.

The green flag dropped. Ashley pulled away from the cars behind him.

"Great restart. You're clear," Cade said.

"I thought so," Ashley answered.

Danni crossed her fingers and counted down the laps.

The starter waved the white flag. One lap to go.

"Hey, can you sing a song or something? I'm getting kinda bored," Ashley joked.

"You have checked out." Danni recognized the slang for running away from the competition. Ashley had nearly a half second lead when the checkered flag waved. A huge margin on this tiny track.

"Yeesss!" Ashley shouted. "The best. You guys are the best!"

"You're not too bad yourself," Kenny said.

"Well, thank you, thank you," Ashley laughed.

Danni bounced up and down on her toes and cheered with everyone else as Ashley did a burnout, then grabbed the checkered flag and circled the track.

Edward and Jane gave her a hug, momentarily chasing away her nerves.

"I want to watch the stuff in victory lane," Danni announced.

"I thought you would." Jane grinned. "Just remember, here, Victory Lane is on the track."

Danni watched as the crew ran up to Ashley's car, which stopped right on the start finish line.

TV camera's and microphones were in Ashley's face as he climbed out of the car. The giant screen in the infield broadcast the pictures. Loud speakers in the stands boomed with the voice of the reporter and Ashley.

His voice washed over her. She could listen to him all day. She watched his face, and her fears about what she would say and how he would react when she found him, resurfaced.

She wanted to talk to him face to face. She thought by showing up now, at a race, she'd prove to him and her, she could do it.

Edward put both his hands on her shoulders. "Remember where I told you to go? You'll have to wait. They have to do all the photos, the hat dance and interviews."

Danni nodded.

Jane took the headset and the receiver from Danni's hand. "We'll just roam around the caravans until you call. Good luck." She kissed Danni on the cheek.

"He's a lucky man today." Edward winked. "I hope he knows

how lucky. Off you go," he said, with gentle push on her back.

Ashley changed into jeans and a shirt for the victory party in one of the suites. It had been almost two hours since he'd climbed out of his car. He walked toward the pit road wall.

Kenny walked up, smiling. "As expected, post race inspection was clear. You still planning on Mexico for your week off?"

Ashley nodded. Next week, Easter weekend, was one of the three weeks off during the thirty-six-race season. He was hoping the time alone would help him get his head together.

He looked across the track to the gated entrance. About fifty people milled around, waiting for autographs.

As rabid as they were, the fans were amazingly respectful. Ashley smiled and shook his head. It had been a good day.

Only one thing could make it better.

Stop it. Just stop thinking about her.

"The multitudes await. Maybe you can pick up a date?" Kenny joked.

Ashley raised his brows, reached into the pocket of his team jacket and pulled out an indelible ink pen. "As I am nothing, if not magnanimous, I will sign some autographs."

Kenny grinned and said, "I'm going back to the hauler." _

A security guard kept the fans off the track and out of the pit area.

He glanced through the crowd, in the late afternoon light, but saw no one familiar.

No. No way. She was in Scotland.

Ashley reached the fence, went through the gate, under the watchful eye of a security guard, then took the program someone pushed in front of him. He signed it, then a baseball hat, a model car, another program.

A child handed him a t-shirt and before Ashley signed it, he glanced down, asked the boy's name. At the edge of his vision a small, blond woman reluctantly backed away, as if she were afraid she would be noticed.

His breath froze. He stared, as she took another hesitant step back.

"Danni?" he whispered.

She stopped.

The fabric of the boy's T-shirt slid through Ashley's hands.

"Thank you," the boy said.

Still staring at his dream, Ashley answered, "You're welcome." She was only a few feet away. She looked like a scared rabbit, about to run.

He made his way to her slowly, like walking through water.

Finally, he was close enough to touch her, but kept his hands balled into fists at his sides. "Danni?"

She was gasping, with tears in her eyes.

"You're in Scotland--or were." He tried to rein in the emotions boiling in him. "Why were you leaving?"

She sniffed. "I thought you saw me, then when you stopped to sign autographs, I thought you didn't want to see me."

If she didn't stop crying, he'd start himself. Pain warred with pleasure, fantasy with reality. He wanted to touch her. Kiss her. Scream at her. He crossed his arms over his chest.

"Why are you here?" he asked quietly.

Danni brushed her eyes with the backs of her hands, as if pressing the tears back in. She sniffed again, then managed to speak. "I owe you an apology."

For kicking him in the gut? Ashley didn't move.

"I lied to you. Well, not a lie, I just didn't tell you. I should have. I hurt you, and I shouldn't have done that either. I love you. I should have told you that day, instead of walking away."

"You love me?"

"But, I was afraid. Afraid of what I felt, what I thought. Afraid to be hurt."

He opened his mouth, but she just kept on going.

"But I hurt, anyway. And I hurt you. I'm so sorry, Ashley. I had to tell you. I hope you don't hate me."

She stood, eyes closed, head down, looking like she'd break. He'd been angry, depressed, realized he was a lot of the cause, then given up hope. But, here she was.

He could stand it no longer. "Danni?"

She did not look up.

Ashley reached out, lifted her chin with two fingers. Her eyes were puffy, red, so was her nose. She'd never looked more adorable. He put one hand on each side of her face. Touched her wet, warm skin. Softly, he brushed her tears away with his thumbs. "We have a lot of talking to do." This was not going to be easy.

"I know we do. I ... have to try Ashley. I love you too much to just let you go."

The words took away some of his anguish. But it was a start. He had to try too. "Apology accepted."

Her arms slipped up over his shoulders. He wrapped his arms around her waist and lifted her off the ground.

She nuzzled her face against his neck. He spun her around, and noticed the faces of several dozen strangers. All of them grinned like happy fools.

One tall, large man drawled, "I guess when she told that guard she knew you, she meant it."

Ashley let Danni slide to the ground, but didn't let go of her.

"Yeah, she does," Ashley answered. He looked down as she looked up and gave her best brave face. He brushed his knuckles along her cheek. "Come with me?"

She nodded, apparently out of words.

But they had much to say to each other. This was just a starting place.

He kept her hand in his, and walked through the small crowd. "If you'll excuse us, please," he said.

Several people had cameras and camera phones out. With photos no one else had, they probably wouldn't mind not getting an autograph.

"Have you been out here long?"

She nodded. "Since the end of the race. I asked the guard to send word, or take a message, but he wouldn't. So I just waited. We couldn't get garage credentials." She sniffed.

He blinked as he realized what she had said. "We? Who?"

"Edward and Jane."

Ashley smiled. Maybe he would get to meet them.

Without letting go of her hand, Ashley made his way to the tower suite where a number of people waited to congratulate him. Danni, understanding what was happening, told him to schmooze, she was okay. They stayed only a little while, then Ashley announced they had plans with some of Danni's relatives. That would either stop or start a number of rumors. Danni wasn't the first woman who'd appeared at his side after a race, but she was the first one he wanted to keep.

Ashley held her rather chilled hand in his, and ran down the stairs into the parking lot, laughing.

"Stop, stop," Danni called.

He pulled her around, into his arms. He realized she looked--thinner. "Are you alright?"

"I'll be fine," she said through shallow breaths.

Her phone rang. She glanced at the screen , then answered. "So far so good. We're in the parking lot." Silence, then, "I'll meet you at the car."

"Where are you parked?" he asked with a smile.

She pulled a slip of paper from her pocket. "Lot, row and space." A lopsided grin appeared. Charming.

He walked beside her, an arm around her shoulders. After a bit of hesitation, her arm went around his waist. It was good.

But for how long?

Apprehension filled him. "Danni?"

"Hmm?"

"What do you want to do?"

She stopped, turned toward him, her hand still resting around his waist. "I've so much to tell you. But, I don't know what <u>you</u> want."

He stood thinking, as smoke tickled his nose. The RV campers had stoked their campfires and grills. The air filled with the smell of roasting meat. He wanted more than he could explain. Unsure how to go forward, he asked, "Are Edward and Jane going to meet us?"

"Yes."

"Do you have plans with them?"

"We have a hotel, but, I guess..." Her voice faded away. She glanced down.

Her shoulders were set and her back stiff. With one hand on each side of her face he lifted it. He stared into the deep blue depths of her eyes and tried to read her mind. "Danni, tell me what you want." So much depended on her answer. "Right now, what do you want?"

She turned her face into his palm, filling it with warmth. "I want to go with you."

"I'm flying to Denver in the morning. Then, day after tomorrow to Puerto Vallerta for a vacation, coming back the Monday after Easter, then, testing in Richmond, appearances somewhere, then to the race in Texas."

A hint of a shy grin appeared. "I don't have a bathing suit with me."

"We're stopping in Denver, you'll have time to pack."

"You want me to go with you?"

Damned right. "If it's what you want."

"It's what I want. But, I'm scared, Ashley."

He pulled her close. She melted against him. He felt the beat of her heart against his chest. "So am I..." The words his brain tried to form evaporated as she looked up at him. She kissed him.

His hands skittered along her ribs. "What happened? You're a lot thinner."

"She was in hospital for a week with pneumonia," a man's voice, with a Scots lilt, said from behind him.

Startled, Ashley turned as Danni chuckled. He looked back at her. Concern bubbled with anger. "Pneumonia? Why didn't you tell me? Are you okay?"

"Yeah, I'm fine." The squeeze she gave reassured him. "Let me introduce you to Edward and Jane Scott."

Both offered him a firm handshake and a smile.

"Are you coming back to the hotel with us or do you have a better offer?" Edward asked Danni, with a crooked smile and a lifted brow.

Ashley's gut tensed. What if Danni had changed her mind, again?

Her fingers laced through Ashley's. He relaxed.

"I have a better offer," she answered.

Jane smiled brightly at him. "Very good. We'll probably fly home in a couple of days. Give us a ring."

Feeling better than he had in months, he smiled back. "We will."

"You need a lift anywhere?" Edward asked.

Ashley shook his head. "No, thanks. I have a helicopter waiting, if Danni feels up to walking a little?"

She squeezed his fingers. "Just don't run."

"But, crazy as this sounds, I'm starving. Change in plans, could we meet at your hotel?"

Jane and Edward smiled. "Sure," she said as Edward nodded.

Ashley put an arm around Danni's shoulders and tucked her in next to his side. This is where she belonged, where he needed her to be. Where he hoped she wanted to be.

"This is the oddest thing."

"What?" she asked.

"Only a little while ago, I won a race, and I haven't thought about it much at all."

"That is odd." He could hear the smile in her voice. "So, what are you thinking about?"

Still walking, he turned his head and kissed the top of her head. "That you're here." There were several other things on his mind, but this had to be done one step at a time.

"Was it easier, or harder than watching an F1 race?" He took a breath, then another, and another before she answered him.

"Easier, it was easier, maybe, because I could see the whole track. I didn't have to guess what was happening."

Breathing was a little easier. "I'm glad."

"So am I."

There were a few cars left in the parking lot. But, he could see fires near the campers and motor homes. Smoke and the smell of food filled the air.

His mouth watered. He wanted food almost as much he wanted Danni. Food first, then, other things.

In the bar, tucked into a corner, Jane and Danni found the gentlemen, who as the title indicated, rose and pulled out chairs for her and Jane.

Danni had thrown all her stuff back in her suitcase and had it ready to go.

Ashley had tonic water with lime. Edward had gin in his.

"They will have a table for us soon. Out of the way," Ashley said.

"I think only thirty people or so have stopped by, fortunately none of them drunk." Edward smiled.

Danni watched as, after a little prompt from Edward, Ashley hit the highlights of the race, told them the things they did not hear on the radio. There was more than one frequency.

Thinking about the race, she knew something inside her had changed, and she had no idea what. Was it maturity? It had been easier and not only because she could see the whole track.

She had been scared for him, but not to the point of panic.

Quietly, the host came and escorted them to a dimly lit table in the very back of the restaurant. Perfect.

Steak all around, though Ashley ordered an appetizer and a salad. "A bottle of champagne and four glasses, please," was the last thing he told the waiter.

Danni raised an eyebrow at him.

He slipped his hand over her fingers where they rested on the table. "I feel like celebrating."

His fingers were warm and she squeezed them.

They ate, talked, and Danni wondered how in the world she had stayed away for so long.

She would try. It was all she could promise right now. But she would try.

Late that night, they boarded Ashley's plane, blissfully devoid of anyone other than Pete and a copilot Danni hadn't met before. She and Ashley settled into a seat for take off. Once they were at a cruising altitude Ashley kissed her cheek. "I'm taking another shower. I'd ask you to join me..." he leaned over close to her. His breath tickled her neck. "The shower is tiny and I want a bed."

The image of making love to him was so marvelous she almost forgot what she intended to tell him.

After only a few minutes, Ashley appeared, thick hair wet, slicked back, curling on the ends. She wanted to run her fingers through it and kiss him until she couldn't think anymore.

He slumped into the seat beside her. "I feel, and smell, human again."

Danni chuckled. "You weren't too bad."

"Thanks. I think."

He smelled of soap and shampoo, and--him. She drew in the scent like a tonic.

She sighed and moved back, so she could look him. She could fall into the depths of those eyes so easily, but it was time to talk.

Her fingertips to his jaw, she said, "Ashley," then paused. She'd rehearsed what she would say, but it didn't seem right. She started again, "I convinced myself I didn't love you. I never wanted to let anyone get close again. When you told me you loved me, I panicked."

His wonderful mouth turned up just a tiny bit at the corners. "I noticed."

She wrapped her arms around her body and tried to hold herself together. "When I met Colin, he was doing Grand Touring series. I wasn't comfortable with racing, but I thought it would get easier. It never did. It got worse." It had taken a lot of introspection to think through all this.

"Colin moved into Formula One in only a year. The press, everyone, talked about how young he was, how much pressure there was on him to win. He worked harder."

She glanced at Ashley. His focus was centered on her. After a couple of deep breaths, she continued. "It was like the harder he drove, the more frightened I became."

"You thought he was taking more chances?"

She nodded. "That's how I felt, whether it was true or not. As the years went by, the fear got worse. I so wanted him to quit." She ignored the stinging in her eyes. "I know he loved me. But, I came to feel I - - I was second."

She forged ahead. "I'd been on bed rest with my pregnancy for weeks. Colin was home when he could be. His team didn't want him to miss anything. He was in contention for the drivers' championship. When Struan was born, I finally had something to hold on to. Then--"

"Danni, I know about--"

She put a hand up, stopping him. She had to say the rest. She rushed on. "Struan died from SIDS when he was a month old. I was so lost. I wanted Colin home. But he had to drive." This time, she couldn't stop the tears flowing, she closed her eyes, and went on.

"Colin called from the track. I told him I was leaving him. He told me we'd talk when he got home. Then, he said, 'I love you'. I hung up on him."

Danni couldn't seem to make her lungs work right. Strangled, she the forced the words out. "Two hours later, he was dead."

Chapter Twelve

Ashley tucked her close. He held her, his warm, solid body kept her from floating off into misery. She didn't know how much time went by before she swallowed hard, and finished. "It's my fault. He was too busy thinking about what I'd said to concentrate on his job."

"Oh, Danni." He shifted away from her, but the warmth of his hands didn't leave her. "I've seen the video. It was a freak accident. You have no responsibility for what happened."

"You don't think our argument had anything to do with it?" she asked.

"No, and you shouldn't either," he said, his voice sincere and full of determined comfort.

Silence fell. After several minutes, he said, "Just in case you're thinking our split was all your fault..." He tipped her chin. She looked straight into his green eyes. "It wasn't. I'm sorry."

"I guess we both messed up." She moved her head, back to his shoulder, where she could hear the beat of his heart.

"Um hum." His hand still moved on her back, soothing. "Why didn't you return my calls?" he asked, a trace of sadness in his voice.

Again, she regretted her decision to not call back, much less leave the country. "I thought if I didn't talk to you, you would forget about me." She snuggled her face against him. "The longer I was gone, the more I knew I was wrong. I just couldn't admit it." It had been hell. "I ran away, because I was scared."

Needing to see his face, she leaned back. His eyes were filled with an intensity she had never seen, as if he wanted to see into her thoughts.

"I do love you," she said.

He pressed his mouth against her forehead. "How could you love an arrogant, self centered, ass like me?"

"You're not any of those things."

"Yes, I am," he said. "You make me better."

His fingertips brushed her lips, and they tingled.

"Ashley, I don't know if I can do this. I really don't. But, I'll try. If I can't handle it, I'll tell you."

"You will not face this alone. I'll help you, every way I can." He squeezed her so tight it took her breath. His scent filled her senses. His soft words filled her mind, and heart. "I love you, Danni."

It was late, but there was still so much between them that they needed to say. They had been talking the whole flight. He reveled in the feel of her soft hair. She lay, half off his chest, her head on his shoulder. His arm wrapped around her waist.

She said, "When I got to Scotland, more people asked me what the heck I thought I was doing, and finally, I knew. I was just running away, because I was scared."

She shifted, stared at him.

He touched the creamy smooth skin of her cheek, still damp from tears.

"I'm still scared, but I don't want to miss a single day with you. I want to wake up and see you. I want to tell you I love you, every day."

The soft tips of her fingers brushed his lips, he shivered.

She was here. They were together. Now, he had to make sure he didn't screw it up.

Danni sat quietly, her body tucked up beside him. He had given a lot of thought to this. He might as well say it and see how she reacted. "Danni, I think we should see a psychologist or psychiatrist."

A very quick turn of her head and she stared up at him. "Why?"

"You said yourself you spent the hours during a race scared and tense. That it was irrational. It makes sense to find someone who can help. I don't want you to be miserable."

Her shoulders slumped a little. "I'm afraid, not psychotic."

Ashley pulled her tighter against him. "You're not. I just think there is a better way for us to cope."

"Us?"

"Yes. Us."

She sighed. "You really think it could help?"

He leaned his cheek against the softness of her hair. "I do."

In Denver on Monday, they'd met Danni's parents for dinner, who'd beamed like a couple of lunatics. Obviously, they thought she'd made the right decision.

Tuesday morning they left for Puerto Vallerta. Good thing they were in Ashley's jet, or else she'd be way over the luggage weight limitations. She'd packed three suitcases, one for Puerto Vallerta, one for Richmond, one for Texas. Ashley spent most of the flight on the phone, doing interviews and managing all the other things he had to do to keep a very hectic life on schedule.

She understood that, accepted it as a part of the life of a race driver. She was happy to be with him.

At three in the afternoon, heat and humidity hit her like a warm wave as she stepped off the plane. The fresh salt scent of ocean tickled her nose. The limo sent by the hotel dropped them off at the end of a covered walkway that led to the open-air lobby. Stucco walls painted a cool tan with red tile floors and a woven palm roof completed the tropical feel. Straight ahead, palm trees, bougainvillea and flowers lined the walkways to the pool. Beyond lay the beach.

The ocean waves lapped in a soft rhythm against the sand. Ashley tugged on Danni's hand, pulling her away from the view.

The only solid wall of the lobby appeared to be the one behind the front desk, to her left. On the right, still sheltered under the roof, were chairs, tables and overstuffed loveseats for the patrons of the bar. A Piña Colada suddenly sounded very good.

The desk clerk said, "Welcome Mr. Jenkins. Your suite is ready."

While Ashley registered, Danni looked around again. She hadn't traveled much since Colin's death. She could afford it, but hadn't seen the point. Ashley had planned to come here by himself. Would he have been as lonely as she imagined she would've been?

Being alone she understood, and appreciated, but lonely was a different matter. Ashley had few close friends. His best friend had been married for several years. A surge of empathy washed over her.

She'd been by herself for a few years. Ashley had spent most of his adult life alone.

"Thank you, sir," the desk clerk's voice drew her from the winding path her thoughts had taken. "The bellman will take you up."

Ashley took Danni's hand, looked at her, then cocked his head to one side. "What are you thinking?"

Filled with so many emotions, she voiced the one that was the least dangerous. "That I'm glad I'm here."

A charming lopsided grin lit his face. "Me, too." They followed in the wake of the bellman with their luggage.

Her jumbled thoughts raced. She loved him so much. She was thrilled to be with him, to absorb his warmth, his scent. But much more, she knew, bubbled beneath his charming surface. His apparent confidence hid self-doubt. The somewhat aloof persona he cultivated kept people from knowing him well.

He was so complex. Like a faceted diamond, and sometimes, she figured, he could be just as hard.

Their relationship would not be easy, for either of them. But damn it, he was worth every drop of effort.

The bellman stopped before the doors of an elevator. She'd been so busy thinking, she hadn't appreciated what was before her.

The center of the hotel was a giant solarium, rising six stories. Trees, plants and flowers filled the indoor garden. At the far end, an artificial waterfall cascaded down the full height of the building, then flowed through three black marble channels to a pond.

The scent of the plants and the music of the water filled her. Both were suddenly cut off as the doors of the glass elevator closed.

On the sixth floor, the doors opened silently and sounds and smells again filled the air.

The hotel was shaped like a reverse "L". The foot held the lobby and restaurant, the long part, rooms. Theirs was at the very end.

The room was immense. They waited while their luggage was placed in the bedroom to her left. The bellman quickly pointed out the features of the room, got his tip from Ashley and left.

Danni finally found her voice, "This is incredible."

He smiled a crooked little grin, making her smile back. "Glad you like it."

The big bedroom had it's own balcony, covered with a wooden arbor, overlooking the swimming pool and the surrounding gardens and fishponds.

Grasping her hand again, he led her back to the living room. "This is my favorite part." He opened the door onto the balcony. It was at least twenty feet from the door to the rail, where plant boxes overflowed with flowers. There were high walls to either side, making the space completely private. At the rail she looked down on the beach and ocean.

It was spectacular.

After a deep breath, she sighed, then laughed as she realized he had done the same thing, at the same moment.

"I love coming here," he said, as he stared out over the waves. "I know there are lots of places I haven't been and probably plenty that are nicer, but...I don't know, I just feel comfortable here."

Danni watched him out of the corner of her eye. He leaned with his forearms on the railing, his fingers interlaced.

"Have you ever felt that way about a place?" He looked at her, his eyes narrowed against the glare of the sun. "A place you'd never been before, but suddenly felt connected?"

Danni took a breath, unsure if he would appreciate her answer, but she'd tell him anyway. "Yeah, Scotland."

Something flickered through his eyes, then he nodded. It had to be difficult for him to be reminded she'd been in love, been married.

Growing up, she'd always thought there was one special person in the world for her, and she'd decided it had been Colin. And now, she'd discovered another person, and she never wanted Ashley to believe he came second. Because, he didn't. There was nothing more important to her, than him.

She ran her fingers along the line of his jaw. "I felt connected to you, with that first kiss in my laundry room."

His eyes closed for a moment, just longer than a blink. A little tension left his shoulders. He ran the tips of his long, strong fingers under her jaw, more than a caress. It seemed to say <u>you're mine</u>.

She leaned her head into his touch, and closed her eyes. Soft, warm lips touched her cheek, then her mouth. Danni drank in his kiss, drowning.

When, at last, he let her go, she held to his waist like he was a life preserver sent to save her.

He'd brought her back to life, to living. The beat of his heart thumped in her ear. His fingers in her hair, she felt as much as heard him say, "I'm here, baby, I'm here."

An hour later, after they'd unpacked, Ashley proclaimed he was ready for a snack, a "fu-fu drink," and a dip in the pool. He looked good in a swimsuit. That lean, well-sculpted body and slightly olive skin made a dynamite package. It might be hard to keep her hands off him.

She'd never been much of an exhibitionist, but being with Ashley might change her mind. After all, she didn't want some other woman thinking he was available. It wouldn't do to hang a sign around his neck saying, Look Don't Touch.

They dumped towels, Danni's beach bag, with books, sunscreen, sunglass cases and other stuff on a small table under a cabana, kicked their flip-flops under the chaises and walked into the water. It was perfect, just enough to feel cool without being cold. They played around only for a couple of minutes before he took off toward the end of the infinity-edged pool, where a realistic looking pile of rocks sat like a small island, complete with waterfalls. As she sidestroked in Ashley's wake, the front side of the rock pile revealed a swim up bar, facing the ocean.

Short of breath from the light exercise, Danni gratefully slid onto the seat of a bar stool that didn't quite rise out of the water.

Her shaky breath drew a questioning look from Ashley. She nodded, blinked. He understood, then, kissed her cheek.

Ashley ordered ceviche for two and the Piña Colada's she'd

dreamed of earlier.

"So, what do you do when you come here?" Danni asked.

"Run on the beach, use their work out room, snorkel, swim in the pool and eat fantastic seafood." He grinned. "Sleep late."

"You always sleep late." She took a sip of the tasty drink. "And you are a bottomless pit when it comes to food."

The smile deepened as he shrugged. "I relax. No temptation to add stuff to my schedule."

"I think I'd feel isolated."

His smile faded. Dark brows rose. "You haven't taken a trip like this since he died?"

Danni almost hated to admit it. "No." It was another example of running away from life.

"That's understandable." His hand, fingers cool from his drink, slipped over her shoulder and cupped the back of her neck. "But, it's behind you now."

"I'm working on it."

Leaning very close, only inches from her, he said, "I know. And I love you."

"I'm glad."

"Hello," a male voice said from directly behind them.

Danni jumped, damned near out of the water. She'd been so focused on Ashley she hadn't noticed the guy swim up.

Ashley jerked around. "What the hell? Were you trying to scare the shit out of me?" Ashley demanded.

The big blond guy answered, "Well, yeah." His gaze shifted to Danni.

Bewildered, she looked from Ashley back to the blond, then noticed a woman, with very long dark hair and brown eyes, who was inspecting Danni as if she might be a particularly low form of parasitic life.

"Who are you?" Danni asked.

"I was about to ask you the same question?" the woman asked, her words clipped, a haughty note in her voice.

Danni considered leaving her comfortable water seat and swimming away. But, she'd run enough, from lots of things. And she wasn't leaving Ashley to these two.

Straightening her spine, she put on her best aristocratic mien like a cloak. "I am Dr. Danielle Hopkins-Scott, and I am not at all pleased to make your acquaintance, whomever you may be."

She started to turn away, but Ashley dropped his arm around her shoulders, stopping her. Taking her eyes off the intruding woman, Danni stole a glance at him. He had a half-cocky grin, his eyes filled with challenge and--humor. Something here was not what it appeared.

"Danni, I'm sorry. The tall blond is Cade Smith and the lady, who puts up with me, is his wife, Pam."

Perhaps a sinkhole would appear and swallow Danni. "What?" She stared at Ashley, who until a second ago, had been the new love of her life.

"Oh, my," Pam said, joined in chorus with Cade's, "Damn it, Ash."

"I didn't have the chance to say anything," Ashley attempted to explain to Danni.

Pam walked through the chest high water, closer to them. "I didn't realize..." She shook her head.

"Cade is one of the team engineers and my spotter."

"And someone you've known since seventh grade. I do pay attention," Danni said, still peeved.

Ashley didn't move his arm, but cleared his throat. "Why don't we start over? Cade, Pam, this is Danni Scott, who I asked to come with me on this trip. What are you two doing here?"

"Well," Cade seemed to shift from one foot to the other while simultaneously moving toward them. "We thought you'd be here by yourself and we came to surprise you." He looked down, shrugged, then glanced up. "Guess it wasn't too good an idea."

Ashley rubbed his hand over his mouth, effectively covering a smile.

Danni pursed her lips to stop the grin she felt coming on and said, "Maybe not a bad idea but, rather, unexpected?"

Pam's lips lifted on one side, a deeper understanding glimmering in her eyes. She chortled and it grew into a wholehearted laugh. Danni found herself smiling in return.

When Pam wound down, she said, "I'm sorry, when we saw the two of you sitting here, we thought the absolute worst."

"I'm sorry, Dr. Scott, Ashley." Cade blushed.

"Please, call me Danni." She held out her hand. Cade took it, almost gratefully. Then, Danni extended the same gesture to Pam, who with another smile, accepted.

"Piña Colada?" Danni asked.

"I think I need one," Cade said.

"I thought for a second or two I would have to stop a fight," said the five foot, three inch tall bartender.

"You are the same Danni who broke up with him in January? Right?" Pam asked.

Danni, stretched out in the sun on the chaise, took a sip of her second drink, and pretended to watch Cade and Ashley play water volleyball with a bunch of other people.

"Unfortunately, yes."

"I know it's none of my damned business, but why?"

She had known this woman for an hour, and if she didn't think Pam had Ashley's best interests at heart, Danni would have told her to take a hike. "I didn't think I loved him."

"So why <u>unfortunate</u> that you split with him?" Pam persisted.

Danni pushed her sunglasses down her nose, and looked over the top at Pam. "Because, I was wrong."

"Fair enough."

Silence reigned for several minutes.

"The first time I met Ashley," Pam said, "he informed me and my friend he was an arrogant bastard. That is a quote. For a long time, I believed him."

He'd said as much to Danni, and it was so very far from the truth. She knew he had a darker side, and there was the competitive part she had only seen glimpses of. "Interesting. I never thought so."

"Please, tell me how you met?" Pam asked.

Danni spent the next half hour going through some of the history. She thought Pam read more into it, in an insightful way, than Danni intended.

The guys rejoined them. Ashley intentionally dripped over Danni, then smiling, he towel dried then dropped onto a chaise. "I have a suggestion."

"Really?" Danni asked, flicking the water beads off her stomach with a finger, pretending annoyance.

Ignoring her, Ashley said, "You two..." he pointed with his head to Cade and Pam, "...go your merry way, a second honeymoon, since you obviously left Erin somewhere."

"My beautiful daughter is with my folks," Cade said.

"Figured as much," Ashley said. "We do what we want, then meet each morning for breakfast. How's that sound?"

"That's a great idea," Pam answered.

Cade shrugged.

Danni still wasn't sure what he was thinking. Pam seemed to be encouraging, but Ashley's best friend seemed ambivalent, at best. "Sounds good to me," he said, at last.

Late in the afternoon, Ashley and Cade left their ladies and went to the concierge desk to make dinner reservations, and then headed toward the bar.

"What's on your mind?" Ashley asked, noticing for the forty-fifth time how thinly Cade's lips were drawn.

He shook his head, his lips rolled in completely. Ashley recognized the stubborn look, he'd seen it a lot in the last twenty years.

"Nothing..."

"Bullshit. What?"

Cade shifted, obviously uncomfortable. "This the same woman you've spent the last three months being pissed at."

The not really a question made Ashley mentally stop. "Yeah, sometimes. But it's not that simple."

"Sure it is. She pulled your heart out and walked all over it. How can you just welcome her back into your life?"

Ashley stopped and lowered his voice. "It wasn't all her fault."

"Come on Ash--"

"Cade, I love you like a brother, but this is not a topic for discussion."

After a deep breath, Ashley spoke what he knew was fact. "I did something stupid and there are things about us, about her, you don't know."

"I just don't understand." Cade glanced away, then back.

Had their positions been reversed Ashley would have felt the same way. "Hang with me, please. I...need your help."

Cade shook his head. "I'll try. But right now, all I can think of is the look on your face at your house a few weeks ago, and how damned miserable you've been."

"I have not been mis--"

"Yes, you have."

Ashley could concede that point. "Okay. I won't argue, but I want you to understand. Her appearing after Martinsville may be the single most important event in my life."

Cade took a huge, deep breath. As he exhaled, his body relaxed, a little.

He'd been Ashley's bodyguard, figuratively and literally, for so long Ashley could hardly imagine life without the stable, solid presence.

"Okay," Cade said.

Ashley ordered the next round.

While they waited for the drinks, Cade said, "I'm not the only one Ash. You'll have to fight this with every member of the team."

Ashley had known that, but had buried the thought. "I guess I'll have to convince you, so you can help me convince everyone else."

Cade stared, boring a hole deep into Ashley's head, and then said, "You have a long way to go."

Ashley had awakened over an hour ago, and had been staring at the ceiling ever since.

He and Danni had had a romantic dinner at one of his favorites, Le Bistro on the Cuale Island. The sound of the river burbled through their conversation. Candles lit the restaurant and her face.

But he couldn't escape the problems Cade had brought to the forefront. Judging by the number of questions Danni had asked about his crew, she foresaw the same thing.

His team was tight. Ashley hadn't done much explaining, and no one had prodded him about his moods. But they'd resist Danni, on his behalf.

He slipped out of bed, pulled on his underwear and walked silently through the living room to the balcony overlooking the ocean. At the rail, he gripped the slightly cool metal and breathed in the salt air. Slowly, consciously, he relaxed his body, trying to do the same for his reeling mind.

Cade had been right. Ashley had been miserable the last few months. Now, Danni had slid back into his life, almost as if she'd never left. The question was would she stay? She'd said she'd try. But, could he really trust her?

Anger bubbled, rose, and steamed to the surface.

"Are you alright? It's not like you to be up this early." There was concern and humor in Danni's voice.

Stars blinked over Banderas Bay. The lights of a few boats moved over the dark water. The soft <u>shush</u> of the ocean waves mirrored the rhythm of his breath.

She stopped beside him. Her short nightgown was pressed against her body by the light breeze.

"Just thinking," he said.

"'Bout what?" the question was soft, barely above a whisper.

He did not touch her. If he felt her skin against his, he wouldn't say what was on his mind. In the same quiet tone, he answered, "I'm trying not to be angry."

The waves lapped the edge of the sand where it dipped beneath the ocean. "I keep thinking how you...left. It hurt. And here you are, back in my life, as if the last months didn't exist."

A stab of pain knifed up from his right palm. He let go of the rail. He'd squeezed it so hard, he'd abraded his hand.

He looked at her, only a foot away, her head down, hands clasped in front of her.

She nodded. "I understand. I never meant to hurt you. I'm sorry." Her head came up and she stared straight at him. "You can throw me out, if that's what you want. But, I'm not walking away." Ashley had never heard her sound so fierce. "I'm fighting instincts and demons you can't even see. I'm fighting... for you, because you're worth fighting for. Will you fight? Will you fight for me?"

She stood up straighter, lifted her shoulders and said softly, "I'm going back to bed." In a swirl of vanilla colored lace and silk, she turned and went back inside.

Stunned, Ashley watched her move through their suite toward the bedroom before the darkness made her disappear.

Fighting? She was fighting for him? He'd not thought of her reappearance that way. The idea turned his anger on its head. She'd left, but it hadn't been as sudden as he liked to imagine. Insight into his personal relationships had never been a strong point. Suddenly, he knew he expected her to walk out this time, too.

Because that would be easier, for him.

That's what she'd meant. He had to fight, not Danni, but himself. He had to fight himself to be free, to love her.

The realization left him gasping. He sank onto the chaise lounge and tried to breathe. It took awhile.

Finally, he rolled his shoulders, stood and opened the door. How could he explain this?

Good as her word, she was in bed, obviously awake. He walked to her side then flipped back the covers.

"What?" she asked.

He didn't hesitate. He swept her up into his arms and strode to the door. He deposited her on the chaise on their secluded balcony, and ordered, "Stay there."

He grabbed an extra blanket from the closet and went back outside. He pushed her over a little on the chaise, threw the blanket over them both, and pulled her curvy body into his.

Yeah, he'd fight for her and with her, if he had to. Because there wasn't anything he wanted more.

He held her there, absorbing her warmth, watching the stars wheel by in the sky. Finally, the words appeared in his mind, and he was able to speak them. "I wanted you so much, I didn't stop to think what you needed. I pushed too hard. If I hadn't demanded you come with me, would you have left for Scotland?"

"I don't know," her words were broken. "I thought I was doing the right thing."

"Maybe it was," Ashley said. Truth did sometimes come in flashes of brilliance. "If you hadn't left, I'm not sure either of us would know how much we mean to each other."

The silk of her gown slid beneath his fingertips as he moved his hand down her back. He wanted so much to calm her, give her the reassurance she needed, that he needed. He just didn't know how.

Words weren't his strong suit. Hell, emotions weren't his strength either. He'd spent years channeling whatever he felt into one thing. From the pain of his parents' ultimatum to the loss of his grandparents, he'd poured what he felt into proving his parents wrong, and his grandparents, right.

He needed something different now and had no idea what. So, he simply spoke the truth, "Danni..." He stroked her back, as much for his comfort as for hers. "I need you. I love you."

The weight of her head against his chest had never felt so welcome. They held each other as the stars dimmed, the sky lightened from blackest night to deep blue. The sun rose, to lighten the sea.

They landed in Richmond early Monday evening. His car was at the private portion of the airport, on the east of the city. They headed west into the lowering sun.

Richmond was an old city with a rich and varied history. Danni looked forward to exploring it, but at the moment, she was excited about seeing Ashley's home. She had no idea what to expect.

They crossed I-95, then 195 and turned left into a residential area. The layout of the streets, the size of the lots, varied. The houses were far apart. The architecture was a blend of Georgian, Colonial Revival and Cape Cod. Small parks appeared in oddly shaped corners.

"Is it a development?" she asked.

He nodded. "Windsor Farms. It was started in the mid nineteen twenties and based on an English Village."

It sort of reminded her of one, with much newer, larger houses and straighter streets.

"My place is newer, closer to the river."

The neighborhood had charm. She noticed the name of the street, Long Lane. "It's beautiful. All the trees..." It was obviously an upscale neighborhood. The kind of place she could only dream of as a child. The view to her left stopped her survey. "What in the world?"

"What does it look like?" he asked through a chuckle.

"A Tudor house," she answered as they drove by the entrance to the parking lot for the place.

"That's what it is. Agecroft Hall. Fifteenth Century, if I remember right. Moved here piece by piece in the Twenties."

Danni shook her head. She'd seen plenty of authentic English villages and many, many old homes. She caught Ashley looking at her, expectantly. She smiled. "I guess that's one way to see what they look like."

Ashley's smile dimmed a little. Then, he pointed with his head toward the end of the street. "Up ahead on the right."

They drove onto a slightly curved driveway, and hidden behind a screen of trees was a beautiful Georgian, brick home.

"This is what you bought after your address showed up on the Net?" she asked.

"Yeah. I used to live a few miles from here, a district called the Fan. I bought this about four years ago."

Ashley and Danni hauled their suitcases-- mostly hers--, to the front door.

Trepidation and excitement went to war inside her. She was glad she didn't have to find a house key, because her hands trembled, along with her stomach.

Ashley slid his key into the lock. She heard a distinct click then he pushed the large wooden door open.

"We're home," he said calmly.

She stiffened her mental spine, wrapped her hand around the handle of her suitcase, hitched her shoulder bag higher and stepped over the threshold.

They got the luggage in the door. Ashley closed it, then said, "Leave it for a bit. I want you to come out back."

Typically Georgian, the house had a central hallway, with rooms on each side, and hugging one wall, a staircase. Ashley had a definite destination in mind, as he led her by the hand down the hall, past several rooms and out the back door.

The manicured lawn ended in a line of huge live oak and southern pine trees. Beyond, the sun glinted off water. The air, perfumed with the scent of the opening night blooming plants was heavy and balmy. Despite the humidity, Danni instantly loved it.

He threaded his way through the trees, then stopped, and Danni's heart nearly did the same. They stood high on the bluffs above the river.

Ashley said, "The James. Pretty isn't it?" He dropped an arm over her shoulder.

She leaned against him. "Beyond pretty. It's incredibly beautiful."

The setting sun turned the sky to gold and seemed to infuse the river with a glow of its own. "I see why you like it," she said.

They stayed there until the sun had dipped beyond the western horizon. As they walked back through the yard, Ashley pointed out the few flowerbeds, the gazebo and the brick patio.

"Shit," he suddenly exploded.

The warmth of his arm around her disappeared.

He shook his head, staring down at the ground. "You idiot!"

Not understanding his sudden outburst, she asked what she thought was an obvious question, "Why are you an idiot?"

A sigh burst from him. "Tomorrow's Tuesday."

"And?"

Still shaking his head, he put his arm back around her. A deep frown drew his brows together. "I have a barbeque here every Tuesday night for the whole team."

Danni shrugged. This might be a good thing. "If you're nice to me, I'll help."

"Are you sure? I mean, I sort of hoped to spend the day with you."

"You will. Besides, this way I can meet most of the people in your life in a nice social setting."

His frown faded. "You are brilliant."

"On occasion." She stood up on tiptoe and kissed his chin.

He led her back inside. His home was tasteful with the right colors, Georgian and Queen Anne antiques and reproductions. One of the drawing rooms held a flat screen TV enclosed in a bookcase, and a theatre stereo system. She was sure there was an X Box somewhere.

Upstairs, a large bedroom had been converted to a quasi-office with a computer and shelves of trophies and photos. There were more in his trophy room in Denver.

"It's funny," she said, as they strolled down the hall. "Here you are, a very modern man, with an amazing lifestyle, a demanding career, and your houses are classic, understated elegance."

"You think so?" His voice carried a note of surprise, as if he couldn't quite believe her.

She nodded. "You have excellent taste."

They stopped in the hall, only feet away from the door of what she assumed to be the master bedroom.

"You really think so?"

Arms around his waist, she leaned against him. "Yes. This house, like the one in Denver, is a reflection of you. The real you."

Strong fingers gently massaged her scalp, kept her close against the sound of his heartbeat. "Yeah, me and my decorator."

She chuckled, and wondered if his parents had ever set foot in this sophisticated, yet relaxed, beautiful home. She leaned back, looked at his face and said, "Show me the bedroom."

Tuesday, Ashley teased and joked as he drove around town. They had an early lunch at Sam Miller's in Shockoe Slip, the upscale, urbane, watering hole district close to downtown. It seemed everyone in the place recognized him. They said hello or waved, but no one bothered him. It was nice. Danni still preferred anonymity, but knew it wouldn't last forever.

"Relax, Danni. Everything will be fine."

Despite nerves, she couldn't help but smile. He was getting very good at reading her moods.

"Things will be easier for you if your team likes me. Well, and for me, too."

With a little shrug and a grin, he said, "Just be you. Look at Cade and Pam. You won them over."

"Hot weather and Piña Coladas can do that."

"I'll be there." He leaned back, his eyes full of warmth. "You promised me you'll try, and I made you the same promise. We're a team."

She hoped the rest of the team would agree with him.

He dropped her at home, and went off to the race shop in

Richmond.

Danni went shopping for the party. Once the groceries were put away, she pulled out directions and went to her first appointment with her new psychiatrist.

By six her stomach fluttered nervously. Ashley kept telling her to relax, but she couldn't escape the feeling she was a lamb about to walk into a lions den.

As people arrived, Danni did her best. She knew how to do this. Done it for years when she was married. This had to be easier than Formula One. At least all these folks spoke English. Engineers, tire specialists, shock specialists, the guys who went over the wall at the track, jack man, tire changer, all filed into the back yard, some with their families or girlfriends.

On the surface, everything seemed to be going well. Cade and Pam arrived fairly early and made sure they introduced her to anyone she might have missed. Their support was a godsend.

Then about a half hour late, Kenny Morgan, Ashley's crew chief arrived. He looked down at her, his mouth turned down, with a frown that made her think he'd smelled something awful. Then walked on.

Danni thought about chasing after him, forcing at least a few words, but thought better of it. This was a battle she'd have to win, but how?

The next morning Danni felt very bleary eyed as she and Ashley flew to Kansas for an appearance followed by an autograph session. Thursday they flew to Ft. Worth. Friday was the first practice session, qualifying, then more practices on Saturday, then the race on Sunday. Endless meetings and interviews were squeezed between the times he was on the track,

Danni hung out in the background, letting Ashley do what he needed.

Friday afternoon Danni watched Ashley climb into the car. Hands on the roof, he slid in, feet first.

The butterflies in her stomach turned to bumble bees. Her heartbeat throbbed in her ears. Time to escape. She concentrated on confronting the root of her fear, took a deep breath and worked on calming her anxiety.

Kenny strode up beside her. Danni glanced up at him, and tried to smile. "Hi."

He said, "Listen, I have no idea what went on between you and Ashley this winter, and I don't care. But, I will not have you messing with his mind."

Danni stopped, turned, and wasn't sure if she wanted to punch him, slap him or agree with him.

He towered over her. She was used to that. But, his face was a mask of belligerence. Something in her snapped and anger won.

She pointed a finger at his chest. "You're Ashley's crew chief, his friend, fine. But you don't know anything about me, or my part of the story. And, I don't recall you asking either. So, back off."

She walked away. Kenny grabbed her by the arm, forcing her to turn. "He can't afford to make a mistake out there because he's thinking about you. Where you are. What you're doing."

Danni jerked away. Fury filled every pore. "Don't you think I know that?" The words came out in individual little blasts. She knew it better than he ever would. She'd learned the hardest way possible.

She stalked away. Didn't look back.

When she got inside the motor home, she was tempted to pack

up her stuff and tell Ashley she'd see him in Denver or Richmond.

Her entire body shook.

Danni collapsed, turned her face to the back of the couch, taking huge gulps of air, and lost track of time.

But, she would not run.

"Danni, Danni?" Ashley's soft southern voice came to her. Warm hands touched her shoulder, her head.

From some deep reserve she found the strength to open her eyes. Ashley slid onto the couch beside her, pulled her into his arms and kept her there. She didn't tell him of her confrontation with Kenny and wouldn't. She wouldn't cause any friction between them.

Despite her pledge to Ashley, and his to her, she had to work this out on her own.

She managed to look at him, and see the deep lines of worry around his eyes. That would never do.

Still in the circle of his arms, she lied, "I'll be all right. It's just a headache."

Chapter Thirteen

Ashley's motor home was a hundred and eighty degrees from what she'd expected. She took in the details again, while listening to Switchfoot on her Ipod. The space was appointed in black leather with red and silver accents, ivory granite tile, shot with black, on the floors and matching counter tops.

The bedroom and bath were just as posh.

Though it was very comfortable and quiet, she'd not slept much last night. Kenny's words kept circling in her brain, sending her thoughts in a very unwanted direction. Had she caused Colin's wreck? And, would Ashley be next?

The banging on the door was so loud she heard it over the strains of <u>Love Alone Is Worth the Fight.</u>

"Danni? You home?" Pam's voice called as she opened the door. Kim Morgan, Kenny's wife was with her.

They came up the steps as Pam said, "Come on girl. Get your jeans on. We'll go up to the transport truck to watch qualifying and practice."

Danni had no intention of watching. "Thanks for the invitation, but--"

Kim shook her head. "Danni, did you know that men, especially husbands, can be complete asses?"

Flabbergasted, Danni had no idea what she should say.

With a little grin, Kim asked, "Do you ever do searches on Google?"

Danni lost the thread, if there was one, of this conversation, and answered, "Yes. A lot really."

Kim's pleasant face took on a softer look. "So do I. You looked familiar to me. So, I did a little Internet search." Kim glanced at Pam.

Danni felt a conspiracy underfoot.

"We found more about you than I thought possible." Pam shook her head. "Girl, you either gotta be crazy, or so in love you don't know what to do."

Danni laughed on a shaky breath. "Both, I think."

Kim grinned. "Definitely." With a little flutter of her hands, she said, "Now, go put on some long pants, so you can get back in the garage area."

"What if I fall apart?" Danni asked, her anxiety building again.

"Then, we'll sweep up the pieces," Pam answered, a small smile lighting her face. "You're not alone here Danni."

"I told my dopey husband what I found out about you," Kim said. "If he doesn't behave himself, I will kick his butt."

Texas Motor Speedway was behind them. With help from Pam and Kim, Danni had made it through. Ashley's first words to her after the race had been, "How'd you do?" Nothing about how well he'd done, a top five finish, or anything else, just, how was she? It warmed her heart.

The next race on was in Phoenix on Saturday. Which only meant the schedule was condensed by a day.

The week shaped up. Tire tests Monday, in Indianapolis.

Tuesday, a team meeting in Richmond, press interviews by phone and half a day off before the barbeque at Ashley's house, leaving them time to go to Danni's doctor together. Wednesday, Kentucky, for more testing. Thursday, an appearance in New Hampshire in the morning, then fly to Phoenix. Practice Friday morning, qualifying that afternoon, meet and greet with sponsors after qualifying.

It was like living in a whirlwind. But, Ashley continued to make time for her, for them.

Friday night at some restaurant in Phoenix Ashley knew, she slumped in her chair, almost too tired to be worried. "How do you do this for thirty-six weeks a year?"

He winked at her. "Insanity."

"I believe it."

"That and taking a break every chance I get." He ordered her a glass of wine and a large bottle of sparkling water for himself. "Speaking of a break, the vintage group is racing at La Junta this weekend. Want to drop in there Sunday on the way to Denver?"

Hang out at a racetrack on their extra day off? The vintage racers were her friends too. She'd have a chance to talk to Sally. "Okay, as long as you swear to me you will not drive."

He held up his right hand. "I promise."

"They've been your friends for years," Ashley said. Danni had fidgeted through the whole short flight from Phoenix to Otero County Airport in La Junta, Colorado. "It'll be okay."

"It's just, I haven't talked to them since I came back."

"Well, now you'll have the chance."

Once the jet rolled to a halt, Ashley dropped the stairs down. The track was literally next-door.

Cars, campers, motor homes, canopies, trailers and racecars

were scattered over the concrete pit area. With Danni's hand in his, they walked around. People waved, said hello, but it was all casual, with underlying excitement.

It hadn't escaped Ashley that Colin had known these same people. For all Ashley knew, one of them had bought Colin's vintage racecar when Danni sold it. The sense of déjà vu must at times, be overwhelming for her. He held her hand a little tighter. There were small lines of tension around her mouth. "You sure you're okay?"

She squeezed his fingers and nodded.

The high-pitched whine of motors told him a formula Ford group was on track. Judging by the activity around the MG's he could see, they must be up next.

Several voices reached them at the same time.

"Hey, look who showed up."

"Hi, Ashley--Danni!"

"Danni's with him."

In seconds there were handshakes, hugs and back slaps.

There were no pit crews or car chiefs here. These guys did their own work for the most part. No prizes, no trophies, racing just for fun.

What Ashley did was fun, if it wasn't, he wouldn't do it, but this was different. More like what he did as a kid. But even then, he'd wanted to win.

Ashley lent a hand with car prep, while Sally and Liz dragged Danni off to the shade under the canopy between their motor homes.

He checked tire pressures, added gas to the fuel cells, and double-checked hood and trunk latches. Three drivers, Mark, Bryan and Doug, climbed into their cars and went off to the grid. Anne would race later with the student group.

Danni didn't object when he pointed his head toward the grandstand near the start-finish line.

He'd seen more seats at a Little League field. People sat or stood along the concrete barriers. After the open wheel cars came in, about thirty small-bore cars hit the track.

Danni had her bottom lip firmly under her front teeth, then she took a deep breath and slowly released it.

"You sure you're okay?" he asked again.

She gave a tight series of nods. More tense than relaxed. "Quit asking me that." She glanced at him, a tiny smile turned up one corner of her mouth. "I think this could be good for me."

He patted her leg. She put her hand over the top of his, and kept it there.

It was like the beginning of any race. The starter pulled out the green flag and the cars surged forward. In no time, he was caught up in the race. This was recreational sport, but most of the drivers were very good. Even the slower cars were well driven. His three friends were doing well. Doug was battling another MGB. He'd get right on the bumper, but couldn't seem to find the right line to pass.

"Crossover. Crossover," Ashley said.

Liz laughed. "Since he can't hear you, tell him that after he comes in."

Maybe ESP worked. The next corner, Doug feigned right, the car ahead went the same way, leaving the door open for Doug to tuck under to the left and make the pass.

"Yeah!" Ashley smiled.

At the end of the twenty-minute session, the spectators stood and applauded as the cars came off track and onto the pit road. The drivers, most in roadsters, waved back.

It poignantly reminded him of simpler days, with his grandpa, when racing was what he did because he loved it. He still loved it, but it carried pressures he'd never dreamed of ten years ago.

Danni reached for his hand again as they stepped off the bleachers. "Maybe aversion therapy will work," she whispered.

He put his arm over her shoulders. Talk of the race buzzed around them as they walked back to their little corner of the pit area.

Drivers climbed from cars, stripped off helmets and fire suits and immediately rehashed the race.

Food came out of coolers and motor home refrigerators, grills were fired up, everyone pitched in and soon lunch was served. This was almost as much a social event as racing.

"So, where'd you find Danni?" Anne asked him.

Danni laughed.

Ashley answered, "Just after Martinsville. It was better than getting another grandfather clock."

"Why would you get a grandfather clock?" Danni asked.

Ashley laughed. "That's the Martinsville trophy."

"You need to study up some Danni," Mark said with a grin.

"Ashley?"

He turned toward Doug.

"Second?" Doug added.

A sudden hush descended on the group.

"Passed on the last lap?" Doug prodded.

Ashley had answered all the questions last night during the interviews. His tires were twenty laps older than the winner's, and he just couldn't hang on to the lead.

Ashley answered in his best media interview voice, "I did it on purpose."

There was a small gasp from some people.

Ashley nodded. "True. Every year all you hear at Phoenix is how the he's never won a cup race there. I'm sick of hearing it, and I know he's sick of hearing it, so I let him by."

After five seconds of stunned silence, Anne said, "You are so full of shit."

Ashley laughed with everyone else, then said, "Makes life more entertaining."

He found himself helping Sally put food away. They were alone in her motor home, as he handed things to her and she put them in the refrigerator.

"How'd Danni do at the tracks?"

What he knew was second hand, he'd been busy, so he reported what she, and others, had told him. "Okay. She watched the race in the motor home in Texas. I think she was behind the pit box during the race in Phoenix. She watched practice and qualifying from the hauler. She listened to the in car radio. She said being able to see the whole track helps."

The door opened. "Conspiring against me?" Danni asked with a slightly crooked grin.

"No, but we were talking about you," Sally said.

Ashley's heart thumped in his throat. Danni would tell Sally the truth. He asked, "How has it been? Brutal honesty, please."

"I did...alright." She frowned. "The relaxation techniques Dr. George taught me have helped."

At Sally's quizzical look, Ashley added, "Dr. George is a psychiatrist we've seen."

Sally nodded. "Good."

"It was Ashley's idea," Danni's brows lifted. "Though today feels kinda weird," Danni said.

"That's understandable," he said.

Sally lips turned up in a very slight smile. "Forgive me Ashley, but I wasn't sure why you would want to come here. Colin liked being the center of attention."

"He did," Danni added.

That was news. Ashley glanced at her.

Danni's smile was small and gentle. "He also liked picnics and creeping around old graveyards."

Sally smiled softly at Danni, then said to Ashley, "I thought maybe that was why you wanted to come here today." She shrugged. "You know, to grab attention. But it's not. You're here to be one of the guys. I've watched you, helping with the cars, talking just like everyone else. It's like you're here to be... well, normal. Am I wrong?"

Ashley looked at Danni, and found the smile still lingered in her eyes. She understood, truly understood him.

Apparently, so did Sally.

"No, you're not wrong," Ashley said.

"How you getting home?" Sally asked them.

Danni laughed. "We have a plane."

"So, send it home, ride back with us and have dinner."

Something normal people did. Damn, he was glad he'd bought a house in Denver.

The grass was green. Daffodils bloomed. Sprigs of green shot up from the ground everywhere. Even the roses had fresh, deep green leaves. He had never seen her yard in bloom, it must be a riot of color. The weeping birch tree that guarded the sidewalk had a definite green cast.

Danni turned around, walking backward, tugging her small, wheeled suitcase with her. "I love this time of year. Everything waking up and coming to life."

She fished in her purse. Ashley pulled his key ring out of his pocket, her house key still hung on it. He pushed it into the lock and swung the door open.

"I hope everything got here," Danni said.

Boxes were stacked on the floor of her Great Room. Sturdy wooden crates and the big barrels packing companies put dishes in.

Danni pulled on his hand, urging him to follow her. She opened the garage door and flicked on the light.

An ice blue Aston Martin Vanquish sat like the ultimate thoroughbred it was, under the florescent lights.

"Do you like it?" she asked. She grinned at Ashley, still pulling on his hand.

"It's terrific."

She walked slowly around the machine. "No damage at all. They did a great job."

She dug into her purse, pulled out a key and punched a button. The car alarm chirped, confirming it was off.

"The factory converted it from right to left hand drive, then shipped it here." She sat down in the now drivers seat. "Dad made sure everything, including the car, got delivered."

At long last she was letting go.

Ashley knelt down beside her, and peered into the car. "Wow, it's something."

She touched her fingers to his cheek and felt a bubble of pleasure rise in her. Ashley was here, and she was with him. Still, a hint of sadness tinged her emotions. "This was my twenty-ninth birthday present."

His day's growth of beard lightly scratched as he turned his head, and kissed her palm. Quietly, he said, "From Colin."

She nodded, despite the fact it had not been a question.

"Moving crates, cars. What have you been up to?" Ashley looked a bit uncomfortable, squatting on the garage floor. She swung her legs out of the car. He stood up and moved back.

She wrapped her arms around his waist, leaned back to look at him.

"Before I left Scotland, I packed up all my stuff and had it shipped here. I gave the cottage back to Jared and Augusta. I still want to visit, but when I do, it will be as their guest." It had been hard to do. Tears rose. She blinked, tried to bat them away.

His thumb brushed against her cheek. "Why?"

"It's my past. A past I treasure, but it's time to move on. I need to be here. This is where I belong, with you."

The May race in Richmond was the same week as Ashley's birthday. He had no excuse not to meet his parents. <u>Oh joy</u>.

"Why are you so tense?" Danni asked. "You talk to them once a week."

"Yeah," Ashley said, then turned the steering wheel to the left. "I say, Hello. How are you? I'm fine."

"They've never come to a race?" her voice filled with disbelief.

"Not since I started doing it full time." It still hurt. He nosed the car toward downtown.

"Not even when the race is here in Richmond?" She sounded incredulous.

"Nope. Especially not here." He swallowed the bitterness. "Some of their friends might see them."

His folks, Ron and Violet, had wanted to make dinner reservations at their country club. Figured. That way they could explain away being seen in his company. After all, most of that set knew Ashley was their son.

But Danni had insisted on picking the spot. The Jefferson Hotel dining room, <u>Lamaire.</u> It was a very fine restaurant.

Through dinner, while Ashley quietly fumed, she was charming, acting as though there was no difficulty between them and their only child. It was such a charade, Ashley damn near laughed a half dozen times.

They quizzed her over her background and education, and were impressed with her doctorate.

Ever the social climber, his mother was awed by Danni's relationship to a Duke and Duchess, never mind they were her late husband's parents.

During dessert, Danni sweetly handed garage credentials to his dad for the race Saturday night. "This way you can come through the garage, see us and still sit with Ashley's sponsor in the Dogwood Suites in turn one."

Other than swallowing their tongues, there was nothing they could do but accept.

Ashley thought about standing up and cheering, but that would be overkill.

Then, his mother said, "It seems so simple, driving around in circles for hours."

Same thing he'd been hearing for years. <u>Bunch of rednecks running around in circles</u>. <u>Low class.</u>

Danni leaned back in her chair, and in her best aristocratic tone asked, "Have you ever read Sharon McCrumb?"

Ashley thought it was one of Danni's lightening quick changes of topic.

Violet answered, "Well, yes I have."

Ashley privately thought she had no idea what Ms. McCrumb wrote. Where was Danni going with this?

She said, "One of her characters commented that writing wasn't very hard. After all, it's just juggling those same old twenty-six letters over and over again in various combinations."

His mother was obviously, completely, mystified.

Danni continued, "She wrote the simplicity of racing is merely the incomprehension of those who fail to understand the sport. But rather than attempt to understand it, some would rather feel superiorly smug about their lack of understanding." Danni put her spoon down on the plate that held her chocolate Crème Brulee, and looked at Ashley. "She called it <u>stupidity as a status symbol.</u>"

Ashley nearly choked on his key lime pie.

He wanted to pick her up and spin her around in his arms. She was a freaking genius.

July 4th weekend, and they were back at Daytona for the Pepsi 400. He was leading the points race. The way the year was going, with any luck, he would win the championship this year.

She stood beside him on pit road, awaiting the end of all the pre-race ceremonies. The pieces his life had changed from a puzzle into a settled picture. He'd never felt this content.

Over the last months Ashley had picked her up and slid her into the car, buckled all the restraints, tightened them and asked her to try to move. She'd had a hard time just shifting her weight. He'd explained what everything was and what it did.

She'd sat in the garage at the tracks, out of the way, and watched the crew. The guys had seemed to take it all in stride. When they had time, they would bring her over and show her what they were doing and explain why.

At the shop in Richmond, Kenny had showed her the car frame, the strength in the roll cage. Pam and Kim took her to pit crew practice, where Danni watched the team jump walls and do everything they would do during a race. Josh Pierce, Ashley's teammate, took her for rides in two-seaters, though at slower speeds. The whole team had come together, just to help her, and Ashley.

She felt like she belonged.

At every track, he'd gotten some open track time and driven her around in a street car. Then, he'd made her drive. It was all getting easier for her.

The touch of her lips against his cheek brought him out of his thoughts. The kiss was part of their routine on race day. With the cars all lined up on the pit road, she kissed him, told him to drive good, and went on her way.

With a hundred laps down, another sixty to go, he'd had gotten better, faster through the day. Three more cars and he would be back behind Josh. When he got there, they planned to do a bit of bump drafting and get them both into the top five.

Just ahead, one car hit another, too hard. Ashley knew it in the split second he had to react.

"Go high, high!" Cade's voice instructed.

Ashley had no time.

The spinning car hit him, forcing him up the banking.

He hit the wall, felt his car absorb the G forces. Metal collapsed. Tires smoked.

Sideways, he slid back down the track. Was hit again on the left side. Something hit his left arm, but he didn't know what.

Damn it. He spun into the grass. He flipped into the air, and tumbled. The world spun. The car landed hard.

"Ashley. Ashley. Talk to me," Kenny's voice crackled on the radio.

Danni strained to hear an answer. Silence. The wreck had taken less than a few seconds. The sight of Ashley's car rolling over and over and over, with parts flying off of it was horrific.

"Ashley, talk to me," Kenny ordered again. "Key the mike."

Panic filled her.

Ashley hadn't put the window net down. That would signal the workers he was okay.

"Danni!" The team owner, Evan Murphy, stood beside her,

hands outstretched.

Her entire body shook. Evan took the radio off her head. Kenny's voice still rang in her ears. Evan guided her quickly through the maze of people and equipment. As soon as there was room, they ran.

The stitch in her side almost stopped her, but she made it to the emergency center. Evan was right behind her. He yanked open the door as she reached for it.

Danni looked around, bewildered. It could have been a top flight ER in any city in the country. Bright lights, antiseptic smell, people moving everywhere. It just happened to be trackside.

A muscular, rather short man stepped in front of her, his face serious.

Oh. My. God. Danni swallowed, tried to squash the terror.

"Wait here, please," the paramedic said, his voice solicitous.

Evan's arm slid around her waist. That was all that anchored her, the only thing that kept her standing.

It was horrible. She wanted to pace, but couldn't move. Wanted to scream but couldn't find breath.

She closed her eyes and prayed. Please, please, help me. I can't do this alone. Please let him be all right.

A painful swallow brought her back to herself.

Breathe some part of her brain told her lungs.

Evan did not leave her side. But she was petrified, so scared.

Ashley's car had been on its top, the wheels skyward, like a turtle on its back, and just as vulnerable, when Evan had helped her from the pit box.

Any number of things could have happened after she'd started running, fire being the most dangerous.

Stop inventing problems. Ashley could be just fine.

Or not.

When the paramedic finally reappeared, she didn't know what

she would do. He gestured for them to follow him.

The warmth of Evan's arm disappeared. He gave her a little push in the small of her back, propelling her forward.

A huge door opened.

Ashley lay on a stretcher, covered with blankets. Her mind noted the IV bag, the bandages on his upper left arm, then the slow lift and fall of his lashes as he blinked.

A woman in scrubs smiled, and with her fingers motioned , Come over here.

Panic faded, a little.

Ashley's dark hair was darker, with sweat. The incredible green of his eyes looked unfocused, but very much alive.

"Danni." It was not a question, only a simple acknowledgment of her presence, though only a hoarse whisper.

No longer frozen in place, Danni took the few steps to his side.

The IV needle in his hand did not stop her from slipping her hand under his. She even managed a smile.

"You all right?" he asked softly.

She brushed her fingertips over his forehead. Felt the clammy warmth of his skin. "Isn't that supposed to be my line?"

A slow smile lifted the corners of his mouth.

The world tipped back into its proper place.

"I'm okay now," she answered. No sense in telling him how she'd really felt. Later, she would tell him later.

The doctor said, "He has compound fractures of the humeral head and clavicle, and I suspect some internal derangement in the left shoulder."

"Say that in English?" Ashley's words were a bit slow, but it was exactly what Danni was thinking.

The doctor gave them an understanding grin. "Your upper left arm, at the shoulder joint, is broken, the skin has been pierced. The left collarbone is broken and you probably have a torn rotator cuff or other damage to the shoulder joint. That's the bad news. The good news is nothing else seems to be wrong." She shrugged. "The safety equipment did its job."

Relief was a strange emotion to attach to hearing about compound fractures, but that was what Danni felt.

"He's going to the hospital for some surgery." The doctor looked at Danni. "You can ride along."

"Thank you," Danni said. Somehow she held all the emotion she felt in check.

She wanted to crawl on the bed beside him, hold him, feel his heart beat, listen to his breathing. Instead, she leaned down and kissed him gently. "I love you."

His eyes opened. Well, not really open, they fluttered several times. His face was the only thing clearly visible in the soft light coming from the light above the bed. But the movement drew her to him, from where she sat in the recliner near his bed.

Lightly, she touched Ashley's cheek with the back of her hand. The skin felt like it always did. It relieved her.

"Danni?" he asked, barely murmuring.

"It's me. How do you feel?"

"Like hell."

"Are you in pain? I can call for a nurse."

"Yeah."

Danni hit the call button. Then, she went back to lightly stroking his hair. That usually relaxed him. Maybe he could go back to sleep?

The nurse arrived, gave Ashley two pain pills and checked all his vital signs. He, the nurse, gave Danni a wink, then left the room.

She kept her fingers in his hair, hoping to send him back to sleep and calm her own nerves.

Ashley's eyelids dipped and his breathing changed. He was asleep. But she couldn't stop her soft strokes just yet. Each movement took away a bit of her anger.

Almost against her will, while sitting for hours in the waiting room, she'd watched the news, with the replay of the "big one" as they always called it, from the race.

She'd gotten so mad she thought would spit nails. Angry, not at Ashley, but the moron who'd caused the crash. That emotion had warred within her while she worried about Ashley.

And, she'd thought how her life was running in circles.

Colin and Ashley. They were so different, and yet...not. Competitive...driven...loving. In her most honest moments she knew Ashley was much more giving. More honest about himself. But that could have been a function of age.

She and Colin had been so young when they married. She hadn't thought she was immature then. Now, she knew differently. The horrible truth was they had grown apart instead of together. But, they had still loved each other, deeply. Something inside both of them died with their son.

Ashley shifted, drawing her attention back to him alone.

As she brushed her fingers through his hair she wondered if the injuries would keep him from driving again. Part of her hoped it would give him a reason to quit. But another, smaller part of her wanted him to get back in a racecar and drive the competition into the ground.

With the morning sun shining through the flimsy blinds, the nurse had come in, covered his arm, got him in the shower, then he'd shaved, brushed his teeth and was rewarded with a fresh uncomfortable gown and two more pills.

He was half asleep when the door opened. He turned his head on the pillow, hoping for Danni. It was Kenny, Josh, another driver, Peyton, who'd driven the car that hit Ashley in the door.

It was a nice break, though Ashley wasn't in a good humor.

The four of them talked for a while, told him what had happened while he was in drug-induced neverland.

"After Josh won, he had the best quote of the night," Kenny said.

Josh's shoulders moved as he chuckled. He was known more for his short answers than for being a great interview.

"A bunch of reporters were outside the hospital, waiting for us," Peyton added. "They asked what we thought about the crash. Josh told him, quote, <u>when someone is on testosterone overload, they become a danger to themselves, their crew and the professional drivers on the track</u>, unquote."

Josh shrugged. "I stole it from Danni."

"What?" Ashley asked.

"Danni said almost exactly that last night to Taylor, with her finger jabbed in his chest."

Stunned, Ashley tried to think of something to say. His Danni had a wicked sense of humor, could hold her own in a conversation with anyone, but she was <u>not</u> confrontational. She was the least confrontational person he knew. Then he thought of how she'd handled his parents. What Kenny had told him about his talk with Danni at Texas, and her response.

When had she changed?

"She didn't tell you?" Kenny asked.

Ashley shook his head. He envisioned Danni doing what Josh reported, imagining her sticking her finger into the chest of a man about a foot taller than she was. It made him feel less angry.

But where the hell was she?

As if reading his thoughts, Kenny said, "She's been here all night. Cade came over with us a few hours ago, he took one look at her and took her back to the hotel. He and Pam had rented a room for her."

She'd been here all night? He didn't remember.

Feeling like a complete ass, he tried to compose himself.

Peyton continued his story, "Taylor was stunned. I've never heard such a dressing down, and not one single cuss word. It was amazing," he said.

Ashley could not help but try to smile. "She has an excellent vocabulary."

"Maybe I could take lessons from her," Josh added.

"Josh's quote was on Fox and ESPN. The other drivers and a few owners have added their take on what happened. There is a lot of pressure to suspend Mr. Taylor for the rest of the year, and maybe part of next," Kenny said. "From his conversation on the radio, he meant to wreck the twenty car."

"Little good that does you," Peyton said. "Ashley, I'm sorry." He shook his head. "I want the championship this year, but I want to beat you, fair, racing, on track."

"It's not your fault," Ashley said.

Peyton shook his head. "Still. I'm just so damned mad. What Taylor did, wrecking someone intentionally, starting the whole mess. It's...it's..."

"Unconscionable." Danni's voice came from the doorway.

Ashley turned his head toward her. His wordsmith. Despite pain, disappointment and anger, he smiled at her.

A few days later, Evan sent the team jet to fly them home to Denver. Odd, how Ashley now thought of it as home. Richmond was where he was <u>from</u>.

He had no idea a simple trip could make him so tired. They had dinner, then Danni helped him out of his clothes and he went to bed.

Early in the morning, Ashley awoke, restless and distraught. He slid out from under the covers, went downstairs and opened the door to what he always jokingly called the <u>it's all about me</u> room. The dim light of the moon glinted on the trophies. He sank down on the sofa. Disappointment filled him. Frustrated tears blurred his vision. Months of work destroyed, and there was not one fucking thing he could do about it.

A shape shifted in the shadows near the door. Danni's nightgown shimmered as she moved. Without a word she settled, nestled her upper body against his right side.

After several minutes, the chill in the air made her shiver. He kissed her jaw.

"You'll get it next year," she said, her voice so filled with confidence, he almost believed it, just because she said so. "You'll have to work harder than ever. You probably won't have full strength in your arm until well into the season. But, I'll help you."

No words of commiseration, no sympathy, just determination to start again and win. "You sound pretty sure."

"I am. I'm certain of your abilities, certain I can help you, and certain I love you."

"And I'm certain I will be a complete pain in the ass the next few weeks."

Her chuckle moved her against his chest. Despite the pain, he circled his good arm around her and pulled her head against his shoulder.

"I'll survive," she murmured.

It had only been two weeks since Ashley's accident and Danni was certain he was going crazy.

He was still in a lot of pain. She kept reminding him he'd had major surgery, multiple breaks and a lot of stitches. None of that seemed to matter.

Scrupulously, he followed the doctor's orders, not taking any chance of re-injuring his arm, or delaying his recovery. Another driver had taken his ride, and while Ashley understood it, intellectually agreed with it, he was not happy.

Danni couldn't blame him. He'd shown every sign of having a championship year, and unless you were Jimmie Johnson or Jeff Gordon, those did not come along too often.

Dealing with the accident had been cathartic for her. She'd made it through. She'd felt fear for Ashley, but anger at the idiot who'd caused the accident had overridden it.

Ashley had pronounced he wanted steak for dinner. Danni grilled nice ones, did baked potatoes, salad and some fresh grilled zucchini, then wondered how she would remind Mr. Gorgeous Macho that he couldn't cut a steak.

She'd been cooking finger foods and things that could be cut with a fork.

Plates ready, he sat down at the table and stared at the piece of beef for a good thirty seconds. Then, he glared at her and said, "Would you cut it, please?"

"Sure," she answered as politely as she could.

His sigh nearly rattled the silverware.

Danni cut the meat, judging his temper.

Nasty.

Out of the corner of her eye she watched as he slowly reigned in his frustration.

She heard two more sighs before the steak was cut in neat, bite-sized pieces. She slid his plate in front of him.

"Thank you." It did not quite sound like he was biting through nails to say it.

"You're welcome." Thank goodness most of the day he could take care of himself, allowing her to escape into work, or go somewhere. Otherwise she'd be just as irritated as he.

They ate in silence, other than Ashley saying, "It's really good."

One handed, he helped her clean up. He was getting more co-ordinated.

"Let's go sit outside. You want a glass of wine?"

Ashley nodded.

Danni poured then led the way out, down two steps, off the porch and into the yard. She settled on the bench under the maple tree and soaked in the sights of the mid summer garden. The sound of crickets and frogs came from the stream that flowed into the small pond at the back of the property. The air was slightly perfumed with the scent of freshly cut grass--courtesy of the gardener.

Ashley sat on her left, took his glass from her and stared off to the west. The sun stood a few degrees above the mountain peaks, the thin clouds burnt orange and gold in the fading light.

"I'm sorry, Danni. I warned you I'd be a bastard."

True, he had. "I know. I keep reminding myself of that."

"Got an email from my publicist, she's getting a lot of requests for interviews." Emotions ebbed and flowed across his face. "But I am so pissed off, I don't think I could be civil."

She shrugged. "So don't do them. Wait a while, till you feel better." It sounded sensible to her. It was so hard for him to talk about the accident, missing the rest of the season.

"The Association has asked me to do them."

Still attempting logic she added, "Ashley, you can still say no. Tell them the truth. You're not ready to discuss it."

He couldn't talk to her about it. How could he make it through an interview?

She did understand what he was thinking. His career was dependant on his accessibility, to his sponsors, the press. But this was different.

She watched his lips thin, he closed his eyes, lowered his head. "I want to get out of here."

"Isn't that usually my line?" She grinned.

He did two interviews, and politely said no to everyone else. Three weeks after the injury the doctor put his busted arm in a new lightweight removable cast, and made him promise not to take it off, except to shower. He had to put it back on before he took one step.

A fall could re-break it.

Danni told him to pick a place to go to and they'd go.

Weird, he wanted to see the places she talked of so much. So, they were on their way to England and Scotland. First class on British Air to London.

Danni said quietly, "You have to see this."

"What?" he complained.

She pointed out the window. "Ireland. There's a reason it's called the Emerald Isle."

Land was land. Ashley looked out and down. Broken gray clouds floated between the plane and the greenest green imaginable. "Wow," he muttered.

He heard Danni's chuckle, and quickly turned to her.

"Told you," she quipped.

The rest of the flight was spent watching the Irish landscape, the Irish Sea, then the coast of England appeared.

"Is that...?" he asked, still peering out the window.

"Yep," she answered. "The white cliffs of Dover."

Minutes later they touched down at Heathrow. Customs

cleared, the limo Danni had arranged for drove them into London.

It was late morning when they got to their hotel. Danni let him sleep for a couple of hours.

"Reveille!"

Ashley woke with a start. "What?"

"Time for some exercise. Believe me, it will help with the jet lag. Though you, lazy bones, slept through most of the flight."

"Where we going?"

"For a nice walk."

They walked. Oh, did they walk. Ashley soaked it in. From their hotel to the east side of Hyde Park, past Wellington Gate, then Apsley House. Danni pointed out the highlights as they went. He was surprised at the beauty of the parks, and how many people were in them. In Green Park they stopped, sat on a park bench, people watched, and bought water from the vendor cart. Ashley had tried to keep track of the number of different accents and languages he'd heard, but lost count.

"Are you tired?" Danni asked quietly, brushing a wisp of hair behind her ear.

Though his arm hurt a bit, he was enjoying the walk, and the views. "No, not really." He smiled at her. "And I have my own personal tour guide."

"Okay, then we go from here down the Mall to Trafalgar Square. What ever you do, <u>do</u> <u>not</u> feed the birds. I swear the pigeons pooping on Nelson are the most vicious creatures on the planet."

Ashley chuckled. Then he was there, in the Square, one of the most photographed places in the world. It was a place he had not dreamed of seeing. Not for a long time anyway.

It was nearly eight, the sun more than two hours from setting, when Danni steered them into a pub. She led him to the bar, where she ordered a Plowman's for herself, which was a salad, several big hunks of cheese and some bread, and for him and fish and chips.

"So when we go home, you'll know what they're supposed to taste like," she told him.

Ashley probably would have sat at one of the tables expecting someone to come wait on him.

The beer was great, the food delicious. He picked her brain about her favorite places here, and places she hadn't been she wanted to see.

Thirty-six races and weeks of testing had never left him much time to travel. Since he was usually off in December and the first week of January, going to the Caribbean or Mexico had always been an easy decision. The ocean was always a fun place to play and it was warm.

He'd never thought of Europe. Of course, maybe it wouldn't be so wonderful in winter.

They strolled along, through the streets and the dwindling light. Despite being tired and a nagging sense that he should be some-where else, he felt relaxed. More than he had in... he had no idea how long.

Danni headed north. "Welcome to one of the most famous shopping streets in the world." She pointed with her head to the sign on the side of a building. Regent Street.

A grin lifted his lips. "Cool, but all the shops are closed," he teased.

"Much better for the pocket book that way."

A block later, just after full dark, he was startled for the third time in less than twelve hours. Bright lights flashed, flowed, com-peted for his senses with the hum of voices, cars and music that filled the air.

Piccadilly Circus.

Danni smiled at him. He smiled back. Almost overwhelmed, he felt like a country boy gone to the big city for the first time.

They roamed through it all for a little while more. Then, with the same surety she had shown all night, remarkable for someone who claimed to get lost in a paper bag, they went to the Underground station, took the Bakerloo line to the Central and got off at Marble Arch, a total of two blocks from their hotel.

It was nearly eleven.

"Ready for bed?" she asked quietly as they rode up the elevator.

He was tired, and his arm had begun to throb. "Yeah." He kissed her, just a brush of lips. "Thanks."

"For what?" she asked as the doors opened.

The well-appointed hallway seemed nearly sterile after the glories of the streets outside. "Showing me something you love so much."

He felt lighter, less disappointed. This trip was going to be good for him. And them.

They spent two more days in London. They walked to Westminster Abbey, then followed the Thames along the Victoria Embankment all the way to St. Paul's, then the Tower of London. That took one day. The third day was less ambitious, they went west, to Notting Hill and Kensington. Then back through the heart of Hyde Park.

Danni's relaxed and smiling face, the lightness of her steps, showed him how different she was here.

He certainly understood how someone could become fascinated with London. It was so immense, filled with history, and at the same time pulsing and modern. She'd given him the choice, to take the Night Scotsman, an overnight train to Edinburgh, or take the train to York, then rent a car, and drive into Scotland.

He could stay in London for a long time. But, she appeared ready to move on. He asked, "Why not rent a car here and drive up?"

Danni raised both her brows, nearly to her hairline. "I do not drive in London. That's for the truly insane."

Chapter Fourteen

York Minster floored him. The old walled city was fascinating, but the Minster? He'd been stunned at the overpowering sense of <u>Church,</u> something ancient and in its way, holy. Danni stood by his side and he felt for maybe the first time in his life, awe at something manmade. At Westminster Abbey, the sense of history was overpowering. St. Paul's was beautiful. But York was something else entirely.

"Every time I come here, I feel as though I should go to my knees," Danni said quietly.

Ashley agreed, and still under the spell of the ancient building when they left, he was glad they had come.

"There's so much to see. You could spend years here," he said.

"It's why I keep coming back. There is always something I haven't seen."

In a rented Mercedes, Ashley sat on the left side of the car and felt stupid, having nothing to do. Danni drove confidently, comfortable, on the wrong side of the road. He was in charge of the GPS and directions.

She didn't seem to mind that he got frustrated because he tired easily. They developed a routine. They'd decide where they wanted to go, what sights to see, then she'd stop early at a bed and breakfast or hotel.

They had the time to do whatever they wanted. Even take a nap. His usual schedule didn't allow for leisure. When he took a break, he still played hard. This whole trip was different, and good.

From York, they toured around the Borders, then north, into the Highlands. At the Great Glen, they turned south along Loch Ness, which was incredible, to the little village near Fort William, where Danni had made her home.

She stopped in the drive of a stone roofed, whitewashed, flower bedecked, two-story cottage.

It was idyllic. It was deep summer. The fragrance of plants and flowers filled him as he opened the car door.

Before they got to the cottage, a smiling, gray haired woman came out of the house and said, "Lady Danni!"

The thought had never before crossed his mind. He knew, but not anywhere near the front of his brain, that Danni was titled, thanks to her marriage to Colin.

Danni embraced the older woman, then stepped back. "Mrs. Murray, this is Ashley Jenkins."

She waved a hand dismissively and said, "Do call me Bea." Then she jabbed Danni with an elbow. "You usually do."

"I was trying for decorum," Danni said, grinning.

Bea smiled brightly at them, then said, "Please, come in. I'll make some tea."

Danni hung back for a second. Ashley took her hand. Slowly, they went through the house, spaces he now thought typical of the older places they had been in. Smallish rooms, clean, with a homey feel.

He watched the blink of Danni's eyes, the way she tipped her head. Letting go of her hand, he slid his arm around her waist. She leaned into him, still for a moment or two, as if gathering herself. "I want to show you the garden."

The back of the cottage was a wonderland of plants. A small creek burbled through, only twenty or so feet away. He had no idea what fragrance he smelled, but, it was sweet and light and wonderful.

Bea, the now retired head housekeeper at the keep, as she'd called it, brought out small sandwiches to go with the strong black tea, served with milk, of course. He was developing a taste for it.

The garden buzzed with the sounds of birds and insects. Danni leaned back, and Ashley realized how relaxed she was. There was not a hint of tension in her. He pictured the way she looked when he was racing. It was the antithesis of what he saw now.

Big white clouds boiled up, followed by a shifting breeze. They said their good-byes to Bea and walked back to the car.

It was obvious Danni loved it here. "Sure you don't want to keep this place?" he asked.

Danni stopped, turned and looked back at the house. Her eyes were touched with sadness as she shook her head. "Too many ghosts."

Ashley would do a lot to remove that look from her face. He kissed her temple, and a small smile lifted the ends of her lips.

Once more in the car, they drove a little north and west, then turned on a gravel drive, past huge, open, wrought iron gates. The road beneath them dipped down a hill, and a stone tower appeared, then more stone, all of it connected.

The place was literally a castle. Complete with crenellated walls. Impressive.

At the door, they were greeted by Augusta and Jared Scott, who turned to him with a little wink.

"Welcome to Corpach Keep," Jared said as he shook Ashley's hand.

Though he was dead tired and his arm hurt, Ashley looked around. He'd toured all sorts of places with Danni, but this was a new experience. The people he'd just met lived here. It reeked of history, and felt old and drafty.

"You look all in," Jared commented.

A dry chuckle stuck in Ashley's throat. "That obvious?"

"Danni wearing you out?" Jared asked, in his soft Scottish accent, a wry grin on his face.

"She told me we've been doing the ABC tour."

Jared chuckled softly, "Another bloody castle or cathedral. Well, now you can take a bit of a rest."

They followed Augusta and Danni through a dark wooden paneled corridor, with wide, wooden floor planks. Chairs and small tables lined the way. Portraits hung on the walls. A fireplace was visible at the end of the hall. They entered a comfortable sitting room. Tall windows faced south. Jared closed the door behind them, and immediately the air felt warmer, the draft, gone.

Jared strolled to the bar and hefted a decanter, one eyebrow lifted, inquiring. The light, filtered through the crystal and amber liquid, fractured into fragments drifting in the air.

Danni said, "Oh, yes, please," before Ashley could open his mouth.

He smiled at her and looked at Jared. "Me, too, please."

"Ice?" Augusta questioned.

"Ah, no," he answered.

"Good man," she said. "She's got you trained."

"She tries."

Augusta invited them to sit in the big overstuffed chairs near the empty fireplace. They spent the better part of an hour talking companionably. The whiskey tumbler empty, his eyes drooping, Danni stood beside him.

"I'm going for a walk. Stay put." The backs of her fingers were warm where she brushed his cheek. "Take a nap."

That was irresistible. "Okay." His lids dropped again.

The room was empty when he awoke. A light blanket covered him, courtesy he assumed, of his hostess. The sky was leaden silver, promising rain.

Awkwardly, he stretched his right arm and rolled his left shoulder as far as he dared, then readjusted the sling. He pointed his toes until his ankles popped, feeling much better.

The door behind him opened with a slight groan. Ashley turned his head.

With a smile and a nod, Jared said, "You're awake."

Ashley nodded. "Thanks for loaning me your sitting room. I hope it wasn't an inconvenience. Is Danni back?"

The smile in Jared's eyes dissipated. "No, and I suspect it will pour soon."

"Do you know where she went?"

He nodded. "It's something she's done for a long time. She's needed to." Jared's brows pulled together in a little frown. "I hope you understand."

Ashley wasn't sure he did. Either where she'd gone, or why she needed to.

A sad smile lifted one side of Jared's mouth. "Let's fetch her, shall we?" A little sparkle came into his eyes. "I'd say you should go, but I don't think you can drive."

"True. And the whole right hand drive thing is confusing."

Jared turned his Range Rover off the drive onto a gravel path, well maintained.

The bell tower on the church peeked though the trees long before the rest of the building came into view. Ashley recognized it from the video he'd seen of Danni leaving Colin's funeral. The family chapel. Hundreds of years old.

Despite his worry for her, the thought crossed his mind that his mother would be very impressed.

Jared parked the SUV a few yards from the arched metal gate that marked the entrance to the cemetery. He gave Ashley a long look.

"She's in love with you, you know. She's managed this far because she's stronger than she thinks. But then, she always has been. Strong enough to do what she needs to, for you. The question is, are you strong enough to do what she needs?"

Ashley swallowed the lump in his throat. He couldn't keep eye contact. With his head pressed into the headrest, he answered, "I don't know."

"Honesty counts for much." Jared paused. "Don't mistake me, I loved my son." Tears appeared, his voice choked, but he went on, "I was not blind to his shortcomings. When she needed him the most, he wasn't here. His inability to understand what Danni needed and why, may have been his biggest fault. I'm relieved to know you try to think of her needs, too."

Only with a touch of guilt, Ashley said, "I try." He looked at the graveyard.

A fat drop of rain hit the windshield. He leaned over and opened the passenger door with his right hand.

He had one foot on the ground when the older man's voice stopped him. "Maybe, she won't feel the need to come here anymore." He clapped a hand on Ashley's good shoulder. "Go find her, lad."

Ashley closed the car door and covered the distance to the unlocked gate, getting hit with the occasional raindrop.

Halfway through the churchyard he spotted her, bent over a plant, pruning it. Roses. Of course, it had to be roses.

She didn't see him.

"Don't you think it's time to go home?"

Danni turned toward him, color draining from her face.

He went to her as fast as his legs would carry him. Pulling her up, he asked, "Are you all right?"

She stammered, then said, "Yeah, you startled me."

The rain suddenly fell faster.

He wrapped her in his good arm. "We're about to get drenched."

"I dropped the pruners."

He glanced around the ground, looking for the object keeping them both from a dry car and noticed the headstone, silent and overwhelming. There were two names on it. Her son's and her husband's.

It felt like hitting a wall, full speed. He had to concentrate to take a breath.

Two, there were two. The ghost he sometimes saw in her eyes wasn't just her husband.

He took a deep breath. "Danni?"

She had to collect her thoughts. Had to. His words had so echoed those of her dream or hallucination or whatever the hell it had been when she sat out here and caught pneumonia, it had scared her. Only the accent had changed. In her dream, it had been Scots. She was so glad he'd come looking for her, she kept one arm around his waist as she looked for her nippers. "I got so busy trimming things up I... I lost track of time."

"And the weather."

The rain was falling harder. She grabbed her sack of cuttings, still looking around.

"I don't think you'll be too heavily criticized for leaving some clippers in the rain."

She dashed to the garden shed at the back of the church, threw away the bag holding the clippings, then stripped off her gloves and left them on a bench. Then she ran back to Ashley, where he stood, still staring at the gravestone.

Damn it. Could she make him understand?

Her fingers were freezing as she grabbed his hand and tugged. "Come on, before we're soaked through." She led him to the church.

"Jared's waiting," Ashley said.

"He can wait," she said, not unkindly. She dropped onto one of the hard wooden pews, and continued looking up at him.

Ashley's deep frown made her stop and think. How could she explain this without sounding like a candidate for the nearest psychiatric hospital?

"Why did you come here?" he asked.

No avoiding it now. Despite having spent the last months in his company, learning more about him, seeing how much more there was between them, she wasn't sure she could make him see. Nothing to do but face it head on.

"I started coming here a few months after Colin died. I was completely alone. I started talking to him..." she looked away from Ashley's green eyes and toward the altar. Truth, a voice whispered through her. "I yelled, sometimes screamed, cried... everything at him. He'd left me. When I'd needed him most, he'd left." Danni closed her eyes, hoping to hide the tears that had risen. "Struan was so perfect. Everything I'd dreamed of. He'd wiggle his hands and feet and make wonderful noises. Then, one morning, I went in to check on him." She shuddered as she remembered that horrible moment. "I touched his head..."

"Danni. You don't need --"

Ashley meant to stop her, but it was too late now.

"He was cold. Every part of him. He wasn't breathing." She risked opening her eyes, but she really didn't see anything. "I froze. I couldn't move. Couldn't believe it, then, I don't know how long later, I pushed on that tiny little shoulder and begged him to breathe. I still didn't believe it when they lowered that little white coffin into the ground."

Something warm touched her hand. Ashley had taken her fingers into his. He was slightly blurry from the tears in her eyes. His head tipped to one side, as if he wanted to say something and didn't know what.

Danni swallowed hard. "You should know, don't you think, you should know, if your baby dies? He'd died in the middle of the night, and I never knew."

She left her hand in Ashley's. She suddenly lacked the strength to move. Hollow, all she could do was talk.

"Colin...Colin stayed home for a little while. But I couldn't let go." The tears started again. How could she still have tears? "I couldn't let go of my son."

"Then Colin was gone too. I had nothing left."

Danni dropped her head, closed her eyes and felt the streams of pain flow down her cheeks. Ashley's strong hand was the only thing keeping her from dropping into nothingness.

"I think out of desperation, I started talking to Colin. After awhile I stopped apologizing for letting our baby die, and getting him killed, and just started talking to him."

"It wasn't your fault, either of them," Ashley's voice was quiet. But, she couldn't look at him.

"Most of me believes that, now." She took a breath, and couldn't manage more than a shaking intake. She wished she had a tissue. "I talked to him almost everyday, telling him what had happened, what was going on. It became less necessary as time went on. In the last year, before I met you, I'd come to the graveyard and fill him in. Tell Struan I loved him, then go home.

"I came today..." She stopped. "I wanted to tell them why I didn't think I'd be back. To tell them both good bye."

Ashley didn't know what to say. The look on her face while she'd talked had nearly cut him in two. He'd felt jealous of Colin's ghost more than once. He'd never thought much about the loss of her son, because Danni never mentioned it.

She seemed boneless sitting there. As if the last few minutes had emptied her.

He put his arm around her, then pulled her close. Wondering what he should say, he looked around the church, noticed the details for the first time. A big clock hung on one side, it's bright brass work contrasted with the dark stone of the building. Iron brackets were still attached to the walls, remnants of when torches lit the building. High windows along the walls allowed a view of the dark clouds outside. There was something here. As if generations of faithful had sanctified it, filled the ground and the rock itself with their prayers.

A simple Celtic cross sat upon the altar. As he looked at it, the fresh scent of Danni's hair mingled with the rain and the slightly musty smell of the old chapel. Tucking her against him, he kissed the top of her head. "You believe in Heaven, don't you?"

She nodded against his chest.

"I think they know," he said.

Lifting her head, she tried to lean back to look at him. Ashley pulled her back against his shoulder.

"Colin and Struan, they know you loved them. You can tell them anytime you want. They'd hear you. You don't have to tell them good-bye."

He felt her shoulders move, whether in tears or laughter, or both, he wasn't sure. He cupped the back of her head in his hand.

"I know," she said. "But--"

"Shhh. I'm not done yet." He added, "You love them, I understand."

"That doesn't mean I love you any less."

"I'm a bit slow. I just figured that out." He stood and pulled her up with him, keeping her close. He lifted her chin. Her eyes sparkled, and not just with tears.

"I don't want you to ever think you are second in my life," she said.

Cade had been telling Ashley he was stupid to be jealous. It was almost as if he couldn't help himself. The last minutes had washed that away, leaving his heart as clear and fresh as the rain would leave the world outside. "I love you."

She sniffed again.

The air in the chapel swirled.

Ashley looked up, just as the church door closed.

They'd been in Scotland for nearly two weeks. Danni was enjoying herself. For that matter, so was he. They had gone to the local pub, where she'd had been persuaded, over almost no objection, into singing a couple of sets. She'd driven him to beautiful, wild, places, where they were totally alone, yet...not. This ancient country held more than he could see.

He hated to end their idyll, but they had been gone more than a month.

The reservations were made for a flight home the day after to-morrow.

They'd gone to Fort William, near Corpach Keep to do a little shopping. Danni wanted to stop at the florist, for fresh flowers to take to Augusta as a small thank you for their hospitality. "Wait for me at the tea shop." Danni said then kissed him on the cheek.

Warmth spread out from his stomach, like a good single malt scotch, and just from her touch. "Okay. What would you like?"

"Strawberry cakes and black tea, with milk, of course."

From his experience with teashops, they'd have enough pastry, cakes and cookies to spoil dinner. Good thing that was hours away, at eight.

Ashley took a deep breath of the incredibly crisp Highland air, then made his way across the street. He'd come to understand why Danni loved it here. The pace of life slowed, people were warm and open. They had their problems. Who didn't? But they seemed to fade to the background. They were both more relaxed, comfortable. He still couldn't answer Jared's question. Though he knew Jared was right about one thing, Danni was stronger than she knew. Ashley admired that strength.

The teashop was next door to the pub. Ashley really wanted a beer, not tea. He pulled open the door to the shop, and found a table by the window, where he could enjoy the bright sunshine.

He placed the order, then asked, "Do you think I could get a pint?"

The owner, Mrs. Ross, who now knew him by name, said, "Well, ya know that's an interestin' question. I suppose as long as I can't tell what's in yer cup, it won't make much difference." She winked, then turned away.

Ashley smiled, dashed out, went next door and wrangled a pint, discretely poured into a big ceramic mug, probably breaking all kinds of liquor laws, then, back to the tea shop, where he tried to settle innocently in his chair.

The village bustled with summer tourist traffic. He dipped his nose toward the rim of his mug and inhaled. He took a sip.

Great beer. When he got home, he was going to install a refrigerator in the basement to keep beer the right temperature, cool, and scope out the local liquor stores to find good Scottish and English ales.

Danni's bright blond hair drew his attention. She came out of the florist, a huge bundle of flowers resting in her arms. She looked like she held a rainbow. Ashley smiled.

Despite the cause of his extended vacation, he was more relaxed than he could remember, even though he watched every race on TV. Danni...

Tires screeched on the road outside. Ashley spun. Flowers lay scattered on the road.

He raced to the door and threw it open.

She lay on her side on the pavement, motionless.

"Nooooo!" Running to her side, some part of his brain noticed a small white car stopped inside the cross walk. The pain as gravel dug into his knees when he knelt beside her.

He reached out.

A man beside him said, "Don't touch her sir, don't move her. We've called emergency,"

"I didn't see her." A woman's anguished voice came from somewhere near the front of the car.

The voices faded. The only thing Ashley could see was Danni. The brilliance of her hair darkened. Blood. Panic boiled from his stomach through his body.

"Danni. Danni?" he pleaded softly, as if saying her name would make her wake up. "Please," he whispered.

He couldn't see through his tears well enough to tell if she was breathing. He touched her hand. She didn't move, didn't moan.

Another hand covered his. "She'll be alright, Mr. Jenkins. The ambulance is coming." Ashley registered the voice as Mrs. Ross, but he couldn't risk looking away from Danni. What if...

No, it was not possible.

Sirens thickened the air.

"Let go of her hand, give us a bit of room," a strong voice commanded.

How could he?

Mrs. Ross tugged him back. The paramedics were there. Ready

to take her away.

"I want to go with her," he said.

Numb, Ashley watched as they placed a cervical collar around Danni's neck, put her on a backboard, picked her up.

"Come with me," a constable said to him. "We'll follow the ambulance."

The constable deposited Ashley at the small hospital, the staff pointed him toward a waiting room. His mind refused to work. All he could think of was the sight of Danni, lying on the pavement, bleeding.

"Ashley?" Jared stood a foot away, Augusta beside him, her hand in his. "The Constable's Office called us."

A young man with dark hair, glasses, wearing blue scrubs, walked toward them, his face impassive. He stopped in front of them. "We are flying her to hospital in Glascow. They have the best trauma unit in the country."

Ashley's heart beat loudly in his ears. Each word hit him like a punch.

Augusta took his hand and patted it. He held on to her like a lifeline, but nothing touched the core of fear that had a death grip on him.

If they were flying her... Ashley's terror mounted, along with panic and exploded. "How the hell am I supposed to get there?"

"I'm driving us," Jared said.

All Ashley could think of was Danni in a hospital, and he wouldn't be there for her.

Augusta and Jared herded him outside. "How far is it? How long will it take," Ashley demanded.

"About a hundred miles. A couple of hours," Jared answered.

Ashley closed his eyes. "Oh, Jesus." How could he wait that long?

"Hold it together, Ashley. I'll get us there fast as I safely can."

Damn it. He was acting like an idiot. "I know. I'm sorry."

They sped off down the road. He didn't notice the countryside or anything they passed. He realized Augusta was on the phone, but nothing else registered.

They were the longest hours of his life, filled with an awful noise in his brain, tension that tightened every nerve and muscle with the horrible fear that he had lost her.

Jared paced. Augusta held Ashley's hand. Edward and Jane arrived, stood around, then sat, then stood again. Ashley had never felt more useless.

He'd called his pilot to go pick up Danni's parents. That was his sole contribution.

He hated this. He needed to see Danni, but there was nothing he could do, nothing but wait, and hope. His thoughts revolved around how she looked, felt, smelled. Then, suddenly, finally he understood. "My god," he muttered. He threw his head back, closed his eyes. The dread he'd known for the last hours had knotted his stomach, now, he felt ill.

"What, Ashley? What is it?" Augusta asked. The sound cut through the unruly, numbing buzz in Ashley's mind.

He glanced at her then stared down, between his shoes, at the white tile, overwhelmed. "This is what it's like," he said, more to himself than anyone else. "This is what she goes through, every time. This--this mindless--fear." This was what she felt when he got in a racecar, when he got hit, or spun or hit a wall.

She'd never told him what she thought or felt when he'd been injured. All she'd talked of was her anger and desire for him to get well. How had she managed it?

A middle-aged doctor wearing a white lab coat walked toward them, Jared by his side. Ashley stood, as if drawn up by invisible hands.

The doctor nodded to Augusta. "Your Grace." He turned slightly. "Mr. Jenkins."

Ashley wanted to shake something, but he froze, unable to do anything but listen.

"She has a subdural hemotoma. We've had to place a drain to relieve the pressure. But, the initial signs are good. Bumps, bruises but no other broken bones. The injury probably occurred when she fell and hit her head on the tarmac."

Ashley wasn't sure which was harder, waiting until they would let him see her or knowing she would be unconscious.

Watching television, mindlessly flipping the pages of a magazine, nothing distracted him. While his fear for her had lessened, the realization of what she'd gone through since January, when he'd first gotten in a car, twisted him into knots.

He'd never truly understood what he considered her irrational fear. He'd thought he understood her better than Colin had, now, he knew he hadn't.

He did now, to the deepest level of his soul.

Unsuccessfully, he tried to hold back the tears that threatened to overwhelm him.

"Come on son. Come with me," Jared said. He lifted Ashley up by the right arm. Ashley paid no attention to their direction. It was simply good to move.

"It's a good thing to remember there are more powerful things than we," Jared said as he opened the door on a quiet room, filled with muted light. It was a chapel.

"It's quiet here," Jared said in a barely audible whisper. "A good place to think." Ashley felt as though Jared could see through him, straight to everything that was really important.

"I don't know about you, but I need to be here just now," Jared added.

Ashley watched as Jared sat on one of the long wooden pews, his face raised slightly to the altar at the front. Ashley had never been one to pray. Wasn't really sure he believed in it, but Danni did. At this moment, that was enough. He sank down on the wooden seat, and slowly words formed in his mind. Words asking for help, for her. He was honest enough to know the request was a selfish one. He couldn't bear the thought of losing something invaluable, especially since he's just found it.

Ashley lost himself, beseeching help.

"You ready to go?" Jared asked. Ashley had no idea how much time had passed.

Stiffly, awkward without the balance of his left arm, he unsteadily rose. Once more he looked to the plain altar, with its bouquet of heather and roses. Something in him had changed. Not just the understanding of how much Danni meant, what she had been through, but the incredible sensation that he was no longer alone.

Had he glimpsed into the source of Danni's strength?

Jared stood beside him, with an open, clear look that seemed to confirm what Ashley had been thinking. Jared gave Ashley the kind of fatherly hug he'd longed for, for years.

It wasn't pretty. There was a drain in her head. Danni was hooked up to IV's and all kinds of equipment.

"She'll be sedated for a bit. Keep her quiet."

She looked like a blond angel, sleeping.

Ashley stroked her hair, what hadn't been shaved away, and with a clearness he'd never felt before, knew what he needed to do. For her.

Ashley shifted, trying to get the pillows behind him a bit more comfortable, without waking Danni, who was curled up beside him, her head on his lap. He picked up the remote next to his leg, and flipped channels. He found a U.S. sports channel, the sound on just loud enough to hear. He adjusted the light quilt that covered her. It had lightly rained earlier, the sun was shining now, but there was a bit of a chill in the air.

His leg was asleep but he wouldn't wake her for anything.

She was doing remarkably well. The bumps and bruises healed in no time. The brain swelling had been, thankfully, minimal, and the drain and holes they bored in her skull to relieve the pressure had worked. She'd been in the hospital for two weeks. There would be no long-term problems. Ashley had been so relieved, he'd almost dropped to his knees.

He looked up as a shadow appeared in at their bedroom door. It was open, so he nodded in acknowledgement.

"She sleeping?" Ron Jenkins asked softly. He stood by the doorframe, fingers in the front pocket of his jeans.

Ashley nodded.

"I'll talk to you later"

Ashley shook his head. "It's okay, just talk softly."

Ron walked into the room. "Violet and I are leaving day after tomorrow, same plane as Danni's folks. I'm glad we came," he continued in the same soft voice.

"Me too. It was nice to have your support," Ashley said.

"You should say, about time you had our support." With a sheepish smile, he continued. "I had my own dreams for you. I never considered how different your dreams were from ours. By the time I did, you were out of the house and out of our lives. Thank god Mom and Dad were there."

Ashley didn't know what to say. All the hurt he'd felt, for years, surfaced, then he looked down at Danni. The anger popped like bubbles in the wind. She'd told him they loved him, maybe didn't understand him, but they loved him. He looked back at his dad. "They were wonderful to me. Kept me out of trouble for the most part."

"This is going to sound really crazy. But until dinner the other night, I had no idea how successful you were."

"What?" Ashley nearly whispered.

"We knew you did well, but, when Violet joked that, at first, she was concerned that Danni might be after your money." He grinned, rather shamefaced. "I looked up your net worth on the internet."

Ashley chuckled. "You could have asked."

He grinned. "Really gauche," then said, "so I back doored it. Then, I looked up Colin Scott."

"You had my best interests at heart." Ashley smiled, then said, "Maybe you should tell Mom I was after Danni's money."

Ron's grin widened. His brows went up. "That has some possibilities."

Danni stirred. Ashley looked at her face as she started to blink. "She's a remarkable woman."

Ashley nodded to his dad, then, said, "Yes, she is."

"We'll talk to you later." Ashley nodded.

He couldn't resist stroking her hair. It woke her completely.

"Hmm. Nice nap, nice pillow, too."

"My leg is asleep."

"Too bad. You're the one who offered." She grinned up at him.

"Was that Ron I heard?" her voice a bit rough from sleep.

"Yeah. We just had the most extraordinary conversation."

Danni's brows rose, questioning.

"He just told me he loved me. Not in so many words, but..."

"Never had a doubt. It was just hard to see."

Ashley smiled. "Have I told you in the last few hours or so that I love you?"

"Yeah, but you can tell me again."

Chapter Fifteen

Ashley stood, rolled his shoulder back then spent five minutes doing the gentle flexing of his left arm the therapist had taught him. Exercises finished, he placed his arm back in the sling. He checked his pocket one more time, then walked through the house.

He and Danni were living at her house while the kitchen at his place was brought up to Danni's standards.

Soon, they would have a comfortable space for the two of them, with lots of room to entertain, without knocking down any of the walls that had been finished the year before.

He'd not asked her the pivotal question. She'd not pressed the issue. It just seemed they belonged together. They'd been living together since Danni said she would "try" to make their relationship work. Something formal hadn't seemed necessary. That was about to change, he hoped.

"Danni?" he called out.

"Out back," her voice answered from the back yard.

He opened the screened portion of the double French doors and stepped onto the deck. What he saw stopped him. He would recall this moment for years to come, like a photograph in his mind.

Danni stood at the edge of the flowerbed encircling the fountain. Blond hair shone bright in the sun. Her sassy new cut hid many of the traces of her ordeal.

She was dressed in shorts and a sleeveless top, wearing rose gloves that came up to her elbows. A bag for clippings hung from her arm. She smiled at him, then bent to snip a spent bloom.

Surrounded by color, the melodic tinkling of water spilling down the fountain, and the soft buzz of bees, he knew this was where she belonged.

Where he belonged.

There were more pots of flowers and plants on the deck than there were chairs. The small areas of grass in the yard were surrounded by plantings.

Something purple was in almost every bed and every pot. And roses, red, yellow, pink, white, copper, even several kinds that were multicolored, climbed trellises, covered fences, filled whole corners and little nooks.

This yard was the main reason he'd had a debate with himself about which house they should live in. They still hadn't officially decided. But there was no reason to keep two. Danni had said it really didn't make a difference to her. He wasn't so sure about that. This house had its ghosts, too. But, the yard almost made him want to live here.

He had talked to a good nurseryman. Her plants could survive a move. The roses she had trained along the fences would have to be cut dramatically, but they would recover in a new home, as would the others.

Ashley smiled. A year ago, he didn't care much how his yard was landscaped. Now, he was intensely interested in having a low, stonewall built around a generous area in back, adding sitting areas under trees, building an arbor for wisteria. "When you're done, I want to talk to you," he said.

"Okay," she said, bent over inspecting a purple mountain aster. He went inside, filled two large glasses with ice water and managed to get back outside without spilling them.

Ensconced comfortably under the fabric shade of the covered swing he slowly moved back and forth. He should have been nervous, but somehow the quiet outdoor sounds soothed him. The slight snip of Danni's clippers drifted away.

The swing moved, waking him. Danni sat beside him. "Thanks for the water," she said.

He opened one eye. "You're welcome."

"What did you want to talk about?" She leaned back, and put her hand on his thigh.

"I've been thinking, and I want your opinion."

"Ooh, two dangerous things. You thinking and my opinion." Her eyes crinkled with humor.

God, he loved her. After a chuckle, he said, "The last months have been... peculiar." Months without a race to be in. "I never tried to imagine what life would be like if I wasn't racing."

Her expression was thoughtful, serious, inviting him to go on.

"Aaron's done really well in the car," he added.

Blue eyes narrowed at him. The wheels in her head were turning. "You said he would."

Aaron was one of Evan Murphy's younger drivers and had taken Ashley's seat when he got hurt. While the kid hadn't made the top ten, he had shown real potential. "Evan and I have talked for a while about starting a another team. I'd be the majority owner."

Danni's head tipped to one side. "Soooo..."

"So, maybe its time to plan life after racing."

She lifted her hand from his thigh, put it in her lap, then chewed her lip. He recognized the signs. She was thinking real hard. "Go on."

"Aaron takes my seat permanently next year. We start up the new team. I do more driver development." He took a sip of water and watched her face, then said, "I retire."

"No," she said decisively.

He'd expected her to be ecstatic. "What do you mean, no?"

She put her hand on back his thigh. "You're not ready. You could race for years," she said, her tone firm.

Ashley took a second to reconsider his approach, then nodded. "Yeah, I could." He had to touch her. She had to feel the truth of what he was about to say. He picked up her hand. "That's one of the things that's made this so weird. I thought I'd go crazy. I wanted back in the car. That's why I had to get away. And getting away worked."

Danni smiled. "Only to an extent."

He smiled back and nodded. "True, but I wasn't aching for it. And what I've been doing since has been fun. Look at what we've been able to do. Went to Europe, despite the unfortunate incident," that's what Danni had taken to calling her accident, "take a road trip with the MG club, spend evenings sitting in the garden under the tree and have a glass of wine."

Not once had he ever dreamed that such simple things could fill his days.

"You're too active, too much a do-er."

"I finally know the hell you go through when I race. I can't keep doing that to you."

She blinked, then her eyes narrowed. "Your accident was liberating for me. I learned I could live through it. You love driving. You're not ready to quit, And..." she sat up straighter, squeezed his fingers hard, "...neither am I."

The words were soft. She meant it.

"I do love it. But, there is something I love more. Something that takes my breath away."

Birds sang. The water in the fountain tumbled along. The scent of roses tickled his nose. Cupping her cheek with one hand, he searched her eyes. "I have the means to spend every day and night on this earth with the one person I love more than anything else. Why shouldn't I? I don't want to spend the next fifteen years traveling through a cement and asphalt world. You belong in a green and growing place."

She shook her head. "You can't give it up for me. I couldn't live with that."

Ashley touched his lips to hers. "There's nothing more important to me, than you. I've figured out, I am strong enough to do what's best, for both of us."

He felt her resistance, the gentle pull of her thinking <u>you are so full of it</u>.

"Besides, I told you I'm a selfish bastard. I'm not giving it up for you. It's for me. For the way you make me feel," he added.

They could argue about retiring later. "We'll talk more about it. I just want you to know that is what I think."

She nodded.

Now, there were other things to discuss. Filled with an absolute sense of the rightness about what he was about to do, he slid off the swing, onto one knee, pulled the ring box out of his pocket, opened it and lifted it toward her. "Will you do me the honor of being my wife?"

Tears sprang into her eyes. "Leave it to a guy named Ashley to be so romantic."

She took the box from his hand. "Yes." She smiled.

His hand shook as he slid the ring onto her finger.

Ashley had never felt so blessed.

She lifted his hand and brushed his palm, her lips soft and warm. "You understand me, and I understand you." Tears glimmered in her eyes. "I'm strong enough to do what you need. I know I can. What you do is part of you, a part I can live with. Are we still a team?"

"More than ever."

She looked up at him, her eyes filled with a glorious, defiant gleam. "Then, speaking as half the team, you can't retire, not yet. I won't let you."

December: A year and a half later

Ashley smoothly shifted the Aston Martin and they sped onto the freeway. Danni smiled in the dark, remembering again how pleased he'd been the first time she had handed him the keys.

The night was clear and cold. She looked out the window at the stars blinking like tiny pin pricks in the inky sky.

"Any regrets?" Ashley's voice was soft.

Turning her head, she saw him glance from her to the road and back. Could he see how she felt? "No, not a one." She put her gloved hand on his thigh, felt the slight tension of his muscles as he moved his foot on the gas pedal. "How about you? Want to change your plan?"

He shook his head.

"We plan two years out, and decide as time goes along. When we are both ready, then I'll hang up my helmet."

Danni chortled. "And when you do, you'll race something."

Ashley's laugh answered hers. "Yeah, but not thirty-six weeks a year."

At the restaurant, Ashley got the big case out of the trunk. Despite it's weight, he carried it like a baby, safely cradled in his arms.

She wrapped her fingers around his right arm, and enjoyed his strength. "I'm kind of glad I fell in this parking lot."

"So am I." She heard the smile, the joy, in his voice

They were early, as planned. Danni settled in the bar and

ordered a glass of wine for each of them, while he delivered his package to the manager, with instructions.

Ashley smiled as he walked back into the bar, and took the seat next to her.

"Relaxed yet?" she asked.

He waggled his head from side to side. "I'll be better this time next week, and so will you, I hope."

"I will be." She leaned over and kissed him softly. His smile warmed her, from tips of her toes to the ends of her hair.

"Hello you two," Sally said from the door, Mark, a step behind her. They settled in at the table with them.

"You both look composed," Mark said.

Ashley chuckled.

"I can not understand how you've done all this without a wedding planner," Sally said, then adjusted the long sleeve of her dress.

Danni smiled. It hadn't been hard at all. "Who needs a wedding planner? I have a mother and a duchess."

"But planning a wedding of this size, while you're traveling all over everywhere?" Sally persisted.

"We had a choice, real small, or really big."

"And when we got my mothers guest list," Ashley chimed in, "we knew it had to be big."

The four of them shared a laugh. Ashley's mother had been very impressed with some of the names on Danni's list, and responded as Ashley predicted, by making it a competition. Maybe that was where his competitive streak came from?

The quarter hour before the official start of the MG Car Club Christmas party went by quickly, as they chatted with Mark and Sally and waited for their other friends.

Once the official part of the evening started, there was a brief award ceremony, where all the folks who had planned or helped plan an event in the past year were recognized. Then Ashley took the opportunity to stand. He nodded at the manager. Danni didn't know exactly what Ashley planned to say, but the reveal at the end was going to be a good one.

"A couple of years ago, I joined this group, not really sure what I would experience. What I found were great friends and," his voice broke, "the love of my life."

Danni bit her lower lip, in a valiant, but hopeless effort to hold back tears. She was so proud of him, and so grateful for her second chance at love, at life.

He swallowed, glanced down at the floor. His shoulders rose and fell with a big breath. "There are no words to thank you for your friendship."

Danni looked around the room. Some people seemed to have an inkling of what he was doing, most didn't seem to have a clue.

The manager carried in the steel case. She knew the inside was filled with foam to protect the contents. He set it at the center of a table covered in a black tablecloth that was tucked to the side of the room. The box fit, just perfectly. They had planned well.

"Danni?" Ashley held out his hand toward her. Her heart nearly bursting with happiness, she stood, walked the short distance to him, and took his hand. He raised it to his lips and kissed her fingers.

He looked around the room. "You all helped me through the last year, whether you realize it or not. So, thank you, very much."

The manager opened the box, held it while Ashley took out the shimmering silver mass that was the Cup Championship trophy. A gasp ran through the room, with smiles, then applause.

Ashley set it on the table "Share this with us tonight," he paused. "And next week, we'll celebrate the most special event of my life.' His smile was dazzling. "See you again at our wedding."

About the Author

Rebbecca MacIntyre was born in California and transplanted to Colorado at a very young age. She still lives there with her husband and their 1952 MG TD Mark II and 1960 MG A.

When not inventing stories, MacIntyre sings, travels, drives around with friends in their Little British Cars, and somehow manages to hold down a full-time job.

Racing Luck is her first published novel.

Made in the USA
Middletown, DE
04 November 2023

41691529R00156